"I've come to fin
why you killed my nephew."

Fury blazed from Luke Jefferson's blue eyes as he stood before her.

For an instant, Heidi couldn't respond. She stared blindly around the prison room. "You wouldn't understand," she finally whispered. "You couldn't. You weren't there."

"Because you didn't tell us!" Luke said angrily. "Didn't you think Peter's family would want to know? That we'd do everything in our power to help Timmy?"

"Your brother denied the baby was his...."

"Peter may have acted like an idiot, but who gave you the right to decide?"

"I did it because I loved Timmy more than anything in this world." She turned away, hoping he would leave.

"This isn't over yet," he said.

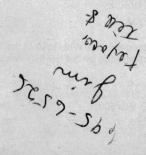

ABOUT THE AUTHOR

Lynn Leslie is the nom de plume for sisters-in-law Sherrill "Lynn" Bodine and Elaine "Leslie" Sima. Both women have been writing most of their lives and are avid researchers. Their investigation for *Defy the Night* actually included a day in prison, which Sherrill says was "an eye-opener." Their interest in such situations is not a passing one. Both Sherrill and Elaine sit on the boards of social service groups and are active participants in their communities. They also like to travel and spend time with their families. Their activities have all provided authentic background and atmosphere for this, their first Superromance novel.

Books by Lynn Leslie

HARLEQUIN INTRIGUE
129—STREET OF DREAMS

Defy the Night

LYNN LESLIE

Harlequin Books

TORONTO • NEW YORK • LONDON
AMSTERDAM • PARIS • SYDNEY • HAMBURG
STOCKHOLM • ATHENS • TOKYO • MILAN

Published January 1992

ISBN 0-373-70485-2

DEFY THE NIGHT

To Warden Jane Higgens,
in appreciation for her time
and her special insight.

And to John O'Malley,
lawyer extraordinaire,
and a hero in anyone's book!

PROLOGUE

HEIDI ALLAN PRESSED her nose to the nursery window. He was beautiful! All around her parents were comparing the relative merits of the babies, but there could be no doubt: her nephew, Timothy Lawrence Allan, was the cutest of the bunch. Wrapped tightly in his white blanket, snug and warm in the safety of the hospital nursery, he was pink and perfect.

If only Faith were strong enough to visit the nursery.

One small fist emerged from Timmy's blanket, and he made a funny little movement with his mouth, almost like a smile. Intellectually Heidi knew it couldn't be. Still, it engendered such a wave of emotion that she gasped.

Was this what a mother felt when she looked at her children? This all-consuming love and devotion?

Since their parents' death she'd loved and cared for Faith, but the fierce surge of protectiveness she felt for this tiny bundle was even stronger.

Perhaps it was because he was so tiny. Perhaps it was because he came into the world with only Faith and herself to give him love. Perhaps it was because, deep down, she felt such anger at his father that she wanted to shield him from the world and all the pain she'd been unable to keep from Faith.

The nurses started wheeling each bassinet into the hall for the proud parents to take into their rooms for feeding. Heidi was happy to push Timmy down to Faith's room, but she wished her sister would walk to the nursery herself and feel this special joy.

She couldn't resist touching his pink cheek with her fingertip, even though he slept. His eyes opened in response, a blue stare, still unfocused and glassy. "Yes, sweetie, it's Auntie Heidi. How's my little precious today?" She made cooing sounds, unembarrassed when a passing visitor looked at her oddly. Babies did strange things to even the most sophisticated adults!

The door was shut tight, the room dark; once again Faith was sleeping at an inappropriate time. This behavior couldn't be healthy, Heidi thought. "Faith! Feeding time. C'mon, you've got to try at least."

Faith rolled over in bed, her pale face contrasting starkly with her unkempt black hair.

"Isn't he just perfect, Heidi?" Faith smiled sleepily, reaching for her son. "I wish his father could see him. I thought he might come once the baby was born." As quickly as she had smiled, tears welled in her eyes, sliding down her ashen cheeks. Suddenly she was not a proud parent, but a lost child.

"Faith, how could he know about Timmy? You promised you were going to forget him after what he did to you." Heidi carefully watched Faith's stricken face, uneasy about her sudden shift in mood. "Did you call him?"

Sniffling, Faith shook her head. "I wrote him about a month ago, right before you came. I wanted to give him one last chance. But I haven't heard a word. You...you were right." She broke into sobs. "I should just forget Peter Jefferson." She looked down at her son, then thrust him into Heidi's arms. "Here, you hold him."

Timmy's spiky black lashes lay against his pink cheeks. That great rush of love Heidi had first felt when she saw him came again, stronger, more powerful. Suddenly she remembered what her mother had once told her about children: when you had them your life was never the same. Now she knew exactly what that meant. Her life, Faith's life, had a whole new dimension—loving and being loved by this child.

Faith drifted back to sleep, so Heidi encouraged Timmy to take the bottle into his mouth. He was just finishing when Faith's doctor breezed in. "Getting the hang of being an aunt?"

Smiling, she nodded, but watched carefully as he turned to the bed. Faith barely stirred as he leaned over, quietly asking how she felt. When she closed her eyes and turned away from him, Dr. Vogland stood. "As soon as you're finished here, I'd like to speak with you," he whispered to Heidi.

She carefully burped Timmy and placed him in the bassinet. When they were both asleep, she slipped out to find the doctor.

He was waiting for her at the nurses' station. "It's about your sister. I don't want to alarm you unnecessarily, but Faith is exhibiting classic signs of postpartum depression."

"What does that mean?" Heidi heard the fear in her voice. Faith had been through so much already. She didn't need any more pain.

"It's a hormonal change that causes depression. It's not unusual with young mothers. After she's settled at home with the baby and adjusts to the routine, it should be fine. It usually lasts three or four weeks. I'm going to keep her here for a few more days just to make sure there's nothing physically wrong."

"What can I do for Faith?" Heidi asked, eager to do whatever it would take to help. "I've been hoping she'd snap out of it, but she isn't getting any better. She seems to swing from one mood to another at the slightest thing."

"That, of course, is one of the symptoms. Dr. Dawson, Timmy's pediatrician, is ready to release him. But I think we'll hold off until Faith is ready to go home, too. One thing you might carefully consider, Miss Allan. Faith has to be Timmy's primary care giver if she's going to recover properly. Back off a little and give her some space, okay?"

His smile softened the words, but it didn't stop the burning rush of shock tightening her chest. Was she overprotective? Was she stifling Faith's natural feeling for her own baby just because she loved him, too? Slowly pushing the door open, she found Timmy still asleep, although he was fussing slightly. Faith was awake, watching him from her bed.

Heidi sat down beside her. "Yell if I get too overbearing, will you?" She laughed, trying to ease her own conscience. "I'm sorry if I've been pushy, taking over while you were so weak. It's just habit…being your big sister. And I feel so close to Timmy. But you're the mom!"

"In a way he's yours, too." Faith swallowed, looking up at Heidi with trusting eyes. "If it weren't for you, I couldn't have gotten through all of this. I mean it! If you hadn't found Mrs. Copt to stay with me until you could come home, if you hadn't put your career on hold, I'm not sure what would have happened to me. Or to the baby. So you see, in a way, he does owe his life to you.''

Wishing she could take away all her sister's pain, Heidi pressed a kiss on Faith's wet cheek, just as Timmy's whimpers grew into real cries. Heidi stifled her first reaction to rush to him, waiting until Faith flung back the covers and slid out of bed to lean over the bassinet.

''Heidi, he probably needs to be changed. I'll do it, but I'd feel better if you stayed and watched. This is all so new to me.''

Heidi had changed him several times in the past few days, and until now she'd been unable to interest Faith in doing it herself. Now the hot, tight feeling in her chest relaxed as she watched Faith change her son for the first time. It was going to be fine. Heidi and Faith would both find their way through these burgeoning maternal instincts.

Faith did a good job. Timmy blinked up at her, and she gathered him in her arms, leaving Heidi to clean up. As she pushed the wet diaper into a plastic bag, she noticed an overpowering sweet scent. That was odd...she'd never noticed this odor to the diapers before.

It was so odd that she waited to talk to Dr. Dawson. Even though he was his usual stone-faced self, his insistence on an immediate battery of tests frightened her. Surely there couldn't be anything wrong. Timmy looked so healthy. It couldn't be serious. Still, there had been something very threatening about that odor.

Vague uneasiness drove Heidi to pace around the hospital halls. It was probably nothing, she told herself. Timmy would be fine, and Faith, too, as soon as they settled into a routine at home. She took a deep

breath, just as her voice teacher had taught her. She
should be calm when she talked to Faith. Tomorrow
everything would be back to normal. She and Faith
would meet with Dr. Dawson and everything would be
fine.

DR. DAWSON FLIPPED open a file and stared at the lab
sheets. "I'm afraid it's bad news."

Faith crumpled in her chair, tears bloating her tired
face. Heidi was practically numb with fatigue. She'd
tried to reassure Faith during the interminable wait, but
as the hours marched by she had become more and
more frightened for Timmy.

She sat up straighter, holding her breath, and concentrated intently on the doctor's face.

"I'm sorry." He finally continued. "Timmy's tests
show he has a generalized deficiency of the enzymes
that catalyze the basic amino acids in his body. In consequence, these acids accumulate in excess throughout
his body, in his blood and urine."

Beside her, Faith began to sob softly. Heidi gripped
her hand to offer comfort, but she directed her questions to the doctor. "What do we do now? Is there a
treatment for this disease?" Her mind grasped at the
miracles she'd heard about, but Dr. Dawson's stern
face slowly eroded what little hope Heidi had left.

"There is no cure for this syndrome, Miss Allan.
However, there have been some gratifying results in
certain cases by careful dietary control. It is a simple
theory, but difficult in practice because of the com-
plexity of the enzymes and acids involved. I would
recommend starting the therapy immediately." He
looked at Faith.

"Yes. Do whatever is necessary." Heidi answered finally, for Faith, sobbing, had buried her face in her hands.

"Timmy has been moved to neonatal intensive care. You can follow me there. I'll be starting an intravenous feeding and enzyme regulatory right away."

TIMMY LOOKED much smaller in the large crib. He was surrounded by equipment: tubes were attached to two different drip bags and a monitor beeped continuously.

Faith refused to get too close to the bed and leaned weakly against the wall, peering unbelievingly at the setup. Heidi couldn't believe it, either. How could a beautiful baby get so ill so quickly? She wanted answers!

Heidi followed the doctor back into the hall. "How soon will we know if Timmy's condition can be controlled?" she asked with a firmness she was far from feeling.

"Almost immediately. Certainly within the next few days." Dr. Dawson jammed his hands into his coat pockets.

Needing to have all the facts, she forced herself to ask the question. "And what if it doesn't work? What will happen to Timmy?"

The doctor hesitated slightly, looking beyond her to the room where Faith was now huddled beside the crib. "Since it's obvious you will be dealing with both your sister's health and Timmy's, I'll be frank, Miss Allan. Timmy's case follows the usual pattern of the condition. Patients, normal at birth, soon develop the sweet odor in their urine that you noticed. Statistically the earlier the condition is identified, the better the chances. Fortunately we caught this before he left the hospital. However, until we see if he responds to this therapy, I can't really give you any answers.''

Blood pounded in her ears, in her throat, behind her eyes, nearly blinding her. But she had to cope with this, she had to stay strong . . . for Timmy and Faith. ''How long till we know?''

Dr. Dawson shifted back a step, clearly uncomfortable with what he had to say. ''A few days should tell us the story, but even if the therapy works, Timmy will have to endure a complex and expensive feeding ritual throughout his life. If the therapy doesn't work, it's readily apparent. Lethargy and feeding difficulties set in, followed by seizures, decorticate rigidity, intercurrent infection and, finally, coma.''

The first seizure began shortly after midnight two days later.

CHAPTER ONE

THE FOCUS of Heidi's life now was waiting. Waiting for a miracle. Waiting for some glimmer of hope. She sat alone in the private room on the pediatric floor where Timmy had been for more than a month. Time ceased moving. Every day was a repeat of the day before.

She didn't even have the solace of seeing Faith and sharing her grief. When the doctors diagnosed Timmy with a rare amino acid disorder, her life fell to pieces. Within days Faith's depression deepened until the doctors finally recommended she be hospitalized. The visits the doctors allowed to the mental health wing were short, and Heidi was cautioned not to mention Timmy until Faith did.

Still numb with disbelief that sweet, beautiful Timmy was so ill, Heidi felt nothing but fear and loneliness. Fear for Faith. Fear for Timmy. Fear she would be able to do nothing to help him. Memories of other hospital rooms when her parents were ill haunted her. Now, as then, she called upon some inner strength she'd never known existed until those terrible days. Maybe it was courage, maybe just stubbornness, but she would face this and beat it. And she would help Faith and Timmy do the same.

She sat quietly in the easy chair the staff had moved into Timmy's room when they realized she was going to stay with him all the time. Today he was a little worse than yesterday, although slightly improved from the week before. Not that he was getting better, or ever would. But at least he wasn't on the dialysis machine anymore. After his feeding, Heidi held him, singing softly until he fell asleep. She really should run across the street to check with Faith's doctor rather than sit here where she could do nothing but watch Timmy, as if her vigilance could keep him safe.

Forcing herself out of the chair, she wandered to the window. Spring had arrived without her realizing it. She didn't even turn when the door clicked open and shut.

"You look like hell. If this is what three months of country living does, I'll take Chicago's air pollution every time."

She spun around. "David!"

"You've lost five pounds at least," her agent and friend, continued in his usual blunt fashion.

"Thank you!" Somehow Heidi managed a shadow of her usual spirit. "I'm glad to see you, too." And it was true; it was good to have him here.

His answer was to engulf her in a tight, comforting hug. Even after five years singing on the nightclub circuit in Chicago, she was always amazed that this big teddy bear was one of the shrewdest managers in her business. He'd been an All Big Ten linebacker but had turned down the pros to get his MBA at Northwestern. "I decided I wanted to be able to walk without a limp when I was forty," he'd explained succinctly one night.

She pushed him away and touched his temple with one finger. "You are definitely going gray."

"You helped put every one of those hairs there." His wide face broke into a smile, crinkling his eyes into green glints. "So I hightailed it down here to find out what's going on. Your phone calls have been damn uninformative. Any improvement in Timmy's condition?"

"No. He developed pneumonia again last week, but the antibiotics cleared it up." Moving to the crib, she touched Timmy's hand, and he turned his head, looking up at her.

"Hi, big fella," David said from behind her shoulder. Timmy responded to the booming voice by focusing on David and blinking a few times before his lids drifted shut again.

"What do the doctors say?" He followed her as she backed away from the crib and went to the window to stare over at the park. Somehow it was comforting to watch all the children at play.

"The doctors say they're doing everything possible."

"Damn all doctors and their euphemisms! And the specialist?"

"He was wonderful, David, but the results were the same. Although he used slightly different terminology." Her voice cracked. She couldn't even think the words, let alone say them. "He said Timmy is terminal." She twisted around. "I won't give up hope. Something will happen, you'll see. Timmy will get better."

She walked over to the crib and bent down, studying Timmy's fragile body. He was asleep and peaceful for the first time in days. Her fingers stroked his wispy hair into place. "Looks like he'll sleep for a while. Why don't I buy you a cup of coffee?"

The cafeteria was small but almost deserted. A young couple Heidi vaguely recognized from the pediatrics floor sat over soft drinks in a far corner. Gratefully she sank into a chair and let David wait on her. She was so tired these days, as if a numbness had settled into her mind and body. She smiled faintly as David set down the tray.

"Thanks for getting the specialist down here from Chicago so quickly. I wanted to make sure Timmy was getting the best care." She stirred her coffee absently; she really didn't want it. She'd lost her taste for most food days ago.

"No problem. He's a friend of one of my old professors. He's the best there is." He hesitated, shaking his head. "You know me, Heidi. I'm not very tactful, but if Bill said there's not much hope..."

"While there's life there's hope, David. I just have to believe that."

"Is Timmy in pain?" David asked.

"They don't know." She lifted her hand to rub away the faint throb in her forehead that appeared every time she thought of Timmy in pain. Pain she could do nothing to stop. "He makes little whimpering sounds in his sleep sometimes. But they tell me they just don't know."

"Well, you have to be satisfied with that, don't you? You've done all you can."

Sighing, she closed her eyes. "It must be reassuring to see the world in black and white, David."

"Life usually turns out that way. Look at me, Heidi." He waited until she complied. "I can't do anything to make Timmy well, but I can help you. You're exhausted. I can see it in your eyes. Making yourself sick isn't going to help Timmy or Faith."

"I'm worried about Faith, David. She's really sick." Heidi picked up two packets of sugar and dumped them into her cup.

David looked unconvinced. "Okay, but you said yourself the doctor thought she would be over this depression by now."

Heidi reached to take his hand across the table, pleading for understanding. She was alone and frightened. If she could make David understand, at least that would be something. "Most new mothers don't have to face what Faith has—first, Peter Jefferson's desertion and now this...illness."

She was relieved when David relented.

"I'm sorry. It's just that every time Faith has a crisis you're there trying to protect her. I've seen you put your own life on hold over and over again. Remember you *do* have a life of your own. And a career!" he insisted. "With a good future. You've worked hard at your music, but it won't wait forever—or until Faith can stand on her own two feet."

"Faith is the only family I have." She pulled her hand away sharply, fresh anger replacing her momentary relief. "And there's no one else to deal with this."

"What about Timmy's father? Or his family. Certainly they should be doing something. They have a legal obligation, let alone a moral one. I can get a lawyer to contact them and—"

"No!" Surging out of the chair, Heidi faced him with new energy. "They have no rights where Timmy is concerned. Peter and Faith aren't married. Peter relinquished his rights when he denied the baby was his. We don't want anything to do with Peter or his family. Do you understand, David?"

"Damn right I do. Glad to see some of your old spirit back. You looked beaten when I walked in here. Now that you're more yourself, I'll head over to see Faith. Maybe I'll be able to understand if I see her myself. I'll be back to take you to dinner."

Smiling, she gave him a quick, fierce hug. "You know me too well. Yes, go see Faith. It will do her good to spend time with you."

He cuffed her lightly on the chin before stalking out, leaving the room strangely empty without his comforting bulk. She left the untouched coffee, anxious to get back to Timmy's room.

Two hours later Dr. Dawson found her staring out the window at the park. There were swings and a glider full of children. Two women sat on a park bench, one rocking a buggy as she talked to another bouncing a toddler on her knee. The children looked happy, and even though she couldn't hear them, Heidi knew they were laughing. When Timmy got better, she would take him to that park and swing him on that glider, she promised herself. Yes, that was exactly what she and Faith would do—together.

"I have some new lab reports on Timmy, Miss Allan." Even after all these weeks Dr. Dawson was still strictly formal. Perhaps doctors did this—kept their distance while they fed you bitter doses of information you didn't want to hear.

"Would you like to sit down? You look tired."

She squared her shoulders. "Just tell me, Dr. Dawson. Is it bad news?"

Ramming his fists into his pockets, he nodded. "We must put Timmy on dialysis again. The amino acid buildup in his kidneys is dangerously high."

She turned back to the window. Suddenly it was vitally important to concentrate on the gentle movement of the swings in the park. "He cries when he's on dialysis," she said softly.

"I know. However, we have no alternative."

There were only two children left in the park, swinging. "He's in pain all the time, isn't he?"

"I've told you, Miss Allan. There is no way of knowing. Timmy can't tell us how he feels."

"He's in the greatest pain when he's on dialysis," she said flatly. "I know. I'm here with him all the time. Don't try to protect me from reality, Doctor."

A woman pushing a buggy came to the swing set and took a little girl with braids by the hand. "I want to take Timmy to the park, Dr. Dawson."

"That isn't possible."

She couldn't see his face, but she didn't need to; she heard the exasperation in his voice.

"Timmy could have a seizure at any time. In fact, as the stress on his body becomes greater, it will happen more and more regularly."

"After the dialysis, will he be better? What would happen if we just took Timmy home?"

"I'm sorry, Miss Allan, but you can't take Timmy out of this hospital. He needs constant medical attention until—"

"Until..." she interrupted, unaccountably relieved as the last little boy was fetched from the swings by an older sister. "Until he dies. Never having been out of this hospital. Never having seen the world he was born into. Never feeling a breeze on his face or being able to swing in the park. Is that what you're telling me?"

There was utter silence in the room except for the rhythmic sound of the ventilator. For an instant Heidi forgot to breathe.

"Yes, I regret that is exactly what will happen, Miss Allan," the doctor finally replied.

Heidi took a biting breath of hospital air deeply into her lungs. Now the alternative which she had tried to push away cried out to be spoken.

"No, that will not happen!" At last Heidi, knowing what had to be done, turned to confront the doctor. "Timmy is not going to die in this room. However briefly, Timmy will see his world. He will have at least a moment without pain. Timmy *is* going home. I know that's what Faith would want for him."

IT WAS SO LONG since Faith had seen her baby. She thought of all the happy plans she'd made with Heidi to bring him home. The blue-and-white nursery with marching soldiers stenciled on the wall seemed unreal. But this was real. This hospital, and Timmy across the street in his hospital bed, were real. Today she would see him again. Faith showered and pulled her hair back into a ponytail before walking across the street in the early summer sunshine to where she knew Heidi was waiting.

Timmy was very sick, she remembered. The doctor had warned her, but he'd told her she could handle it. She was his mother, after all. Yes, she could handle it.

But he was so tiny, so very tiny, in the large crib. Tinier than she remembered. And now his translucent baby skin was faintly black and blue from the IV needles. It was necessary, Heidi said. Necessary to help him get better. But he didn't look better. She remembered him all pink and perfect, the day she had finally picked him up and carried him to the window.

She hunkered down beside the crib, reaching a hand in to stroke his fist. "Timmy, it's Mommy. I'm here."

Suddenly Timmy's elbows bent rigidly toward his chest and his tiny body shuddered in a convulsion. Jerking back, she screamed, but no sound came. The cries were inside her, filling every cell of her body, echoing louder and louder in her head until she covered her ears with her palms.

Two nurses pushed her aside as they rushed to inject something into the IV line. Heidi put her arms around her, pulling her away from the bed.

"What's wrong with my baby, Heidi?" The press of people prevented her from seeing. Dr. Dawson appeared when another nurse rolled in a ventilator and taped a tube into Timmy's mouth.

"No! Don't do that to my baby! You'll hurt him!"

Heidi turned her from the bed. "Let the doctor do what's necessary." She spoke calmly, as if to a frightened child. "C'mon, Faith, let's wait in the hall."

This couldn't be happening! Her baby was fine and she was fine. They were going to go home soon. Everything would be just fine.

The walls began to close in on her—the walls of the room and the walls of her mind, trapping her inside with the pain. She fought against it.

"What's happening? This isn't fair, Heidi! Make the doctor get Timmy well! I want to take my baby home!" Now the screams broke free, loud and piercing. "Away from here!"

Out of nowhere Dr. Vogland appeared. Faith found herself loosening her death grip on Heidi and turning to him as a source of refuge.

Yes, away from *here* Timmy was only a vague happy memory. She wanted to go back to that place.

A pin pricked her arm, and she was pushed gently into a wheelchair. Yes, she would go back to peace and forgetfulness. But she was Timmy's mother....

"Heidi!" Desperately she fought the effects of the shot. "Help Timmy. You're the only one who can. Peter's gone... and I... can't. I'm sorry." A sob broke from her throat. "Take care of my baby, Heidi, the way you always take care of me. I know you'll help him. You're strong. You always do the right thing. I'm counting on you."

From a great distance she heard Dr. Vogland saying, "I'll take Faith back across the street and settle her into her room. As soon as this crisis passes, I'll need to talk to you, Heidi. I'm afraid this is a major setback for her."

No, he was wrong. Forgetfulness was survival, Faith wanted to scream, but instead, surrendering to the floating peace, she closed her eyes.

HEIDI PACED around the small room. She knew every mark on the wall and how many tiles there were in the ceiling. She heard the soft whoosh of the ventilator everywhere, even in her sleep. The pediatric staff had become her closest friends.

How many nights had she stayed to make sure Timmy survived another crisis? How many feedings and changings and baths?

At times like this it all threatened to overwhelm her. Faith had improved, her doctor insisted, but she still wasn't ready to face the harsh reality of Timmy's illness. Heidi was on her own.

When would it end? How much longer could Timmy's tiny body endure the pain? Shaking her head, she dashed away fresh tears. No! She wouldn't give in to these feelings. She still believed in miracles. Even if the only miracle Timmy would have was time away from here; time at home in the room they had created so lovingly for him.

Heidi was expecting the doctor, who faithfully checked on Timmy every night. But when the door opened it was David.

"Well, I've talked to the hospital administrator again. The hospital ethics committee is going to consider your petition to take Timmy home."

Her knees gave way and she sat down abruptly. It was done. Would she be strong enough to face the inevitable?

David sat on the floor beside her. Timmy was restless tonight, crying and fussing at the shunt. Dialysis was always the most difficult time. She put her hand through the crib slats and stroked one tiny arm comfortingly.

"Damn it, Heidi. Look at me."

"I heard you, David. Thank you." She reached to touch David's cheek and discovered that her fingers were trembling.

"Heidi, are you sure this is what you want?" Gripping her hands, he held them tightly between his wide palms. "I've got to tell you, in my opinion, that the ethics committee is going to drag its feet until it's too late. They don't want to deal with this decision."

"I know. Neither do I. But it isn't fair that Timmy has to spend every moment of his life in pain in this room. If I can give him just one day—one hour—of something else, I have to do it." It was the only thing keeping her going: the hope that she could give Timmy a moment of happiness and keep her promise to Faith.

"Heidi, listen to me carefully." David leaned closer, clutching their entangled hands to his chest. "According to Dr. Dawson, if you remove Timmy from the ventilator, he might have another seizure or just stop breathing. Are you prepared to deal with that? And Faith, what does she say?"

Heidi searched David's face for a spark of compassion. "It's all up to me. I'll handle the consequences."

She had never seen David so serious. Deep creases scored his eyes and mouth. She knew he cared about her, and she was sorry to be causing him all this worry. She tried to smile. "David, try to understand. I once vowed I would never give up hope as long as Timmy was alive. If I could give him a part of me... a part of my strength to help him get better, I would. Gladly. But all I can give him is freedom from this...this pain. And a glimpse of the world, the beauty outside this hospital, however brief. To do that I'm willing to accept anything that might come."

Frowning, he stared at her out of shrewd eyes. "Damn it, Heidi, you shouldn't handle this alone." His grip tightened, numbing her fingers. "You're going to be mad, but I've made inquiries. I can't locate Peter Jefferson, but I found out his father passed away three years ago and his mother lives in Palm Beach, Florida, now and is very well off. Peter's older brother, Luke, is one of those crusading lawyers. He's internationally known for championing the underdog. He's been in South America for the past six months securing the release of some activists. This guy is in a position to help you."

"David, I don't want him or any of them involved." She tried to keep the anger out of her voice. He was right; regardless of his well-meaning intentions, she was damn mad.

"Heidi, those people should shoulder some of this responsibility!"

Pulling away, she stood, leaning her head back, meeting his eyes as he rose slowly. "This has nothing to do with them. They haven't been here all this time, hoping and praying. Watching other babies, smaller than Timmy, grow and survive and go home. Watching Timmy struggle to breathe. Listening to his cries. Being so helpless as he gets weaker and weaker. My decision is made."

He stared into her determined face for a moment and then, without a word, walked away. She almost called out to him to wait, not to leave her like this, but at the door he turned.

"God help me, Heidi, but I hope this poor baby's suffering ends before you have to face that decision."

David's harsh words haunted her all evening as the dialysis finished and the machine was rolled out of the room. Still Timmy whimpered, crying in his sleep. She brushed her fingers across his forehead and was surprised at how warm he felt. The night nurse confirmed another fever, another lung infection.

Once again Heidi stayed all night, leaning over the crib, holding and rocking him as best she could. By morning, with the help of antibiotics, the fever broke. Until the next time.

TIMMY WAS WEAKER; she recognized his increased lethargy. His color had faded long ago from pink to a sallow ash. He still seemed to know her, though. When she touched his hand, he stared up at her with his baby blue eyes.

But there was no doubt that, with each passing hour, Timmy was simply growing smaller and weaker. It would be soon. No one said anything, but Heidi could see it in the nurses' faces every time they walked into the room to check Timmy's vital signs.

By the end of the week she realized David was right. The ethics committee would keep putting her off with excuses and postpone their decision until it no longer mattered.

Then, for the first time since Heidi petitioned the ethics committee, Dr. Dawson spoke to her. "I've notified your sister's doctor that Timmy's condition has been downgraded to extremely critical. However, in his opinion, she isn't emotionally well enough to see him."

Disbelief froze her into utter stillness.

He coughed and backed away at her reaction. "In the morning we'll have to put him back on dialysis, although I can't offer you any hope that it will improve his condition."

"Then why do it? Hasn't Timmy suffered enough? He's in such distress when he's on that machine." She couldn't contain her anguish. It trembled through her body and spilled out into her voice.

For the very first time she saw a flicker of emotion on his face. "It will all be over soon, Miss Allan."

Wordlessly she stared at him. He started to say something else but instead looked away, shaking his head before he left her.

Silence settled into the room. The silence of the hospital at rest: patients asleep, visitors gone, fewer staff, quietly at their duties. Late at night, like this, it was as if she and Timmy were all alone in their own special world.

She touched his hand and he slowly lifted eyes that now appeared huge in his shrunken face. He was so frail that she could see his veins starkly blue beneath his translucent skin.

Timmy was going to die. The finality of it shocked her. She should have been ready to hear it, but she wasn't. It seared through her, burning her throat so that it was hard to breathe.

At last she was sure.

She couldn't let him die like this, here in this sterile, impersonal room with the distinct hospital odors and the sounds of machines. She'd made a promise to herself and to Faith weeks ago. There would be at least one moment of freedom, one instant of joy for their baby before he died.

The park beckoned to her in the moonlight. She stared out the window, then back at Timmy. He wasn't sleeping, yet wasn't fussing. He looked up at her with eyes that had never seen anything of beauty or life. She had promised never to give up hope. Now she faced the absolute certainty that there was no hope left.

There was only one thing she could give Timmy.

Carefully peeling back the tape, she removed the ventilator tube. She held her breath, only beginning to breathe again when she saw that Timmy was doing the same.

His lightness terrified her; he was nearly weightless in her arms. But it was wonderful to hold him again, with no tubes or machines, nothing to lock them into this room. She pressed her lips to his forehead.

Checking carefully both ways down the hall, she made sure the nurses were occupied before making her escape to the stairwell.

It was a typical midwest summer night, and the air softly caressed her skin, soothing and welcoming. She had never noticed the flower beds in the park. Now the fragrance of roses and lilies wafted delicately on the breeze.

"Doesn't it smell wonderful, Timmy?" she whispered, pushing back his blanket as they settled onto the glider. "Look. There's a full moon, and all those little lights are millions and millions of stars."

His eyes were wide, looking up into the sky. His head moved ever so slowly from side to side as the breeze bore the scent of the wonders of nature.

It wasn't fair! The rage she had suppressed for months threatened to escape. She couldn't allow it. This was Timmy's only glimpse of the world, and she must make it perfect for him.

Gently rocking the glider, she whispered the words of lullabies...songs her mother had sung to her, songs she had taught Faith. Her voice broke, cracking more and more as she sang, but Timmy didn't seem to mind. He just stared up at her with his huge blue eyes.

Then he made a funny little movement with his mouth, and this time Heidi knew it really was a smile.

Tilting back her head, she could no longer control her pain or her tears. She held nothing back as she cradled Timmy in her arms, humming brokenly, gently rocking, until at last his eyes, filled with the wonder of the night sky, closed.

CHAPTER TWO

LUKE JEFFERSON WALKED into his younger brother's apartment and stopped dead in his tracks. It smelled like a pigsty. In the sink grease congealed around a stack of dirty dishes, and food rotted on the kitchen table.

God! He was too exhausted to face this! He'd only been home twenty-four hours. Six months in South America working eighteen-hour days to make a dent in a system that fought him every inch of the way had drained even his extraordinary energy. But it had been worth it; both activists were out of prison and free, or as free as they could be under the circumstances.

Maybe before he decided on his next case he should take a little time off and reacquaint himself with life's little pleasures while he still remembered what they were. Cleaning up his brother's mess wasn't one of them, but he'd never been able to turn down his mother. She had been frantic about Peter's disappearance, and Luke had promised to fly from Chicago to Champaign immediately, take care of the two months' back rent the landlord demanded and look into Peter's whereabouts.

From the look of the place, Peter hadn't been home for longer than that. A quick check of the closets revealed what Luke already suspected: Peter was gone, off on another of his spur-of-the-moment gallivantings. Damn him! Just like him to think of no one but himself!

Kicking some old newspapers out of his way, Luke prowled around looking for a hint as to where his brother might have gone this time. Suddenly he remembered the last time he'd seen Peter. As usual they had been fighting.

"You're not my keeper, Luke!" Peter had sneered, pacing Luke's office like a caged animal. "I don't have to jump every time you snap your fingers. Why the hell did I have to come here for another of your lectures?"

"Peter, I don't want to fight with you," Luke had sighed, trying to control his own temper by relaxing back into his swivel chair. "I'm just concerned about your future. So is Mom. Are you going to stay in school and finish the semester?"

Peter's careless shrug had brought Luke to his feet.

"What kind of an answer is that! When are you going to grow up?"

A funny look crossed Peter's young face—a face much like Luke's, but without the strength and determination. "I may be more grown-up than you think."

"What exactly does that mean?" Luke demanded.

"I mean I don't know what I'm going to do!" Peter answered. "Maybe I'll hitchhike across America. Maybe I'll be a fisherman in Alaska. Maybe I'll do anything I damn well please!"

"You're wasting your life, Peter." Luke heard the disgust tinge his words but couldn't repress it.

"Maybe some of us don't want to be on the fast track. Maybe some of us don't want to have our own law firm when we're thirty and run all over the world being 'Crusader Lawyer.' Maybe some of us want to live. And maybe it's none of your business!"

His face flushed beet-red beneath curly blond hair, and resentment flashed from his blue eyes. Luke wanted to take those slim shoulders and shake some sense into him, but instead turned away. "Fine. I wash my hands of you!"

The office door slammed, and Luke wearily threaded his fingers through his wavy blond hair, rubbing the temple, where just a smattering of gray was beginning to show. He didn't have any more time for the kid; this job in South America was too important. He had to concentrate on getting his clients out of prison. Peter's problems would have to wait. When he got back, he'd talk to him again, he had decided.

But now he couldn't even find him!

Ticked off at his brother and angry with himself for getting involved, once again, where Peter wouldn't want him, Luke continued to search the apartment but found nothing.

The only thing left was a mound of mail, most of it junk, piled up beneath the slot in the door. For just an instant he hesitated. There had always been an unspoken bond between the brothers that kept them from crossing the invisible line between concern and interference.

But even as he vacillated he noticed a small blue envelope sticking out among the pile of third-class mail, magazines and advertisements. It was written in a neat, feminine hand. He tapped the letter thoughtfully against his palm, noticing the postmark. It was five months old.

He made his decision. Ripping open the envelope, he began to read.

"Damn!"

Seeing it, rereading it again and again, Luke still couldn't believe it. Peter couldn't know, he told himself! But, according to this letter, Peter did know, and he'd left town, anyway.

When Luke found him, he'd flay him alive for this! He could hear the desperate plea in the words of this terrified young girl about to have a baby. Peter's baby!

Anger rolled over him, and he took a deep breath. Maybe, for once, Peter had done the right thing. Maybe he'd gone to be with the girl who was having his child.

He turned the letter over. It was simply signed Faith. No last name. Impatiently he picked the envelope up and, miraculously, there was a return address—in Bloomington, only about an hour away. If he left immediately, he might find this girl and a new niece or nephew. And, hopefully, Peter.

HEIDI SAT in the glider, the baby in her arms quiet. She sang her favorite lullaby from *Mary Poppins,* the one that insisted the children weren't tired and should stay awake. The glider moved in time, gently, smoothly, back and forth.

The stars twinkled at her as the song ended, and she looked down at Timmy, safe in her arms. She heard footsteps sound behind her and held a hand up, signaling silence. Faith, smiling, came around the side of the glider. She leaned forward to take her son.

He wiggled in Heidi's arms and reached for his mother. "Mm...mmm," he gurgled.

The imp! He hadn't been asleep at all. He'd only been fooling...fooling...

Heidi awoke to the taste of salt on her lips. Tears of joy! Timmy was better.

Then an insidious drip from the faucet in the corner intruded into her happiness.

Drip...drip.

Her pillowcase was damp. Uneasily she moved her head from side to side.

Drip...drip.

The last remnant of the dream fled, taking with it her moment of joy.

Timmy wasn't better. Timmy was dead. And Faith was still in the hospital. She didn't know if Faith was better or worse. She hadn't seen her since the trial. And she was in prison. Elmwood Women's Prison.

Fresh tears sprang to her eyes, but she dashed them away, blinking into the darkness. It was early. The officer wouldn't be here for at least an hour yet. Then the routine would begin. A short walk to the showers, then back to this small room to wait for another test or interview or examination. The information required by this place was formidable. They wanted to know everything about her: her childhood, her relationships, her health, her state of mind, her hopes, her dreams, her plans. Pretty soon they'd have it all—and she'd have nothing left.

They wanted to determine where she fitted into the system. According to the officer, it would take another week to place her.

At times it didn't seem real. She'd been locked in this room for one whole week, and it still didn't seem possible.

Officer Needham was friendly enough and offered encouragement in subtle ways, giving her bits of information and advice, such as "Just fit in." "Don't make trouble." "Don't ask questions."

But Heidi had no questions to ask. The psychologists had determined that she wasn't a threat to anyone. She'd be given a roommate in medium or minimum security. Another person in a room this small, with a toilet and sink and no privacy. Just a door to lock them in together. Even so, being forced to share cramped quarters with a stranger would be better than remaining in this cell alone.

Being alone gave her too much time to think. She wanted to be busy. She wanted to forget the anguish of Timmy's funeral and Faith's continued illness.

That pain had carried her through all the legal proceedings, numbing her to everything except her lawyer's protests when she insisted on pleading guilty. She had known exactly what she was doing for Timmy. She would make no excuses for what she had done out of love. Her lawyer's loud objections had been overruled, and the judge had had no choice but to sentence her.

She was guilty. She knew that and accepted it. She was guilty of keeping her promise to Faith, of giving Timmy a brief moment of happiness. For that she had always been willing to face the consequences.

She had done the right thing. She would do it again, even knowing how it would end.

Then why did she still have the dream?

Suddenly restless, she flung back the sheet, sat up and slid out of bed. The tile floor was damp and cool on her bare feet as she padded to the sink and pulled the light chain above it. She splashed cold water on her face before burying it in a small white towel which, although worn, smelled fresh and clean. Automatically she glanced up, but there was no mirror above the sink. It was just as well. She wasn't sure she'd like to see how she looked. No one in Chicago would be likely to recognize this Heidi as the sophisticated chanteuse she had been. Even her hair had been cut short for easy maintenance.

Maybe here at Intake, as Officer Needham called it, there couldn't be any mirrors. Maybe "they" were afraid the new inmates would hurt themselves out of despair or rage. But, she reminded herself, this wasn't like the Hollywood B movies of the fifties. This was clean and neat and...adequate. No one threatened her and she wasn't chained behind iron bars; this wasn't a snake pit.

She turned, looking into the small room that had been her home for the past week. The bed was a standard twin, and there were shelves for her personal items, such as were allowed her. There was even a desk with a light on the wall over it. It was better than she had envisioned, if she had envisioned anything through her mind-numbing grief.

She accepted that this effectively administrated institution was systematically and carefully running her through "the system." She had to accept that. What she couldn't accept was the nightly dream.

Sagging against the edge of the tiny sink, she closed her eyes. It was easier to deal with the reality that she would pay her debt to society by being locked away from her family, her friends, her life, than to deal with the emotions behind the dream.

LUKE GLANCED at his watch. It was almost five. If traffic wasn't bad, he might be able to find the house by dinnertime. And if Peter wasn't there with Faith, at least he could help her out. For some inexplicable reason he was anxious to see the baby.

He was an uncle. The thought made him smile. It was good to have something to be happy about besides his work.

He stopped at the second red light on the outskirts of Bloomington. The gas station attendant gave him directions.

Pulling back out into traffic, he finally realized what he was doing. He'd actually driven here to Bloomington without a plan of action. Organization was his life! He lived by a schedule and goals and spent his life trying to make things right, to make the world the kind of place it should be. His life was really quite simple and he lived it accordingly; injustice was intolerable and Luke tried to do his part to rectify it where he could. Damn it, why couldn't he fix what was wrong with his relationship with Peter!

The car behind him honked, and Luke turned onto the access road leading to 1465 Richmond. There was a For Sale sign in front of the neat Tudor. Faith must live with her parents; this neighborhood was too expensive for a young girl alone.

Dusk and the proliferation of huge oak trees darkened the street, but the house was unlit. Luke determined to give it an hour; if no one showed up, he'd check into a motel for the night and call in the morning.

Every time the headlights of a car appeared around the corner Luke sat up straighter, but none stopped at 1465.

Leaning his head back against the seat, he stared through half-closed eyes at the house. He was acting like a damn fool! There was always the chance that Peter's Faith didn't live here any longer. There was certainly no sign of a baby anywhere. There was even the chance Peter wasn't the father of this child. Perhaps his brother had run away for a good reason. But the letter in his pocket refuted that idea. It wasn't the letter of an experienced woman who knew the score. There was an underlying naïveté in her words that bespoke sincerity.

It was really the tone of that letter that had sent him hell-bent-for-leather on this chase after the baby. That, and some vague premonition he couldn't even explain. Maybe it was just jet lag. Maybe the strain of the past six months was finally catching up with him. Maybe he just needed a good night's sleep.

He settled deeper into the seat, trying to formulate the best scenario. Was springing himself on Faith and her family really fair, especially if Peter hadn't lived up to his responsibilities? Should he go away and call, giving them a chance to get used the idea of his visit?

Luke glanced again at his watch. Time to call it a night, anyway. The house sat silent and empty of life. Yawning, he started the engine. Logic told him to find a place to stay and start fresh in the morning.

The Sunset Lodge was clean and spacious. There was plenty of hot water for a long shower, and room service delivered dinner. Wrapped in a bath towel, he ate it while he sprawled across the bed with the phone at his ear. After the fifteenth ring of the sixth call, he gave up. No answering machine. Nothing.

Well, there was nothing to do now but wait for morning. But in the morning he was definitely going to make sure the child was getting the proper care. Regardless of what his brother was up to, Luke would make sure this girl and the baby didn't suffer because of him.

His body ached with fatigue, but his mind wouldn't let him rest. The hours ticked away on the bedside clock, and still he tossed and twisted beneath the sheet. Shutting his eyes, he willed his mind to let go, but it refused, replaying again and again his final scene with Peter. Had he known about the baby then? If so, why hadn't he told Luke?

Just before dawn he was still staring blankly at the ceiling, trying to work out exactly what he would do upon his return to 1465 Richmond. After a shower and a cup of coffee in the lodge café, he decided there was only one thing to do. If he left now, he'd be at the house in ten minutes. He wanted to do this face-to-face, not over the phone. Eight might be a little early for an unannounced visit, but he could wait no longer.

His impatience was rewarded. A black Jaguar with a Chicago sticker sat in the driveway.

He jabbed twice at the doorbell before the dark wooden door was flung open. Whatever he'd expected, it wasn't this!

A huge man filled the doorway, not old enough to be Faith's father, but probably too old to be her husband. Belligerence blazed from his eyes. "What do you want? And let me just say that if you're a reporter, I'll have you arrested for trespassing," the man snarled, his wide face scarlet beneath salt-and-pepper hair.

Luke did what he always did when faced with adversity: he met it head-on. He thrust out his hand. "I'm Luke Jefferson, Peter's brother."

The man's face changed, all color fading except the dark shadows that indicated he hadn't yet shaven. Slowly Luke let his hand fall back to his side. The man just stood in the doorway staring at him.

"I've come to see Faith Allan," Luke said at last, his patience worn thin with fatigue. "Is she at home?"

"Is she at home?" the man repeated, still staring at him. "Aren't you a little late?"

Instinctively Luke went on the defensive. "I just found Faith's letter. I assume Peter's not here. Regardless of that, I'm here to help. I've come to see Faith and the baby."

At last he seemed to get through to the guy, who stepped back and motioned Luke into the house.

"Come in," he said gruffly.

Early-morning light streamed through French doors at the end of the living room. The walls were light yellow and cheerful. A brick fireplace flanked by overflowing bookcases dominated one wall. The Oriental blue-and-yellow chintz couch was comfortably worn. This was a nice house. He needn't have worried that Faith and Peter's child was in need. If they lived here, they were comfortable.

Then he noticed the boxes, some already packed and labeled, others still empty, scattered everywhere.

He turned to the man who had taken a stance in front of the mantel, his legs spread, his arms folded across his wide chest. The awkward silence lengthened as they stared at each other.

Luke worked out every day, but this guy was hefty enough to play for the Bears. He wondered if Faith lived here with this guy, after all.

"I'm David DeVries, a family friend. I'd like to know why you've come now, after all this time." The tone was crisp and held the same edge of anger Luke had heard in his own voice.

Luke pulled out the letter. "As I said, I just found out. I haven't spoken to Peter in more than six months, so I didn't know about Faith."

Reaching out, David took the letter, scanned it and thrust it back at him. "Faith isn't here," he said coldly.

He was being deliberately evasive. Luke's defensive edge once again veered toward anger. "Perhaps I could speak to someone in her family then."

The giant shifted ominously. "The only family Faith has is her sister Heidi, who is also unavailable."

Luke had never cared for double-talk. Why was DeVries being so difficult? Luke fought down his anger and focused on a calm, considered line of questioning, much as he used against hostile witnesses.

"Could you at least tell me what's going on here?" He looked pointedly at one of the boxes.

"It's really not your concern, Mr. Jefferson. I've been authorized to sell Heidi and Faith's parents' home. I'm just packing a few things, so if you'll excuse me, I have a lot to do."

Perversely Luke sank down on the blue-and-yellow couch. "I'm not leaving, Mr. DeVries, until you tell me where I can find Faith and the baby. I believe it's my right as Peter's brother to know the whereabouts of the child."

"Your brother doesn't recognize Faith's claim, so you really have no rights at all."

David's tone was bland, but Luke realized there was something going on he should know about. Yet DeVries was right. Peter had walked away, damn him! Desertion abrogated rights. Still, he hadn't come here just to walk away.

"Believe me, I regret Peter's actions and that so much time has passed," he said quietly. "I only want to speak with Faith and see the baby. Was it a boy or a girl?''

''A boy.''

Luke couldn't help smiling. He'd be a good uncle for a boy. "What's his name?''

''Timmy.''

Luke saw something flicker in David's stony countenance. He'd seen that look on too many faces not to recognize it. He rose slowly to his feet, ready for DeVries's next words.

David shook his head, heaving a great sigh. "Jefferson, I regret to inform you that your nephew, Timothy Allan, died two months ago.''

He'd been right about the look, wrong about his ability to deal with it. Strange crawling sensations crept up his spine and down his arms and legs. Shock and disbelief quickly gave way to pain, then aching regret that he hadn't known sooner. Two months ago his nephew had been alive. Now he was dead. And Luke would never have the chance to see him.

"How?'' he asked, his voice a thread of sound.

Strangely enough David shifted out of his aggressive stance and folded his hands behind his back. "He had a degenerative condition diagnosed shortly after birth.''

Turning so David couldn't see his face, Luke paced to the French doors and stared blankly out at the flagstone patio. "What about Faith?''

"She's in a hospital recovering from severe postpartum depression complicated by Timmy's death.''

Guilt joined the feelings warring inside him. "Can't I talk to Heidi then?'' Luke asked, swinging around. "I'd like to know about my nephew. I want to understand everything that's happened.''

"You can't," David choked out, his jaw clenched.

"What do you mean I *can't?*" The vague premonition that had driven him here flashed bright and cold. There was something more going on. "I need to see someone. Talk to someone."

David's only answer was a hard stare, the veins in his neck cording into knots.

"No matter what Peter did, surely I have a right to find out about my nephew!" Luke bit out through a red haze of anger and frustration.

"You can't see her," David repeated coldly.

His stony facade only fueled Luke's determination. "Look, I'm an attorney and if you won't cooperate, I'm prepared to take legal action."

"That won't do you any good. You can't reach Heidi in prison unless she wants to see you. And I assure you, she doesn't!" David said flatly.

"Prison!" Luke's numb mind couldn't quite handle the new curve DeVries had thrown him. "For God's sake, why?"

Without answering, David walked abruptly away, back through the foyer to the front door, and Luke followed automatically.

"DeVries, I need some answers!"

"I've already told you more than I needed to." David flung the door open. "You're too late. There's nothing more to say. Goodbye, Mr. Jefferson."

This time Luke braced his legs and folded his arms across his chest. "I'm not leaving until I get the truth. Short of tossing me out, you don't have many options."

David's laugh was mirthless. "I wouldn't lay a hand on you, Jefferson, but I'd be happy to have the cops haul your ass out of here."

"Go ahead. Maybe I'll get some answers from them. What the hell did this sister do? Murder someone?"

Luke braced himself for the blow he saw coming, but instead David slammed his fist into the wall inches from his face.

"You son of a bitch!" David's scarlet face twisted in rage. "What kind of game are you playing? Heidi didn't murder the poor kid. She ended Timmy's suffering and gave him a moment of happiness."

Stunned, Luke didn't resist when David shoved him through the door. "Now get out of here!"

For a full five minutes Luke stood frozen outside the paneled wooden door. He wasn't stupid. Why couldn't he grasp what David DeVries had implied, that Heidi Allan, Faith's own sister, had somehow caused the death of her own . . . his . . . nephew. And had gone to prison for killing him.

CHAPTER THREE

THE RHYTHM of the music was inside her, flowing through her arms and her legs, giving them life, movement. She was one with the beat, a part of its magic. Angel never felt so alive as when she danced.

"Hey, Ramon, give us a break, will ya!"

Angel Ramon opened her eyes to stare at the seven women laboriously trying to follow her movements. She blinked and stopped. For just an instant she'd been back at St. Bart's with Miss Juliette—not here at Elmwood.

She paused long enough for Maxime to flip off the record player. In the silence all the women groaned, collapsing on the tile floor of the all-purpose room.

"I've been shoutin' at ya for five minutes to slow down." Maxime already had a lit cigarette dangling from her mouth. "This here's jazzacise, not a friggin' marathon."

Angel laughed, flinging a towel around her damp neck. "If you'd give up those coffin nails, you wouldn't move like a slug."

The other women sniggered but shut up quickly when Maxime glared in their direction. Smiling at Angel, she inhaled deeply and, pursing her lips, let the smoke out slowly. "But, babe, in this joint, it's my only pleasure. Unless you want to make me an offer I can't refuse." She winked, glancing at the other women, gauging their reactions.

Today Angel was in no mood for Maxime's games. "Give it a rest," she sighed, leaning over to touch her toes. "You guys better cool down or you'll be stiff tomorrow," she warned the women sprawled across the floor.

"I ain't never moving again," Letty groaned, pushing to a sitting position as she brushed thin gray hair off her forehead. "I'm too old for this stuff, Angel. I'm asking the warden if I can spend my rec time in a wheelchair sipping tea."

Reaching out a hand, Angel yanked Letty to her feet. "You're never too old to exercise. You'll live longer."

"Yeah, Letty. Ya'll be real healthy the next time yure up before the parole board. The cops will be so friggin' impressed ya might get outta here again."

The older, smaller woman shrank away as Maxime swaggered toward her. Angel stepped between them.

Maxime could bully anyone who would let her, but not here. This class was Angel's pat on the back for four years of good citizenship. A model prisoner, Warden Howell had called her. Angel's mom would be proud if she were still alive. Maybe that was why Angel had done it: to somehow make up for the years her mom had worried, the bad years that had landed her in this dump.

She faced Maxime with her hands on her hips and her chin thrust out. She'd known lots of bullies growing up on Chicago's South Side.

"Pick on someone else, Maxime."

"Babe, I'm quakin' in my sneakers," Maxime twittered, rolling her eyes and shaking her broad shoulders. "My right thigh weighs more than you do."

It was true that Maxime was a behemoth and could easily knock her over with one swing of those beefy arms, but it was also true that Santos and the gang had taught Angel some particularly nasty tricks, and Maxime knew it. Angel had used them four years ago to make it clear she wasn't interested in Maxime's brand of friendship.

"Maxime, even you aren't dumb enough to try that again." Angel spoke softly so the others couldn't hear.

Maxime caught her meaning. She hesitated, her pale blue eyes shifting beneath colorless lashes.

"Yeah, you remember real good, don't you?" Angel sneered. Maxime's eyes snapped with hatred, but it was better that she take on Angel than poor old Letty.

Only a week back from detox, with twelve months added to her sentence for breaking her parole by robbing a store for fix money, Letty was in no condition to go a round with Maxime. Not that Angel particularly liked Letty, but she was nowhere near as bad as Maxime. And she refused to let the fat pig screw up the one hour a day she could dance.

"What's going on here, ladies?" Officer Connell stood in the open doorway, a ring of keys in her hand. No one had noticed the guard unlocking the door as Angel and Maxime faced off.

"Hey, ya just missed Angel dancin', Officer Connell. She's a regular primo ballerino," Maxime shouted across the room.

Officer Connell adjusted her glasses and sent Angel a long look. Angel ignored it, glancing away and pretending to retie her gym shoes. Maxime wasn't worth making trouble for. She could handle her, no problem. What really worried her was the pink slip tucked into her jean pocket. Why did the warden want to see her today?

"Okay, ladies, class is over. Barb, Violet, Sally and Chloe, you're due at the kitchen in ten minutes. Maxime, Letty and Doreen, it's time for your shift at the shirt works." Officer Connell's crisp commands brought everyone to their feet as they prepared to file out.

Routine. That was what prison taught you. Everyone had a job, everyone knew where they were supposed to be every hour of the day, day after day, week after week. Angel didn't even mind anymore. It was sort of nice, comfortable even, to know how each day would go. Now that she had her GED and didn't go to high school anymore, she went to a college course in music and taught this class. Every day except Sunday was the same, so why change it?

But today, instead of going to the Watkin State Continuing Education Building, she was being led into the administration building, past the two secretaries and into Warden Howell's small office.

The warden looked up and motioned Angel to sit down.

Warden Howell was a tough dame, but fair. Maybe that was why Angel had decided to cooperate with the system—because the warden played fair. It was the first time in her life Angel had known this kind of security. If she didn't screw up, nobody was gonna beat her up or lock her in a closet for no reason. Nobody was gonna make her steal to eat.

"How are your classes going, Angel? I understand Letty attended today." Warden Howell settled back in her chair, pinning Angel with clear brown eyes. "How did she do?"

"She's weak from detox." Angel shrugged. "Letty'll be all right."

"Good." Leaning forward, the warden folded her hands on her desk. "Angel, I called you here to tell you how pleased we are with your exercise classes and your involvement with Howell's Helpers."

Angel allowed her shoulders to relax. Hell, this was no problem! Warden Howell was thanking her for doing what she loved. Angel hadn't volunteered for the warden's pet project to gain points. She liked entertaining the inmates' kids so the girls could spend time with their men. She was teaching two of Doreen's girls ballet positions. Not that she was one of those goody-goody types. She never did anything except to benefit herself. It was the only way to survive here, and on the outside.

"I like helping with the kids," Angel said because Warden Howell had fallen silent and was looking at her as if she expected Angel to say something.

"Well, it shows. Because of your record here and your involvement with the program I'm recommending you for the Honor Cottage."

Angel went limp with shock. The Honor Cottage was the prize here at Elmwood! There were no bolts on the bedroom doors, and you weren't locked in your room every night at 10:00 sharp. You could stay up and watch The Tonight Show if you wanted, or even make popcorn in the tiny kitchen. You could do your laundry whenever you wanted, because the cottage had its own washer and dryer. But best of all, your weekend visitors were allowed in the cottage lounge. It was a privilege, that privacy—a real treat for the married inmates to pretend for a day they lived like normal people. They could cook for their family, or picnic; and if they were careful, they could steal five minutes alone in their rooms. Angel didn't have a family, and there was no way she would let Santos know if he ever showed his face again. But she wanted the Honor Cottage, the sense of freedom, that tiny moment of privacy.

"When?" Angel asked, still not quite taking it in. There was only one lock in the Honor Cottage—on the front door. When she got out of here, she was never going to lock another thing as long as she lived.

"I'm afraid there's one problem. I would like you to move in with Coralee, but she's still not well enough from her chemotherapy treatments. It may be another six weeks or so, but I wanted you to know it's coming. Meanwhile, your new roommate will be moving in today."

Angel's shoulders grew tense again. She'd been lucky so far; Joan had been her only roommate, and they'd gotten along fine right up until her release last week. She and Joan had kept their own space—friendly but distant. That was how Angel liked it. What if she got an animal like Maxime?

Disappointment made her bold. "Since I'll be moving soon, anyway, why do I have to get a new roommate?"

Warden Howell smiled, pushing herself to her feet, and Angel scrambled up to face her. "There are no private rooms here, Angel. You know the routine. Your new roommate's name is Heidi Allan. I'll notify you about the Honor Cottage."

Two thoughts whirled through Angel's mind on the way back to her room. She nearly had the Honor Cottage in her hands; she'd have to be very careful not to mess it up. Somehow the grapevine always knew this

kind of stuff, and there were plenty who would try to
screw this up for her. And she'd heard about Heidi Allan through that same grapevine. She was a rich high-
class socialite here for killing some kid or something
like that. Angel hadn't paid much attention. She
should have. The more she knew, the better she could
use her to best advantage. Allan probably had tons of
money. That could mean stuff from the concession
stand in the visitors' hall. Maybe she even had a radio.
Angel had never had one in her room like most of the
girls. Hell, Angel had always been one of the poorest
kids on the street, and nothing had changed, not even
in this place.

IT WAS A SMALL SCRAP of comfort, but at last Heidi
was given her own things. She hugged the bundle of
clothes to her chest. The ten outfits she'd been allowed to bring from home had been returned to her
after the two-week evaluation. Now she could discard
the uniform of blue flower-print cotton slacks and
matching overtop.

   She hesitated, glancing around the small room. Both
bunk beds were neatly made. A toothbrush and paste
were stuck in a glass on the tiny enamel sink. To the left
and right of the sink shelves were built in to hold personal belongings. The left side held a hairbrush, and
there was a bottle of shampoo on the top shelf and a
small pile of white underwear, one pair of jeans and
two blue flowered cotton uniform tops on the middle
shelf. The bottom shelf was empty. Someone lived
here, but there wasn't one personal touch—no picture, no bottle of perfume, nothing to give Heidi a clue
as to what she might be like.

"Here they are now," Officer Needham said, turning away with a rattle of keys as two people walked down the hall toward them.

One was a tall woman wearing beige uniform pants and shirt. The other was a petite girl who instantly reminded Heidi of Faith. She had the same thick black hair falling around a small face filled with large brown eyes. But there was no hint of Faith's confused softness about the frank, hard look Angel Ramon gave her.

"Hi, Connell. I'm turning over Heidi Allan to you. She's Angel Ramon's new roommate."

Officer Needham handed some papers to the taller woman, and she nodded. "All right, ladies. You have an hour before dinner to start getting acquainted."

The two officers shut the door behind them, but Heidi didn't hear the bolt fall into place as it had at the evaluation center.

"Here in minimum security our rooms aren't locked until ten," Angel said as she flopped onto the lower bunk, continuing to study Heidi with wide, unrevealing eyes.

Heidi smiled, relaxing a little as she realized this girl had noticed her shock. "You mean we aren't locked in?" she asked, the heavy, sick feeling in her chest lifting slightly.

"Oh, yeah, but not till later. Except for the front door. That's always locked. But it's not like where you've come from. Bad, huh?"

Hesitating, Heidi returned Angel's gaze. She would be living with this girl in smaller and more intimate surroundings than she'd ever believed possible. She didn't want to start off by trying to second-guess Angel's motives. Heidi was willing to be friends. To tell the truth, she was desperate for it.

"Yes, it was bad to be isolated from everyone and everything," she said simply, waiting.

Nodding, Angel slipped off the bed and with amazing grace twirled around the room. "Such as it is, this is home. Top bunk is yours. There's plenty of shelf space for your things. Might as well move in."

Leaning against the sink, Angel watched as Heidi placed her ten pairs of slacks on one shelf and her ten cotton sweaters on another. But when Heidi pulled the radio out of the bag Office Needham had placed just inside the door, Angel straightened and glided toward her.

"You've got a radio!" A smile spread across her heart-shaped face, making her unexpectedly beautiful.

"It was on the list of things I could bring. Ten outfits, necessary toiletries in plastic containers, books, stationery. It said a radio was all right, and they let me keep it."

"Yeah, yeah, it's fine," Angel said quickly, reaching out. "Can I turn it on?"

"Sure." Heidi put it into her eager hands before organizing her few things on the shelves. She watched Angel's face as she tuned the radio. Finally she found a station she liked. To Heidi's surprise it wasn't rock, thank goodness, but a station playing old favorites. She wondered why the girl was here but realized that asking would be a breach of prison etiquette.

Angel closed her eyes, swaying to Henry Mancini's "Moon River." When it finished, she lifted her heavy lashes and laughed. "I love this old stuff. After Miss Juliette left, I used to practice my dancing by watching old musicals on the TV set at St. Bart's Urban Center."

"Miss Juliette was your dance teacher?" Heidi asked carefully, easing onto the side of Angel's bunk, hoping she wouldn't mind.

Angel didn't even notice. She reverently placed the radio on her own top shelf near the sink. "Yeah, she was a real Avenue Strect Dancer. She volunteered at St. Bart's for four years. How'd you know?" she asked, doing a complicated two-step to a Herb Alpert tune.

"Miss Juliette sounds like a dance teacher. My voice and piano teacher was Madame Romonov. It seems they all fit their names."

"You a singer?" Heidi had finally gotten Angel's full attention again.

"Yes, I sing and play the piano." In my old life, Heidi suddenly realized. Here, what was she?

"Hey, I'm a dancer, so I guess we're a pretty good match. You know you can volunteer for Howell's Helpers. The kids would love being sung to."

"Howell's Helpers?" Heidi shook her head, confused, but there was no mistaking the eagerness on Angel's young face.

"Yeah, it's this program the warden started in the visitors' hall. See, all prisoners can have visitors two days a week. You might have one person each day or twenty. So if there are lots of kids, the place gets crazy. After they visit their moms for a while, the kids go into this little room the warden set up and some of us entertain them so their moms can visit with their men and stuff. We play games and I teach them to dance. Maybe you could teach them to sing. There's an old piano in there."

Angel's enthusiasm gave her a first ray of hope. The pain and confusion of the past six months had deadened all of her emotions but fear. Two-week lockup had intensified that fear. How well, really, would she deal with being locked away? Would she lose her identity in this regimented, sterile world? Now at least she could still sing. If this young girl had survived, and even made a life here, so could she.

"There's the buzzer for dinner." Reluctantly turning the radio off, Angel motioned her to follow. "Come on. At dinner we'll tell Connell you want to sign up for Howell's Helpers."

Heidi dutifully followed Angel down the stairs and stood in single file with other women until the front door was unlocked and Officer Connell led them across the yard into the dining hall.

Angel urged her toward the cafeteria line. Heidi was stunned by the noise of nine hundred women all talking at once, the clatter of silverware and dishes on plastic trays, the scrape of hundreds of chairs across the linoleum floor, all reverberating off the concrete-block walls and the vaulted ceiling.

Somehow she found herself at the end of the food line, her plate, divided like a TV dinner tray, loaded with beef and noodles, apple sauce and two pieces of white bread with a pat of margarine on each.

Still disoriented, she felt a rush of panic when she lost sight of Angel, who appeared suddenly, waving from behind a tall, skinny woman. Heidi followed quickly and found Angel had made room for them both at the end of one of the long tables.

"Bad luck, Ramon. Guess you got the baby killer, huh?"

As if a fist had slammed into her chest, Heidi was robbed of oxygen, and she desperately tried to breathe. Quiet reigned in their small space as the few who had heard waited for her reaction. Desperately and quickly she had to decide what to do.

She looked up at her tormentor. The woman was enormous. Almost six feet tall, she had a firm heaviness bulging out of her red sweat suit. A broad grin split her ruddy face as her pale blue eyes rested on Angel.

Before Heidi could act Angel pushed back her chair and stood facing the larger woman, her chin thrust out defiantly. Briefly Heidi thought of David and Goliath. Then Angel said something to the woman in such a low voice that Heidi couldn't make it out. The stranger backed up, flicked Heidi a quick glance and moved away, pushing people aside to make her way to a table across the room.

Angel slid back into her place, glancing at Heidi. She shrugged. "Maxime's a pig."

"I didn't know what to say. Does everyone know?" she whispered, the weight in her chest increasing.

Angel stared at her frankly, with no softness in her expressive dark eyes. "You'll get used to it," she said simply, and then returned to her dinner.

The dining hall was back to normal before the guards even noticed the incident, and the noise grew around Heidi once again. But Heidi's heartbeat grew louder and louder in her ears, drowning out everything else. There was no escape for her. They all knew. And they wouldn't let her forget for a moment.

It still pierced her soul with a deadly shaft to be called a baby killer. A killer. A taker of life. She wasn't that. She'd never wanted Timmy to die; she'd prayed for a miracle. She'd wanted him to live, to do all the things other children did: grow and be strong, play baseball, go to the prom. But Timmy hadn't gotten a miracle. He'd just lain in that bed and suffered. Faith had looked at her with such pleading, had begged her to help her baby. She'd done the only thing she could.

Hadn't she?

For the first time a seed of doubt crept into her thoughts. Doubt that she had done the right thing. Doubt that she had given Timmy something valuable. Had she instead robbed Timmy of his chance for life—however brief? A wave of nausea washed over her, and she sat as far away from her tray as possible, but it was no use. The smell of food was all around her, as was the noise and shifting mass of women.

Did any of them doubt whether their crimes had been worth their loss of freedom? She'd said she would pay any price for what she had done for Timmy. For her own sanity she had to cling to the belief that she had made the right decision.

LUKE PROWLED from the front desk of the visitors' center through the rows of chairs where others waited to visit inmates of Elmwood Women's Prison. He headed toward the coffee machine. He wasn't going to leave until he had confronted the woman who had ended his nephew's life. Fumbling in his pocket, he found some change. The coffee tasted like ditch water, but he needed the caffeine. He hadn't slept in the forty-eight hours since David DeVries's words had changed his life. Luke was running on nothing but nerves. Maybe that was why he still couldn't accept the fact that he was too late.

One minute Luke had a nephew, the next he was gone as if he'd never existed. He'd thought he was teaching his brother a valuable lesson; instead his delay had kept him from finding his nephew in time to help.

Leaning against the concrete-block wall, Luke closed his eyes, letting his mind replay yesterday's interview with Dr. Dawson, Timmy's principal physician. The doctor had been cool and distant as he sat behind his desk and described Timmy's illness. He'd given him all the details but the important one. He had refused to discuss Heidi Allan, except to repeat what he had said during the hearing: "Miss Allan's abduction of her nephew from the hospital led to his death, albeit *probably* only by days."

Which left room for doubt, and that was what Luke couldn't deal with. He drew a newspaper clipping out of his inside jacket pocket. This was the one page he had copied from the *Bloomington Gazette* morgue. He stared down at the grainy three-column black-and-white picture of Heidi Allan splashed across the front page under sensational headlines: Singer Denies Life Support, Baby Dies. Thick bleached-blond hair fell past seductive shoulders, leading the eye to half-exposed breasts draped in a clinging evening dress. Her face was lovely but unreal, the makeup the sort of flawless perfection to be expected in a saloon singer's press kit. He looked at the tiny hospital picture of the newborn next to it. Innocence contrasted with experience.

He reread the story for the hundredth time; still it didn't make sense. Why would a woman who had apparently been devoted to Timmy decide to do what she'd done? There was no doubt she was guilty. She had said so herself, undoing all the good Charlie Goodman had accomplished in his brief. Charlie was a first-rate lawyer. Why had he let her plead guilty?

Why had he let her more or less convict herself, giving the judge no choice but to sentence her to the minimum—a year and a day in jail.

Even so, it rankled. Was that all his nephew's life was worth? If he'd been there, he'd have seen she was prosecuted for murder one!

Stunned at the rush of rage, he crumbled the plastic cup in his fist. Since when had he become judge and jury? Since it was his nephew she'd decided to terminate, he admitted, slamming the crushed cup into the nearest trash barrel.

"Sir..." A deep male voice caught his attention, and he looked up to find one of the guards motioning to him.

Luke moved quickly through the people standing in line at the desk. The guard handed him back the cards from Faith's sanatorium.

"Sorry it took so long, but since Heidi Allan only has two names on her visitor list, we had to clear you. She will see a representative from the hospital. Just take a seat until it's time."

Luke nodded, backing up two steps. He could hardly believe he was doing this—using a subterfuge to get in to see her. He knew there was a list of visitors for each prisoner, which they filed themselves. He didn't have time for the legal red tape to get in to see her against her will, and so he was practicing fraud by producing Dr. Vogland's card and explaining he was from Faith Allan's sanatorium. It wasn't a total lie—he had just come from there. But Dr. Vogland had refused to give him any information about Faith.

He needed to see Faith almost as much as he needed to see Heidi—to understand, to accept. The doctor told him he could see Faith only if Heidi approved it. He hoped that meant the girl was better. He hoped she wasn't emotionally scarred permanently because of his brother's irresponsibility. And his own. He'd known something was bothering Peter; why hadn't he followed up?

A loud buzzing noise startled him, and he glanced around. Everyone else seemed to know what was happening. They stood and lined up in front of a turnstile. He stepped behind a woman holding two little girls by their hands. They were dressed in short blue-and-white dresses that looked freshly starched, and they wore black patent shoes like those he had seen other little girls wear to parties, yet they were visiting someone in prison.

Luke realized he had been so determined to confront Heidi that he'd been blind to everything else. The eager anticipation of the two youngsters in front of him woke him up.

He took a careful look around. There were a hundred people waiting in line. There was no jostling, no complaining, not even from the children. Almost everyone wore that same look—it didn't matter what their age or sex was or even how well they were dressed. As a lawyer, he'd never noticed this side of prison life.

It was his turn at the turnstile. A guard stopped him and checked him with a metal detecting wand, then he was allowed to pass through the double glass doors into the visitors' hall.

A concession stand on his right was like a minidrug store, selling everything from candy bars to deodorant. Already it was jammed.

He made his way around that line and walked into a room that resembled a high school gymnasium, except it was filled with round tables surrounded by chairs.

He passed another guard, this one female, and stopped momentarily to survey the tables rapidly filling with people. At each a woman sat alone, the same eager anticipation on her face that he had noticed in the waiting room.

If he hadn't studied the newspaper picture a hundred times, he never would have recognized her.

She sat alone at a corner table. Her hair wasn't bleached blond, long and seductive now; it was more natural—a honey blond worn shorter, around her chin. The alluring breasts were covered by a demure green sweater. But the face was the same, he realized as he got closer: the wide-set hazel eyes fringed with thick lashes, the short nose, the pouty mouth colored now with only a light lip gloss.

She glanced up when he stopped in front of her. There was no anticipation on her face, only fear.

"Are you from the sanatorium? Is something wrong with Faith? Why didn't Dr. Vogland contact me personally?" she questioned rapidly, rising to her feet.

She was shorter than he had thought from her photo, and definitely more fragile. But it *was* the same woman. The woman who had arbitrarily decided it was time for Timmy to die.

"I'm not from the sanatorium. I'm Peter's brother, Luke Jefferson, and I've come to find out why you killed my nephew."

CHAPTER FOUR

HEIDI'S KNEES gave way beneath her, but she was able to catch the edge of the chair and prevent herself from sliding to the floor. Adrenaline surged through her, accelerating her heartbeat, making it difficult to breathe. In all her nightmares she had never foreseen facing someone from Peter's family. Peter was part of the distant past, before Timmy's illness, when she had been able to feel something besides pain and uncertainty. She vaguely remembered she had felt keen dislike for Peter. Maybe even hate. Hate and disgust.

Now the hate and disgust blazed from Luke Jefferson's intense blue eyes as he stood before her. But there was also pain. His lips were moving, saying something that animated his stern countenance, but she wasn't able to understand his words through the pounding of blood in her ears.

Suddenly his arm shot out, his long fingers fastening around her shoulder. His touch burned her, and instinctively she flinched away. Suddenly the activity around her intruded into her consciousness, and with it his words.

"Did you hear me? I'm Luke Jefferson. Peter's brother."

"Why are you here?" The words rasped through her hot, tight throat.

"You killed Timmy. I want to know why. No—I *need* to know!"

Anguished eyes confronted her. Timmy's eyes—the deep blue darkening to violet during moments of stress. Fascinated by those eyes, for an instant she couldn't respond.

"Say something! Tell me what happened, what made you do it." His words were rushed, pouring out of him as if he'd dammed them back until this moment. "Or is there no explanation for Timmy's death? No reason for ending an innocent baby's life." His voice trailed off as he finally sat, too, across the width of the table, drained of all emotion.

She stared blindly around the room, her eyes seeing nothing and everything—Doreen playing with two little girls in party dresses; Letty devouring a candy bar at the concession stand; Maxime sitting close to a heavyset woman in a dark dress; and Angel ushering a little boy into the playroom—all registered in her brain as she tried vainly to formulate her thoughts into words.

"You wouldn't understand," she finally said, somehow finding the strength to meet his agonized gaze. "You couldn't. You weren't there."

"Because you didn't tell us!" he bit out. "Didn't you think Peter's family would want to know? That we'd do everything in our power to help Timmy?"

"Peter left Faith, denied the baby was his. Legally—"

"Legally!" He leaned toward her, and she pressed back in the chair. "I'm a lawyer! I *know* my brother's rights. I would have assumed responsibility, made the right decision for my nephew's well-being. You denied me that opportunity."

She could do nothing but let his anger wash over her, his bitter words cutting deeply into her soul and tearing at the fraying threads of her confidence. First the dream had undermined her, now his words...

"Peter may have acted like an idiot, but what made you think his family wouldn't care? If I had known, I would have found a doctor who could help him. But you cheated me of that chance. Who gave you the right to decide it was time for Timmy to die?"

His words brought her to her feet. He'd never understand, that much was clear. But she had to try, had to defend her sense of honor.

"I did everything because I loved him."

Slowly he rose to stare silently into her face.

"I loved him!" she repeated, her words urgent. "I loved him more than anything in this world."

"And that gave you the right to let him die." Luke's response was deadly quiet.

Stepping back, away from the waves of his anger, Heidi shook her head. "You don't understand how it was." She turned, unable to deal with him and her own doubts, her only thought to escape.

"Heidi!"

At her name she automatically looked back.

"I'll be back. This isn't over yet."

His stare was filled with hostility, but somehow she found the strength to lift her chin and answer him evenly. "They won't let you in unless you're on my list."

"I think it would be in Faith's best interest if you saw me again," he said, and she was stunned into moving closer to answer him.

"Faith? What do you know about Faith?" she asked eagerly, almost forgetting he was her adversary.

"I know she's getting better. I've been to the sanatorium. I'd like to help her, to make up for Peter. You owe me that much."

Heidi sagged against the back of the chair. She didn't know what to think. "How can you help her? Why would you want to? You don't know her."

"I know my brother is partially responsible for everything that's happened. You cheated me out of the chance to help Timmy. Don't make the same mistake with Faith. You *owe* me, Heidi, and maybe you owe it to Faith, too." He reached into his jacket pocket, pulling out a business card and slapped it onto the table in front of her. "Think about it. I'll be back for your answer."

In a perverse kind of way she agreed with him, even understood his feelings. She had been so sure she needed nothing from Peter's family. She had been certain that she was doing the right thing, taking the right steps, making the right decision—for herself and Faith and Timmy. Had she been fair? She wasn't sure anymore. Of anything.

Maybe she did owe him and his family. Maybe by helping Faith he could heal the hurt and anger he felt. She didn't know what to do. Once she would have known. Now all she could feel was the same confusion she saw in Luke's eyes. That she understood too well.

Drawing herself together, she nodded. "I'll think about it."

His lips twisted in a quirk of acknowledgment before he turned away, threading his way through the tables and chairs. Heidi watched until he disappeared.

She was shaking inside and out. Wrapping her arms around her shoulders, she glanced around the room, straight into Maxime's pale-eyed stare.

She wanted to see Angel. She was surprised at how quickly and completely she was ready to trust her, still a stranger, when she was so wary of the man who had just been here—a man to whom she felt tied by blood. Timmy was the invisible bond between them, yet she knew that because of Timmy Luke Jefferson would always be her enemy.

Where was Angel? She needed to be anchored by Angel's knowledge of this place and these people who were becoming so important in her life: placid Doreen with three kids left behind at her mother's; Letty, sweet grandmotherly Letty, who swore like a sailor and desired nothing but the dreamlike status drugs offered her; and Maxime, who struck cold fear in Heidi's stomach. Although Maxime hadn't said a word to her since that first dinner a week ago, she always seemed to be there, watching.

Heidi crossed the room to the folding accordion doors that separated the visiting hall from the space set aside for the children. Pushing the door back, she burst into the playroom. Only two children looked up; the rest were totally engrossed in Angel.

She was dancing to a heavy Latin beat, her movements quick and athletic, yet so full of grace and beauty that Heidi was mesmerized. For a few minutes Heidi forgot everything in the sheer enjoyment of Angel's gift. She was as good as, better, than most of the professional dancers Heidi had seen, and she told Angel just that.

"Yeah, you think so?" Angel laughed, flinging a towel around her neck. Taking a long sip of water, she gave Heidi a frank look over the rim of the plastic cup. "You all right? That guy your boyfriend or something?"

"What guy?" Heidi asked, beginning to feel safer here in this roomful of playing children.

"That guy who visited you today. Saw you two off in the corner." Smiling, Angel nudged her shoulder. "Not bad. Kinda looks like a young Robert Redford. Not bad at all."

"He's not my boyfriend!" Heidi snapped. Contrite at Angel's shocked expression, she shook her head. "I'm sorry. He's not my boyfriend. He's a relative of my . . . my nephew . . ." she stammered, rigidly holding her eyes open because if she blinked, the tears would overflow.

"Oh, yeah? Is he coming back to see you? Maybe he can get us some things from the concession stand. Maybe some perfume and some candy."

"Yes . . . he'll be back, but not soon. David will be here tomorrow. He'll get you whatever you need." Tears clouded her vision and slid down her cheeks.

"Hey, are you all right?" Angel asked, a fleeting softness in her hard brown eyes.

Flicking a hand over her face, Heidi nodded. "I'm all right. Don't worry about it."

But she wasn't all right. She might never be again. She could fool herself for just so long, and she'd stopped today. Her life would never go back to normal.

She hid it well, even from Angel's shrewd eyes, and managed to smile as she played some simple songs for the children on the tinny, out-of-tune piano. She made conversation at dinner with Doreen and admired the pictures her mother had brought of her one-year-old son. But by the time the bolt on the door fell into place at ten, Heidi was exhausted from pretending everything was fine, and was already beneath the covers of her top bunk.

Below, Angel had the radio tuned to her favorite late-night station for golden oldies and was singing softly to herself.

Heidi closed her eyes. Suddenly it wasn't Angel singing softly.

Heidi was singing to Timmy in the park. She could feel the sweet, warm air on her face. Timmy was gazing at her out of alert blue eyes above rounded, healthy cheeks. He felt heavier, stronger, and she was flooded with such happiness that she hugged him carefully to her. "Oh, Timmy, you're better. I can see it!"

"Yes, Timmy is better." Luke Jefferson stood beside her, but he looked different—younger, happier. The moonlight was a bright halo around his wavy fair hair, and his eyes, so like Timmy's, glistened with excitement. "They found a cure, Heidi. Just today, but in time to help Timmy get well."

Aching with love and happiness, she looked down at Timmy. Then horror numbed her, evaporating her happiness, leaving her hollow and empty. Timmy's eyes were closed, his small face shrunken to icy blue in the moonlight.

"Oh, my God! What have you done, Heidi?" Luke's harsh, anguished voice echoed above her. "If you had waited, he would have lived, Heidi. He would have lived, Heidi . . . Heidi . . ."

"Heidi, wake up! Heidi, come on . . ."

When she opened her eyes, she found she was curled up in a tight ball, her throat and chest aching. Above Angel's voice she heard moans that sounded like an animal in great pain. Not until she focused on Angel's frightened face did she realize the sounds were coming from herself.

Trembling, fighting to control her breathing, she buried her burning cheeks in the pillow already soaked with salty tears.

"Heidi, are you sick or something?"

At Angel's tentative touch on her shoulder, Heidi forced herself to roll over onto her back. "It was just a bad dream," she whispered.

"Hell, I thought you were dying up there. What was it?"

Twisting her head on the pillow, Heidi blinked back fresh tears. "It was about dying. Timmy . . . dying."

In the diffused light from the lamp below, Angel's face looked younger, softer. "I mind my own business. But if you want to talk about it, I'll listen."

"Thank you, Angel, but I don't think so." She said it as gently as possible, not wanting to discourage this new side Angel had let her glimpse.

"Fine by me." Shrugging, Angel slid back into her bunk. A moment later Heidi heard the radio, very low, as if Angel had already put the incident from her mind.

For Heidi it could never be forgotten. Luke had made his point too well. She had robbed Timmy of his chance for life however brief it might have been.

ANGEL YAWNED and looked away from Santos to find Heidi, who sat in a corner across the visitors' room. She looked like hell. No wonder; she hadn't slept all night. Angel hadn't slept much, either. She kept waking up, listening for Heidi. It gave her chills remembering those cries last night. She'd never heard anyone sound like that, as if someone were ripping their guts out.

"What ya lookin' at?" Santos asked, twisting around in his chair.

"My new roommate," Angel said quickly, sorry she'd brought Heidi to his attention.

"That one in the corner with the great knockers? Hey, we could use a looker like that in the business." He whistled, flinging back around in the chair to wink at her. "You and her together could bring in some heavy cash. What's she in for?"

"I don't know. Besides, she wouldn't be interested, Santos." Angel laughed, and suddenly restless, began tapping her fingers on the tabletop.

"Can't ya ever sit still!" He grabbed her moving fingers and gripped them so tight that they hurt, but she didn't try to pull away. She knew better. "Ain't ya glad to see your Santos, Angel?"

The answer came swiftly, but not to her lips. She was too smart for that. Santos had only visited her four times in the past four years, and two of those had been in the first six months. The few letters she got from Maria in the old neighborhood reliably informed her that Santos had quickly replaced her.

"Yeah, I'm real glad to see you. It's been a long time." She smiled and was rewarded by a slight lessening of the hurtful grip on her hand.

"I been busy, ya know. With business. Got some good contacts with garages in high-priced neighborhoods. I drove a BMW out here. Whaddya think of that?" His burst of satisfied laughter drew attention all around them, and Heidi stopped as she walked toward the concession stand with the guy she'd called David. Angel could just see his broad back as he moved through the crowd, but Heidi was staring at her.

At that moment Santos chose to run his free hand up Angel's arm and across the tips of her breasts. It was all she could do not to jerk away, and she could see understanding on Heidi's pale face.

Angel dropped her eyes, shocked she had let anyone see her feelings so clearly. Especially someone she hardly knew. Someone who might be a ticket to a better life in this place.

Knowing how to play the game, she leaned into Santos's hand and didn't even blink when his fingers painfully squeezed her nipple through the cotton top.

"Have you missed me, Santos?"

"Ya know it. Ya always been my girl. Yer one of us. Proved it when ya didn't rat on us when ya got caught. The gang and me, we don't forget. We want ya back as soon as ya get outta this dump."

At last he leaned back, releasing her hand, and she slowly dropped it to her lap, nursing the numb, bruised fingers. "Thanks, Santos. I appreciate that."

"Appreciate nothin'! We want ya back. When ya get out, I'll pick ya up in a Porsche!" This time his loud laughter barely drew a glance, but Heidi paused on her way back to the table and looked toward her.

Angel seized the opportunity. "You need me, Heidi?" Bouncing to her feet, Angel was already away from the table before Santos stood up. "They need me in the playroom, don't they?"

Heidi was a quick learner. "Yes, Officer Connell wants you," she said quietly.

"Sorry, gotta go, Santos." Angel wasn't quite brave enough to leave him with that red flush of anger on his wide face. Santos mad was dangerous. She tripped back quickly and gave him a kiss on the mouth, but broke it off before he had a chance to flick his tongue through her lips. "See you soon, Santos."

Turning quickly, she gripped Heidi's elbow and steered her back to the corner where David stood waiting. He squinted his eyes, studying her as if she were a bug or something and then dismissed her.

"Heidi, what do you want to do with all these things I bought? If I'd known, I could have gotten you better brands in Chicago."

"They're for Angel. David, this is my roommate, Angel Ramon. Angel, this is David DeVries, my business manager."

"How you doing?" Angel said quickly, eager to see what the brown paper bag contained. "Hey, there's everything in here!" She lifted out a bottle of perfume and sprayed it on her neck. "Smells real good."

"Glad you like it, Miss Ramon," David drawled, and Angel realized her first impression was right. This guy, teddy-bear looks and all, had a growl.

She tilted her head back and lazily took him in, from the tips of his polished loafers to where the knit shirt pulled tightly across his muscular chest and stretched over broad shoulders. Very broad. Her appraisal ended at his face, which was wide and strong but saved from being tough by his short pug nose. It gave him a little-boy look beneath the straight dark brown hair, only slightly silvered at the temples.

Their eyes met, and she laughed, looking away first. Yeah, this guy had her number. Nevertheless, she picked up the bag, cradling it in her arms. Heidi had come through, in more ways than one.

"Thanks, Heidi." She nudged her shoulder. "I'll share the candy bars with you."

"Good. I love chocolate." She smiled in that sweet way she had that Angel couldn't understand. Hell, she had the body and face of a movie star but a smile that made her look like a choir girl. Angel couldn't figure out how someone who seemed this nice could have done what she did. She didn't like it when she couldn't peg people right from the start. She'd decided Heidi was a source of goodies, and that was right on. But it made her nervous knowing there was more to her.

She danced back a few steps and did a turn. She always moved when she was nervous. "Thanks for the other, too. You're real quick."

Heidi just nodded, and Angel spun around again, avoiding David's eyes. "I'm going to check out the playroom. See you guys later."

She glanced back once to make sure Santos had really left and felt lighter on her feet seeing the empty table. What had this place done to her, anyway? Once Santos had been her whole world, even with his cruelty and violence. She had simply accepted it as part of her life. Now it scared her. She didn't want to go back to the old life, but what else was there for her when she got out?

She bit her lip and pushed through the door to the playroom. *Nothing* scared Angel Ramon, she reminded herself.

"That one is out for what she can get from you," David declared firmly, tilting his chair precariously on its narrow back legs. "What else has she asked you for?"

"Nothing." Heidi wasn't paying much attention to him. She was watching Angel. For just an instant with Santos, Angel had looked like a frightened little girl. But now, her small figure hidden by the too-large flowered cotton prison top, she was herself again, ready to take on anything.

"Wait, I just thought of something else she needs. Clothes!"

"Clothes? What's wrong with what she's got on?" David shot a look at Angel's back, which was just disappearing through the door.

"David, that's a prison top. And she only has two pairs of jeans."

"I thought everyone could bring ten outfits from home."

"Sure, if they have them. Some don't, so they wear prison-issued pants and tops."

"Don't tell me everyone here is so fashion-conscious." He gave her a narrowed squint that clearly said he wasn't convinced.

"Yes, even here there's a pecking order. Just because these women are locked away doesn't mean they've lost interest in what's going on in the world."

David reached across the table and took her hands, holding them between his own. "I'm sorry. I'm a male chauvinist, but you love me, anyway. Want me to buy her some clothes?"

"Maybe some underwear." She smiled at his look of horror. "I was thinking, Angel and Faith are about the same size. Faith has all those outfits from last year she'll never wear again. You know how particular she is." Heidi's voice caught suddenly as she remembered Faith as she was now—totally disinterested in her appearance. But that would change. It had to.

David nodded, resting his chin on his hands. "Tell me what to send."

"Well, Faith has a white-and-navy striped shirt and navy blazer and pants. Then there's a washable silk jumpsuit. And send the pair of cream knit pants and the cotton V-neck sweater with the cream and teal stripes and the one with the big red poppies splashed across it. A pair of black knit pants and the red-and-black matching top. Throw in the white cotton cable-stitched sweater.''

David nodded, and she had no doubt he would get every request exactly right. He had a fabulous memory. ''Oh, I just remembered! Send the royal blue spandex top and pants with the matching miniskirt. It will be perfect for her dancing.''

''She's a dancer?'' Again he squinted. This time Heidi wasn't going to let him get away with it.

''Well, she should be. Come on, I'll show you.''

Jumping up, she pulled him to his feet, leading him to the playroom. As she opened the door, they heard the soundtrack from *West Side Story*. The timing couldn't have been more perfect. Angel was taking the routine that made Rita Moreno a star and making it hers. Then she improvised with the kids, dividing them into Jets and Sharks.

Only when Angel slid down into a perfect split and gracefully rested her head and chest on the floor did Heidi look up at David. His arms were folded and his face was set in determined lines. After a moment he flicked her a cool look, and she motioned him back out the door, sliding it shut before Angel could see them.

''Well, was I right?''

He shrugged his powerful shoulders. ''She's got talent. But it's raw.''

''She just needs the right guidance and management when she gets out of here.''

''Now wait a minute! I'll buy her all the chocolate bars she can eat. I'll even buy her underwear and send her clothes. But I won't be Professor Higgins to her Eliza Dolittle. Heidi, she's a street punk!''

"But she was lucky enough to get some formal training and talented enough to improve on her own. She just needs some help.''

"And you have to be the one to help her. Is it because she reminds you of Faith?''

She'd always known how shrewd David was, but his quickness at cutting right to the heart still shocked her. "Yes, she reminds me of Faith. But Angel isn't someone you can befriend. Maybe someday we can be friends. Right now we're both feeling our way.''

"Don't let her use you, Heidi. I know what a softy you are.'' He cuffed her chin before embracing her in a tight, comforting hug.

"I need her more than she needs me.'' Resting her head against his arm, she felt it tighten. He pushed her away slightly, his hands gripping both of her arms, and studied her face intently.

"What do you mean? What's going on here?'' His voice rose slightly. Heidi knew he was already worried about her; she didn't need to add to it.

"Nothing. Calm down, David. It's just that Angel is showing me the ropes here. I'm not used to life inside and all the rules.'' She saw him relax.

"You sure there's nothing else?''

"Angel's been the least judgmental of all. That's another reason I wanted to help her out. I need a friend here—someone I can talk to. David, maybe I can repay her by doing something for her when she leaves here. You could help her get started in the business.''

"I'll think about it.''

Think about it. Luke Jefferson had said that.

David pressed her hand. "Heidi, won't you change your mind about an appeal? Just say the word and I'll get Charles Goodman back on your case. You've accepted the consequences of your actions, just as you insisted you should. But you don't have to be locked away to keep punishing yourself."

She touched his cheek, silencing him. "I know, David, but I can deal with this place. There is something else I should tell you, though." Taking a deep breath, she folded her hands in her lap. "Peter's brother, Luke, came to see me yesterday."

"That bastard! I told him to stay away!" David's boyish face hardened.

"You met him? When?"

"He came to the house about a week ago, looking for Faith and Timmy. He claims he just found out where you lived. He didn't know about Timmy."

"You told him." Her voice was flat, quiet, as she remembered Luke's anguished face.

"Just the bare facts. If he knew more, he must have questioned the hospital or looked up old newspaper accounts. Or he used his contacts and got into the court records. What did he want?"

Who gave you the right to decide it was time for Timmy to die?

He had come for answers, and she had none to give him, or herself. She stared down at her hands, and although she tried, she couldn't stop tears from falling onto her fingers.

"I warned him!" David snarled. "Don't worry. He may be an attorney, but I can still get a court order to keep him away if he's harassing you."

Flinging back her head, she met his worried gaze and tried to smile. "It doesn't matter. We talked. He wants to help Faith, and I'm thinking of giving him the chance to do it."

"What! Why?" Worry slowly turned to speculation. "You didn't want help from him before. When I suggested it, you nearly bit my head off."

"I know. Maybe I was wrong to deprive him of...of knowing Timmy. Maybe I can make up for it by letting him help Faith. Maybe I owe him that."

"You owe him nothing! On the other hand, Peter's family owe you some consideration. After all, if Peter hadn't run out on Faith, they would have been there to share some of the responsibility."

"David, I love Faith. I would have been there for her regardless."

"I know." He embraced her in a hug and she rested, sighing, against him. "Just don't worry about Luke Jefferson. If you don't want to deal with him, I will!"

"Believe me, I'm not going to think about him until I have to," she said, laughing shakily. Luke Jefferson had crumbled the walls she'd erected around herself. What she could salvage from the rubble was no longer enough to protect her.

ON THE WAY across the parking lot Luke glanced up at the brown stone walls and was shocked to see barbed wire coiled along the top. He hadn't noticed that when he first came to Elmwood two days ago. Then he had thought the front facade made the structure look like a small castle, but today the barbed wire gave it another appearance entirely.

Today, a Saturday, there was an even longer line at the check-in desk. He took his place with the others. The process was slower, more time-consuming. As he inched his way closer to the desk, his nervousness grew and he checked his watch for the fifteenth time. Would his name be on the list? Would Heidi have kept her word to think about his offer to help Faith? At that moment he'd thought he'd won, judging from her body language. But now he needed her answer. He needed to do something, or he'd go crazy with guilt. He should have been here to help his nephew. He would have found a way despite the odds. Beating the odds was what he did best.

"Next!"

Jarred out of his thoughts, Luke hastily took a place at the desk.

"Luke Jefferson to see Heidi Allan." He could feel his heartbeat quicken as he waited, watching the guard slowly scan a sheet of paper.

He shook his head. "Sorry, you can't see her today."

Luke had been mistaken. "Isn't my name on the list?" he demanded.

"Oh, your name's here, sir, but Heidi Allan had a visitor yesterday and one the day before."

"She's only allowed two visitors a week?" Relief she had kept her word and anger that he couldn't see her now warred within him. "I saw women in there with five and six visitors on one day."

The guard shot him a tired look. "Sir, each prisoner has only two visitor days a week regardless of the number of visitors."

Luke could feel the people behind him in line shifting impatiently, eager to take his place. Here and now there was no way to buck the system. He stepped back, and another man swiftly moved forward.

Frustrated, he prowled around the waiting room, but in the end he had no choice. He made his way back outside. It had started to drizzle, so he turned up his shirt collar before stopping to look back. The rain had changed the brown stone to black, and moisture glistened on the barbed wire, highlighting its sharp, dangerous edges. He shivered from the damp but still stood staring at the high walls.

The chill deepened but not from the rain. Those walls were keeping him from seeing Heidi and putting his plan in motion. And they were keeping Heidi in, not just until next week, but for months.

She wasn't what he'd pictured in the days after he found out about Timmy's death. He had expected someone harder, stronger, unremorseful—not a fragile woman with haunted eyes. But he had let his rage and pain loose on her, anyway. Torn into her without thought or direction, just wanting to hurt her as he was hurting.

It was her eyes that had finally broken through to him, calmed him and restored his ability to think rationally. If you studied the eyes and knew what to look for, you could make or break a witness, or even determine how a jury would vote. Regardless of what his clients told him, Luke always looked to their eyes to tell him the truth. But there was something in the depths of Heidi Allan's eyes that eluded him.

There were too many questions to which he had no answers. Since Heidi was the only person who could provide them, as much as he hated it, he had no choice but to wait until next week to get them.

CHAPTER FIVE

"ANGEL, here's a package for you."

Angel looked up from the floor where she was stretching out to ease the dull ache in her left calf. "What are you talking about, Connell? I never get packages." An odd excitement made her jump to her feet, flexing her leg a few times to be sure the cramp was gone. "Are you sure? Who'd send me something?"

"I did."

Angel looked up at Heidi, who leaned down from the top bunk. "It's only been four days. I didn't realize David would get it all together so quickly or I would have told you."

Angel jumped up and did a wild twirl. "Hey, Heidi, what's going on? That David didn't like me. What'd he send—a lump of coal?"

Angel swung around to Connell, who held out the box. "Here, see for yourself."

Slowly Angel took it from her hands. Before Connell shut the door she smiled in Heidi's direction. In four years Angel had never seen Connell smile, much less heard her laugh. What the hell was going on?

Carefully placing the box on the floor, Angel knelt beside it. She knew it had already been opened and examined once, but whoever checked it had neatly put back everything beneath layers of white tissue paper.

Fearful eagerness rushed through her, warming her throat and chest and making her hands tremble.

The box was full of clothes—clothes like Angel had only seen in the windows of shops she'd never had the nerve to enter.

Carefully she lifted out each piece. There were more clothes than she'd ever possessed, and her fingers reverently examined every detail. They were all so beautiful and felt so soft and pliable in her hands. They were the kind of clothes Heidi wore.

"Are these yours?" Finally Angel tore her eyes away.

Heidi smiled, her legs now swinging over the side of the bunk. "No, they belonged to my sister Faith. I hope you don't mind that they aren't new. But some she never wore before she got sick."

"They look brand-new! Your sister didn't die or anything, did she?"

Heidi's smile vanished, and her eyes glistened with tears. Abruptly Angel's excitement was tinged with something unfamiliar. Could this be guilt making her wish she'd kept her big mouth shut?

"No. She's in a sanatorium recovering from postpartum depression."

"Yeah, I've heard of it. Some lady in my old neighborhood had it once. I remember she had the sweetest baby, but she didn't seem to care about him. And she used to be pretty and then she went around looking like hell. Like she didn't care anymore." Angel knew she was running off at the mouth, but she couldn't stop herself. Is this what guilt did, make you feel funny inside until you talked yourself out of it? "But she got better," she added quickly. "She and the baby went everywhere together then. She was always walking him and talking about him."

Heidi nodded as if she understood, but her eyes, which were sad and scared, didn't change.

It's none of your business, Angel reminded herself. Springing up, she hugged the clothes to her. "You didn't have to do this. I'll take real good care of them so when your sister gets better she can have them back. Thanks."

Heidi's mouth curved gently, and relief surged through Angel, making her almost dizzy as she backed up a pace and turned clumsily away. Hell, she was getting soft! She'd made a friend of Heidi for just this reason. It was all working out. It wasn't so bad pretending to be her friend. But this guilt stuff was for the birds.

Folding each piece as neatly as Heidi kept her things, Angel placed the clothing on her shelves.

She couldn't get her jeans and prison top off fast enough. Her fingers drifted over the pants, the slacks, the sweater, the shirts, then lingered on the spandex top and tights. She hadn't had real dance clothes since Miss Juliette had given tights and a leotard for her ninth birthday. She hesitated. Having a choice was new to her, but she finally made up her mind.

She tried on the jumpsuit first. Two pirouettes relieved some of her excitement. "Do I look stupid in this? Is it *me?*" she hammed.

"You look adorable!" Laughing, Heidi dropped to the floor. She reached out as if she were going to hug her. Startled, Angel jumped away.

"I'm sorry." Heidi said it quietly, her hands falling to her sides. "You just reminded me so much of Faith I wanted to..." Shrugging, she shook her head. "I'm sorry."

That stupid guilt returned. "Me and your sister are alike, huh?"

"Not really. Except she's small and has dark hair." Heidi's pouty mouth curved in a faint, faraway smile, and again Angel felt better. She must be going soft or something!

"I wish Faith had some of your spirit," Heidi added softly.

"You call it spirit. The cops call it something else. Hey, I can't wait for the girls in class to see this. Come on. The bell's about to ring."

Angel didn't have to wait until class—a crowd gathered around her in the downstairs hallway. She didn't mind the other girls touching the jumpsuit. She'd done that herself when someone got something from home. But this was a first for her: there was no home and no one to send things, except maybe Santos. Pushing the thought away, she glanced around for Heidi.

Connell was talking to her, and Heidi wasn't smiling or answering. She just nodded her head. Hell, what was going on? She shoved her way through the women eager to touch a bit of the outside world, but she couldn't get to Heidi until Connell was already gone.

"What'd she want? There's no trouble with the clothes, is there?"

"No, don't worry. The clothes are yours." Heidi adjusted the shoulders of the jumpsuit. "Everyone's allowed ten outfits, so you'll have to turn in your old prison-issued tops, that's all."

There it was again. Hell, how could Heidi look at her and know what she was feeling? Nobody else had ever paid attention to how she felt—except her mom. Life had really been bad after her mom died. Could Heidi hear the fear in her voice? The fear that these treasures would be snatched from her? She'd have to be careful. Angel couldn't let people get close enough to read her. On the street it was dangerous. Very dangerous.

"What'd she want then?" Angel stepped back, not quickly enough to hurt Heidi's feelings or anything, but enough to keep a safe distance.

"Officer Connell was giving me my assignment. I've had enough time to settle into the routine, so now I'm assigned to the shirt works. I guess they make shirts for the men's prison and all the guards."

"Why would they send you to the shirt works? Maxime and some of her buddies are there."

Heidi's eyes widened, but her soft lips settled into a hard line. "Don't worry about it, Angel. You said it on the first day. Everyone knows why I'm here. If Maxime says anything to me, I'll just ignore her."

Angel could do two dance sets she was so keyed up. The line began moving out the door. Pretending to be Heidi's friend didn't mean she was her nursemaid, but Heidi didn't know how the place worked. Angel did.

Connell motioned to them from the doorway.

"Listen, Heidi," Angel said quickly, "Doreen and Letty are at the shirt works. Stay close to them. Tell them if they don't take care of you, they'll answer to me." They were abreast of Connell now, so she couldn't say anything else.

Heidi nodded. "Thanks, Angel. You're a good friend." Turning to follow Connell across the yard, she waved once, then faced the concrete-block factory at the back of the compound.

Angel ran two steps after them before she stopped herself. Hell, what was she doing! If she was late for class, she'd get reported, and a mark on her record might make the difference with the Honor Cottage. She couldn't risk that.

It is none of your business, Angel, she reminded herself, and swiveled to catch up with the others. If it was none of her business, why did she have this sick ache in her gut?

OFFICER CONNELL TURNED Heidi over to Mrs. Blazer, a tall, thin woman wearing a supervisor's ID card. She hardly glanced at Heidi's papers. Folding them in half, she motioned Heidi to follow her. Voices and the whir of sewing machines came from all parts of the long building, but Heidi couldn't see anything beyond the gray wall partitions. One small space was divided into a little boxed-shape room. Inside the cubicle sat a single sewing machine and stool, with a basket of bobbins and blue and khaki thread beside them.

"Sit down, Heidi. Today you work here winding bobbins."

Heidi hadn't worked a sewing machine since high school, and never one this old. She couldn't quite get her hands on the machine and her foot on the pedal to work together. If she pressed the foot pedal too hard, the machine got away from her, gobbling up thread and bending the little silver bobbins. If she didn't apply enough pressure, it made a slow grinding noise.

Finally Mrs. Blazer nodded. "You've got it now. Today you wind. We'll see how you do before I move you out into the shop."

From her place on the stool, Heidi could see the long expanse of the shirt works through a narrow space between the partitions. Halfway down the room, she saw Letty and Doreen sitting across from each other at sewing machines. Beyond them a stranger cut a stack of plain blue material so thick that she had to use a type of jigsaw. Tall stacks of shirt pieces—fronts, backs and sleeves—sat on a table ready to be assembled. Behind one stack Maxime laughed with more women Heidi didn't know.

She wasn't afraid of Maxime exactly, but something about the woman made her flesh crawl. She wasn't about to involve Angel in any trouble she had with Maxime. She could handle it herself.

Mrs. Blazer might think she was doing fine, but she couldn't quite get the machine to work properly. She leaned closer and her foot shifted on the pedal. The sharp needle bit into her hand before she could jerk it away. Hot tears burned her eyes as she sucked at the throbbing fingertip. What was the matter with her?

Once she had been a strong person, strong enough to survive her parents' deaths while caring for Faith and finishing her own education. She'd believed in herself, in her ability to handle whatever life threw at her, to make the right decisions. She'd always been decisive and sure of herself. David said the audience felt it and that was part of her success. He had felt it, which was why he had taken her on straight out of college, even though she had lacked experience. She had gathered every fiber of that strength and confidence around her during Timmy's illness, and at the end had drawn on courage she hadn't known she possessed to keep her promise to Faith.

She'd known clearly, then, what she was doing and why. She'd known that her love for Timmy, her wish to end his senseless suffering—to give him a moment of freedom, held in loving arms—was greater than her fear of what might happen to herself. She'd sustained herself through the entire ordeal with the knowledge that she'd done the right thing, that any consequence was worth it. But that courage had depleted every ounce of strength in her. Now she was an empty shell buffeted by the winds of doubt and fear. The old Heidi Allan had died that night, too.

Mrs. Blazer peered through the door. "How are we doing in here?"

"Fine," Heidi muttered, bending her head to the machine. If she concentrated on the little silver bobbins and the blue thread, she wouldn't have to think.

She forced her mind to go blank, to ignore the voices on the other side of the partition. Obviously there was a watercooler nearby where the women could take a break. Laughter and snatches of conversations echoed off the ceiling and bounced into her alcove. So far she hadn't recognized anyone's voice.

Then Letty's high voice pierced her consciousness. "I heard that Angel's roommate is working here now. I like her. I don't care what she did."

Suddenly cold and very still, Heidi listened.

"She said the pictures of my little Georgie and the girls were real cute. I could tell by her face that she really meant it. But a baby! How could anyone kill a baby!" Doreen's soft voice asked.

Heidi didn't want to hear any more, yet she couldn't stop listening. There was no place to escape.

"It was real sick, that's what I heard. It was going to die, anyway."

"But, Letty, I could never hurt my babies. I love them so. What if it suddenly got better?" Doreen insisted. "No, no matter what, I couldn't hurt my babies."

"I had a baby once."

"You, Letty! You never said! Boy or girl?"

"Girl." Letty's shrill voice dropped to almost a whisper. "Wasn't right. Doctor said it was 'cause I was doing LSD. Used to go visit her in the hospital, but she never knew me. She never grew. One day she died. I was glad she wasn't suffering no more. Terrible to see her suffer. That's when I got myself fixed so I wouldn't have no more babies. Couldn't stand seeing them suffer. Maybe that's how Heidi felt."

"Who ya talkin' about?" Maxime's harsh voice reverberated throughout the room.

"Angel's roommate, Heidi," Doreen answered softly.

"Her and Ramon got somethin' goin'?" Maxime demanded.

"Shit, you know better than that!" Letty's high laugh echoed over the wall. "Besides, two guys have been to see Heidi. Both of 'em lookers."

"Especially the blond one." Doreen's sigh sounded so close that she must have been just outside the partition, and Heidi's hands clenched as she fought the terrible emotions those words evoked.

"I was watching them that day. It was just like a movie. One minute he looked like he was mad at her and the next he was sorta sad. Just like in the movies when the hero grabs the girl and you think he's going to hurt her but he kisses her instead."

"Hell, Doreen, life ain't no movie. I thought the big guy built like a football player was the real hunk. My kind of man." Letty sighed.

"You're both crazy." Maxime's laugh was loud and cruel. "Letty, you're too old and your brain's so fried with drugs no guy'd give ya the time of day. And Doreen thinks every guy is friggin' Prince Charmin'! They give her kids and dump her."

"I love my babies. And I loved their daddies." Doreen argued with more spirit than Heidi had ever heard from her.

"Hey, there's Blazer. We'd better get back to work. I'd like to know where she put Heidi." Letty's voice moved away.

"Tell ya what I'd like..." The end of Maxime's sentence was lost in the distance, but her short bark of laughter was clearly audible.

Heidi stared blankly at the gray walls that surrounded her. She understood Letty and she understood Doreen. She even shared their feelings. She had loved Timmy so much that she would have died for him and, indeed, had died, little by little, helplessly watching him suffer. If she could go back, would she do anything different? If somehow she had another chance, what choice would she make?

Searching her heart, she didn't know the answer, and it was destroying her.

Taking a deep breath, she dabbed at her eyes with the sleeve of her sweater and blearily looked down at the bobbin. She did know one thing for sure: she didn't want to make a decision about Faith and Luke Jefferson. Doreen couldn't have been more wrong: there was nothing romantic about the way Luke looked at her. The only bond they shared was guilt. It was guilt making Luke want to help Faith. And it was guilt making Heidi realize she owed him the chance. She couldn't help Faith. She must be willing to take the chance he might be able to.

A decision at last. But one that made her stomach ache and her hands tremble.

"So this is where Blazer stuck ya!"

Maxime's voice was here inside her alcove! Heidi gripped the edge of the sewing machine cabinet until her hands turned white. If she didn't look up and acknowledge Maxime, maybe she'd go away.

Luck wasn't with her. Wide, flat hands came down hard on either side of the machine. Heidi dropped her own into her lap. Lifting her chin, she found Maxime's face only inches from hers. She hadn't met many bullies in her life, but she knew the only way to handle one was not to act afraid. So she didn't flinch, not even when Maxime's laugh flooded her face with the smell of stale cigarette smoke.

"What ya doin' in here? Got ya in solitary confinement or somethin'?"

"Just for today. Tomorrow I'll be out in the main room." She was glad to hear that her voice sounded even and natural.

"That's good. Oughta get to know some people. Ya ain't very friendly."

The walls seemed to close in, trapping her with Maxime. What had been comfortable privacy become menacing isolation. No one else could see what was going on. She'd have to be very careful. "I spend most of my time with Angel," she explained, taking a deep breath.

Laughing, Maxime leaned closer, and Heidi saw herself reflected in the black pupils of her pale blue eyes. "Angel ain't goin' to be here much longer. She's about served her time. Me, I can be a real good friend, too." Her thin lips stretched over uneven teeth in a parody of a smile. "Ya got pretty clothes. I like that. I like pretty things." One flat-fingered hand brushed across Heidi's throat and shoulder.

The touch made her nauseous, and suddenly Heidi could bear it no longer. She jumped to her feet. "Please take your hands off me."

The sneer still plastered on her face, Maxime shifted, effectively blocking her exit. "Where d'ya think yer going?" she drawled.

"I'm going to get a drink of water," Heidi said, trying to keep the edge of desperation from her voice.

She failed. That was a mistake.

Maxime heard it. The sneer became a look of triumph. She lunged, catching Heidi's right arm. She tried to pull away, but Maxime twisted it behind her back, forcing her up against the one solid wall of the tiny room.

Fear pounded through her, freezing her in terror as Maxime's breathing came hot and heavy in her ear. She jerked the arm even higher so that Heidi had to arch her back, trying to relieve the wrenching ache. She couldn't cry out. Angel had made it very clear what would happen if she ever "ratted" to the guards.

"I like pretty things," Maxime repeated. The woman's finger reached around to stroke the hair coiling at Heidi's throat, and paralyzing fear shuddered uncontrollably through her body.

With a guttural laugh Maxime moved even nearer, and Heidi closed her eyes, hoping for a miracle.

"I like that a lot," Maxime whispered against her neck an instant before a sharp pain ricocheted through her.

Maxime's moist mouth lingered, licking at the bite, while terror settled deep into Heidi's limbs, making it impossible for her to fight back. Tears gathered under her lids, but she made no sound as she tried to force her mind to function. Then she got her miracle.

"Here you are, Maxime!" Letty called from the doorway. "Blazer's been yelling for you. Better get your ass back to the cutting table."

Maxime dropped her arm and stepped back. Heidi's eyes opened and the bobbin room came slowly into focus. She gave a single sob of silent thanks.

"Friggin' Blazer!" With a raw laugh that sent revulsion through every fiber of Heidi's body, Maxime turned back to her. "So long, Heidi. See ya around." A flat finger tapped her cheek. Heidi jerked away, and Maxime smirked before swaggering past Letty into the main room.

"You all right?"

Twisting around at Letty's loud whisper, Heidi forced a smile. "Thanks to you, Letty. I won't forget it."

"I do you a favor, you do me one." Brushing strands of straight gray hair off her lined forehead, Letty rested against the doorframe. "Your neck is bleeding. Maxime do that?" She reached forward, and Heidi flinched involuntarily. "Wait right here till I get something from the first-aid kit."

Heidi sagged against the wall, her fingertips gently probing the throbbing pain until Letty returned. She was learning the rules.

"I hope that pig don't give you an infection." Letty smeared antibiotic over the bite before applying a bandage.

"I owe you for this," Heidi said. "When my friend David comes, I'll get you whatever you need from the concession stand."

"Which one is he? The football hunk or Prince Charming?"

"Football." Heidi laughed shortly, relief slowly draining the pent-up tension from her shoulders and arms.

"Is he your man?" Letty asked, repacking the first-aid kit. "Or the other one? Doreen thinks it's the blond guy."

Luke Jefferson? He was more like her punishment. His eyes were so much like Timmy's—their blueness, the elongated curve of the lid fringed with dark lashes. Timmy would have looked just like that if... Clearing her head of thoughts too painful to deal with, Heidi slid back into her chair. "I don't have a man, Letty."

"Good for you. They ain't nothin' but trouble. Had my first one at sixteen. He's the one got me hooked on the stuff."

"I hope you stay well, Letty." Heidi could never picture this sweet-faced older woman as an addict. No one here was what they seemed. Including her.

"Maybe I will." Letty shrugged. "Maybe I won't. This place, the warden, the doctors, they try to help you. Me, I'm what you might call a lost cause." Glancing around, she leaned closer. "You always smell real good, Heidi. They won't let us borrow stuff from each other, but how about every day at lunch you bring that expensive perfume you wear and give me a few squirts. Then we'll be even."

"All right. I'll bring it tomorrow." Heidi made a mental note to write David and ask him to send more perfume.

Letty nodded. "Gotta get back. Don't forget to tell Angel about Maxime. She'll handle it for you."

Did everyone think Angel was protecting her? There was no way she was going to let Angel fight all her battles. She'd be here for a long time; she'd learn to take care of herself. She had to.

Nevertheless, Angel was waiting for her just inside the cottage door. Officer Connell barely had the door shut and locked before Angel grabbed her arm, pulling her up the stairs.

"Angel, wha . . . ?"

"Wait until we're in our room!" she spit out, her eyes narrowed in her stiff face, her fingers digging sharply into Heidi's arm.

Slamming the bedroom door, she leaned against it. "What did that pig Maxime do to you?" Her small, sleek body quivered, and for the very first time Heidi knew what David meant when he said Angel was a street kid—a fighter. And for the first time since coming to this place Heidi knew exactly what to do.

She hoisted herself up to her bunk and flipped onto her stomach, resting her chin on her hands to gaze at Angel. "What are you so upset about? Maxime only stopped by the alcove where I was sewing to talk for a few minutes. Who told you?"

"Don't bull me, Heidi. That bandage is hiding something! Out with it," Angel demanded. "There aren't any secrets in this place. You'd better learn that first thing." There was real worry on Angel's face. Heidi hadn't been blind to Angel's motives for friendship; she just hadn't cared. Now there was something new in the dark eyes facing her.

"I'm not *bulling* you. Nothing happened that I can't handle. I know you might find this hard to believe, but I can take care of myself."

"Maybe outside, but not here! You probably never met anyone like Maxime or Letty or me in your life. You're different from us and everyone knows it."

"I'm not so different inside, Angel." She smoothed her hair down to cover the telltale bandage. "Thanks for being concerned but there's no need." Heidi dropped to the floor just as the bell sounded. "Great! Isn't tonight lasagna? It's not bad."

Heidi's cheerfulness bounced right off Angel: her jaw remained clenched, her slender arms folded tightly across her breasts in defiance. "If someone doesn't show you the ropes in here, you won't make it." Angel's dark gaze bore into her.

Yes, there was something different there.

"I know." Relaxing her forced smile, Heidi nodded. "I've known it from the beginning. I do you a favor, you do me one," she repeated.

A bright red tinged Angel's high cheekbones. "You got it. It's the way you survive. Everywhere!" Angel's voice sounded raspy, but she turned away too quickly for Heidi to read her mood. "C'mon, let's go eat before Connell comes looking for us."

Even though she didn't question Heidi any more about Maxime, Angel's air of defiance didn't disappear. When Maxime strutted past their table toward the beverage station, swinging her empty glass nonchalantly, Angel glared at her. Heidi couldn't keep from smoothing her hair over her neck self-consciously. That tiny motion seemed to set Angel off. She rose to her feet, following Maxime.

"No, Angel, don't!" Heidi pushed her chair back, but Letty and Doreen simultaneously gripped her shoulders, forcing her to stay put. Frantically she stared from one impassive face to the other. "What's going on here?"

"Just sit tight, Heidi. You'll see," Letty promised, releasing her hold.

Heidi watched fearfully as Angel stopped, not quite blocking Maxime's return. Maxime smirked, brushing past the much smaller woman. Suddenly Maxime's glass flew out of her hand as she tripped and crashed to the tile floor. Angel bent over her, apparently helping her to her feet. But somehow Angel's knee connected with her chin, and she slid to the floor again with a loud thud.

There was an audible gasp, and two guards rushed to the scene. Angel stepped back innocently, obviously concerned. One guard pulled Maxime to her feet.

Her chin was smeared with blood from a cut lip. The look in her nearly colorless eyes as she glared at Angel sent terror quaking through Heidi.

"She's going to get Angel in trouble, and it's my fault." Heidi hissed at Letty, again trying to rise to her feet.

Doreen kept her pinned to her seat. "Angel can take care of herself. Just stay here or you'll make things worse. Maxime won't say anything to the guards. She knows the score. Angel is telling her and everyone else that you're off-limits."

Incredulous, Heidi watched Maxime shrug the guards off, wiping the back of her mouth with her sleeve. Someone thrust a piece of ice into her hand, and she held it to her lip.

The guards, anxious to defuse the situation, encouraged everyone to sit down and finish their meals. Angel quietly returned to the table, a brittle look on her small face.

What had made her grow such a tough, aggressive shell around herself? Heidi wondered. Why had she used that toughness to protect her roommate? And what was it that Heidi saw in Angel's eyes for the first time? Could it be an inner core of goodness, of untouched truth, that fueled this girl who danced with such beauty? Perhaps the little girl Miss Juliette had taught the magic of dance was still there, hiding inside. Maybe she'd been wrong when she told David she needed Angel more than Angel needed her. Today proved she did need Angel; but maybe they had been brought together for a more important reason. The emptiness inside Heidi diminished ever so slightly.

It felt good to believe she might be able to help Angel. But although she tried after dinner, she couldn't break through Angel's protective shell.

"I did what had to be done. Forget it. It's over." Angel rolled over on her bunk with her back to Heidi.

She respected Angel's reticence and got ready for bed. She lay in the upper bunk, staring at the ceiling blankly until Angel finally stirred. Soft strains of Simon and Garfunkel filled the silence.

Unconsciously Heidi sighed in relief. Angel would be all right. The music lulled her, making this tiny room seem almost cozy—a safe haven with the two of them cocooned by the darkness.

Amazingly Heidi slept more soundly than usual, only once waking to lick salty tears from her mouth. Maxime's hulking menace had faded to almost nothing. What, then, haunted her thoughts? She rolled over and pulled the covers around her shoulders. Luke Jefferson's face flashed into her conscious mind. When would he return for his answers?

CHAPTER SIX

HEIDI WAS ASSIGNED to Howell's Helpers in the children's room the next morning. It had been a week since she'd had a visitor. She wasn't expecting David, but if he showed up, she'd talk to him again about Angel. She owed her; more than she could ever repay.

No one appeared with the initial rush of visitors. David was always one of the first through the glass double doors. Just as Luke had been. Luke Jefferson. She'd been valiantly battling the memory of his visit, but she was losing. How long would he wait for his answer? She was ready for him, she kept telling herself, but she had to admit she was relieved he hadn't shown up today while she was still reeling from Maxime's attack. Now she could spend time with the children. That always made her feel better.

There were more than a dozen boys and girls sitting on the floor doing warm-up exercises with Angel. Four older boys noisily played Nerf basketball at the hoop they'd set up in the corner.

Angel glanced over, motioning Heidi to the piano.

Heidi ran her fingers tentatively across the keys. They were a little off, but not bad. To warm up she played Chopin, and two little girls, holding hands, drifted over to listen, but after a few minutes skipped back to their dance exercises. Watching them go, their pigtails bouncing, Heidi noticed another little girl with long, straight blond hair sitting by herself in the corner.

Heidi smiled at her, but she didn't respond. She switched to a medley of tunes from *Cats* and glanced over at the corner. The blond child had risen to her feet, still staring at her, a look of longing on her face. Heidi kept playing, trying not to look toward the little girl, but she could see through her lowered lashes that the music was drawing her.

Finally feeling the child's presence beside her, Heidi tilted her head and met her stare. "Hello. Do you like the music?"

The little girl's pinched face dominated by round brown eyes, nodded shyly.

"Would you like to learn how to play a song?" Moving over, Heidi patted the bench. "Sit down and I'll teach you."

The child sat tentatively at the very edge of the bench and continued to stare. She nodded again.

"I'm going to teach you 'Happy Birthday.' " Taking the index finger of the little girl's right hand, Heidi pushed the keys. The little girl's head jerked up, her eyes dark pools of surprise.

"See! You made music."

Nodding, the child wriggled her finger. Heidi again went over the notes that made up the first song in most beginning piano books. Patiently she helped the tiny finger over the keys. Once she lifted her hand and the child kept playing, her head bent earnestly. Over and over she played "Happy Birthday" by herself.

The door swooshed open, and the sounds from the visitors' hall intruded. A guard stood there motioning toward her.

"It's time for you to go now, Joyce." Angel came across the room and touched the little girl's stooped shoulder.

Stopping immediately, Joyce slid off the bench. Looking at Heidi, her pinched face split into a smile exposing three missing teeth. "Back next week," she promised solemnly before running to where the guard waited.

Angel collapsed on the bench beside her. "I don't believe it! She spoke!"

"Is there something strange about that?" With her index finger Heidi punched out "Happy Birthday" softly. "I hope she comes next week. I could teach her 'The Volga Boat Song.' It's easy, too."

"Heidi, Joyce never talks. Her mom's in the cottage for the loonies. She's chained in one of those little glass-windowed rooms if she has visitors. I've been trying to get Joyce to dance for a year. Before, she just sat in the corner."

"She feels the music in her hands." Heidi ran her fingers down the keyboard lightly. "Maybe music will be the key to reaching her."

Just as it had been for Angel.

The idea came suddenly and naturally to Heidi: with music she could help people open doors to new worlds.

"You have company." Angel's voice caught her attention, and she looked up, straight into Luke Jefferson's blue stare.

Her hands crashed down on the keys, the jarring chord echoing through the room. He had come, after all. Today of all days.

Taking a deep, steadying breath, she willed herself to her feet. When David appeared behind Luke's shoulder, she thudded back onto the bench, pulling her hair down over the bandage. She couldn't let David know what happened.

"Man trouble?" Lifting finely arched eyebrows, Angel grinned teasingly.

"I need your help, Angel. You've met David. Talk to him while I see Luke. I wouldn't ask except it's important."

In spite of all that had happened, her decision about Faith was made. She had to tell Luke before doubt could set in—again. Besides, she wanted David and Angel to become better acquainted.

"Why not?" Shrugging, Angel signaled to another woman to take charge of the kids. "Better get over to them fast. They don't like each other, do they?" And there was no mistake about whether or not David liked *her*, either. When he realized Heidi had sent Angel to draw him off, he looked angry. He stared at Heidi as she led Luke to a table in the far corner, the veins in his neck pulsing so violently that Angel thought he might burst.

"You want to hit something, or can you cool down on your own?"

Shrewd eyes scanned her, much as they had at the first meeting. "You've got a smart mouth, don't you. How old are you?"

"Twenty-two. How old are you?" Her hands on her hips, she glared back at him. Funny, she was all keyed up, but for once she didn't feel the need to fidget. In fact, her legs felt glued to the floor. "Listen, let's get a few things straight. You don't like me, I don't like you, but we both like Heidi. She wants us to talk, so I'm talking."

Ramming his hands into his trouser pockets, David laughed. "Since when did you and Heidi get so close?

Since the clothes arrived?'' His cynical eyes flicked over her body, lingering on the spandex top and tights.

"You do me a favor, I do you one. It's the law of the jungle. *You* should know all about it. I hear show biz isn't exactly a tea party." She returned his cold stare, even though an unfamiliar excitement coiled in her gut.

"Touché, Angel. Since we can't talk without fighting and Heidi obviously bribed you to keep me busy, I suggest you entertain me. Why don't you dance?"

Now she did step back. "How do you know about my dancing?"

"I saw you last time. Go ahead. Those kids are waiting for you."

The other helper had put on the record of *West Side Story*—her favorite.

David shrugged his massive shoulders. "Go ahead. I'll wait."

Five girls, their soft faces eager, had positioned their narrow bodies in the pose she'd shown them. They were ready to follow her lead.

Twirling away from David, Angel kicked her right leg over her head, then slowly sank to the floor in a split. She rested her head on her knee until the beat flowed through every cell of her body, making her part of it. She moved with the rhythm, forgetting everything: her defiance, her excitement, even where she was, as the music consumed her. A leap and flourish brought her to the end of the number, and the little girls twirled, giggling, around her.

David's applause startled her and brought her back to reality.

"Who taught you?" he asked, moving toward her.

"Juliette De Prell from the Avenue Street Dancers, but that was a long time ago, when I was ten."

"I thought so. You need a teacher to develop some discipline and to show you the new stuff."

Flinging a towel around her neck, she dabbed at the drops of sweat running toward the hollow between her breasts. "Oh, yeah, Paul Taylor and Baryshnikov both want me, but I can't fit them into my busy schedule." Now it was her turn to scoff. "How the hell am I supposed to get a teacher when I've been in here?"

"There are ways, Angel—if you're good enough and smart enough."

"Yeah? What's that supposed to mean?"

He loomed over her, her head only reaching midway up his massive chest. "Let me think about it and I'll let you know. Meanwhile, keep practicing." Abruptly turning away, he moved toward the door.

No way would she let him leave like this. "Hey, David!"

He glanced over his shoulder, mildly surprised.

"I don't like mysteries, David. On the street they're dangerous."

"You're not on the street anymore, Angel. Think about that."

He gave her a lopsided grin and disappeared out the door. The coil of excitement tightened in her gut. Angel definitely didn't like it when people couldn't be pegged.

HEIDI WASN'T what Luke thought she should be. She shouldn't have eyes like this—haunted and empty. That look drew him toward her in spite of himself. He pulled back his chair, away from her. "Well, are you going to allow me to help Faith or not?" he asked brusquely.

Heidi nervously stroked the sides of the sweating soda can he had offered. "I didn't think you were coming today. It's late."

"There's construction on the expressway. Traffic was bad. Your manager must have got caught in it, too."

"Yes."

Following the direction of her eyes, Luke saw David lean one powerful shoulder against the wall as he stared at them.

"I'll visit with David when we finish. I won't keep you long."

"Then you've made up your mind?"

"I think so..." Heidi stopped as a pinched-faced child with straight blond hair appeared out of nowhere. The little girl wiggled her finger, her face wider and prettier when she smiled. There was a large gap where her front teeth should have been.

Something clutched in his gut as Heidi slowly reached out with her own index finger and touched the child's. "Next week, Joyce?"

The child nodded once, then disappeared as quickly as she had come.

It didn't feel right to see the sweetness on Heidi's face as she interacted with the child. Impatience drove him to his feet. "You're stalling. Are you going to give me an answer or not?" His voice was louder and sharper than he intended.

Drawing in a deep breath, Heidi stood to face him. He couldn't help but notice her full breasts beneath the light cotton sweater. In his mind he could see them half exposed in the newspaper photo he'd studied over and over.

"Yes, I will allow you to see Faith. I...I can't help her. I understand you feel an obligation to her because of your brother. I'll have to take the chance you're sincere.''

"Fine!" Relieved, he drew a folded sheet of paper from his jacket. "I've drawn up a document stating you give me permission to see Faith. This should satisfy Dr. Vogland.''

It was short and concise, taking her only a moment to read. She signed it just as quickly.

Satisfaction curled his mouth. At last he could do something to set things right; at least for Faith. For Timmy there was nothing he could do, ever.

"When will you be back to tell me how Faith is? I get reports from the doctors, but I need more. When David goes, she only gets upset. Maybe, since you're Peter's brother, it will somehow help." Anticipation brought a light pink to her cheekbones. Her lips parted ever so slightly, the lower one trembling.

Damn it! She looked so fragile with grief she'd shatter if he touched her, but for once he wasn't going to give in to his need to champion the underdog! Heidi Allan might look as if she needed help, but he wouldn't forget it was by her choice that he hadn't been allowed to help Timmy. He would never understand her decision to leave Peter's family out in the cold and then to terminate a precious life.

"Well, when will you be back?" she repeated. Her lashes flickered, and he saw moisture glistening on their tips. Her eyes widened and her fingers trembled as, self-consciously, she touched her neck. There was a small bandage there. Suddenly the look in her eyes wasn't hard to read at all—it was fear.

"Is something wrong?" he found himself asking, hating the sudden rush of concern he felt.

Her eyes focused on a nearby table for a moment. When she turned back to him, her expression was unreadable.

"No," she said softly, then repeated it for emphasis. "No."

He glanced at the woman in the red sweat suit whose sudden appearance at the next table had generated this reaction. What was going on here?

"If something is wrong here, I—"

"What could be wrong? This place is just like summer camp," cracked a tiny dark-haired girl with flashing eyes who appeared out of nowhere.

The reaction the three women sparked off one another wasn't lost on Luke. The large woman abruptly turned and disappeared into the crowded room. Heidi visibly relaxed, although her hands still trembled. She turned to the tiny girl.

"Angel, I'm all right. Really."

Angel nodded, then moved away.

Luke couldn't stop himself. "If there's trouble here, you should talk to someone about it." He glanced to where David stood by a doorway, watching the children's room. He had completely missed this little drama.

"There's no problem," she muttered, hiding the bandage with her hair. "When will you be back with word about Faith?"

"I'll be in touch!" He threw the words over his shoulder, striding towards the doors. He didn't want to look at her right now; he didn't like the feelings it gave him.

For once in his life he didn't want to care about right and wrong or how this woman would survive in jail. He wanted her to pay for the choices she'd made and the anguish she'd caused. Didn't he? So why was he pacing the waiting room like a caged animal? He'd come here for the sole purpose of getting permission to see Faith. Heidi wasn't his concern.

Still, he couldn't go without alerting *someone* to her plight. He couldn't leave until he talked to David DeVries.

Sooner than he expected, David pushed back through the turnstile. He stopped short when he saw Luke. "What do you want?" he asked coldly, squaring his massive shoulders.

"Look, DeVries, we may not see eye to eye, but this is about Heidi. Did you notice the bandage on her neck or the way she was acting today?"

Speculation widened David's clear green eyes as he lifted his chin. "What exactly are you driving at?"

Spreading his legs, Luke faced down the larger man. "Haven't you ever heard places like this can be detrimental to your health? Frankly, I'm surprised Heidi didn't get off with probation or community service, given the circumstances."

David studied him with shrewd eyes. "Heidi insisted on pleading guilty. Our hands were tied," he finally answered, his face hard.

"Why hasn't Charlie Goodman started an appeal?" So much for his resolve not to get involved.

"Because she won't let him!" David bit out, shaking his head. "You surprise me, Jefferson, although I know your reputation. Do you think you can help her?"

Luke shrugged. "My only obligation here is to help Faith. Nothing more, nothing less."

After another long, hard stare, David nodded. "I understand. You've given me something to think about. I hope you can help Faith, but in some ways I think Heidi is hurting even more.''

Luke leaned against the cool concrete-block wall and watched David stride out.

He had a lot to think about, too. DeVries was right. From what Luke had seen of Heidi, nothing could hurt her more than she was already hurting herself.

FAITH THOUGHT she was hallucinating again. Peter was walking across the parking lot toward her building just as he had the other day. Sunlight gleamed off his golden hair, bringing to life dozens of lighter shades. She'd always loved running her fingers through Peter's curls.

She closed her eyes and shook her head. It wasn't Peter. Dr. Vogland had warned her that she must learn to separate reality from fantasy. She'd thought she was better until she started seeing Peter.

Her door clicked open and she turned, sunlight blinding her momentarily. The figure in the doorway was all too real. ''Peter?''

''No.'' The response was firm yet gentle. ''I'm Luke, his brother.''

Faith wrapped her arms tightly around her body. Hardly daring to believe, she finally found the courage to step out of the glare. This man was taller, more muscular, and his hair lacked Peter's riotous curls, but the eyes . . . they were the same—Timmy's eyes.

Emotion drained her hard-won strength, and she staggered to a chair, retying her robe securely. Her hands dug into the softly upholstered arms.

''Why are you here? Did Peter send you?'' No, that couldn't be right, she realized. Peter was gone. Dr. Vogland said so.

"Your sister said I could come to see you."

"Heidi?" Heidi was real, and what she'd done wasn't a bad dream or one of Faith's fantasies. She just didn't like to think about it, but she had to.

"Heidi took my baby out of the hospital and he died. I...I don't know why she did that. She loved him so much. More than I did sometimes."

Brushing her bangs out of her eyes, she squinted up at the man standing beside her. It was Peter's face, or what Peter's face might look like someday if he matured and developed strength and character.

Strength.

Heidi had strength. She wished Heidi were here to help her understand. But maybe this man, who surely must love Peter as much as she had, could help her sort out the ruin of her life. Maybe she could tell him about Peter's son. Maybe then the pain would go away. If Heidi had sent him, it would be all right.

"How do you know Heidi?" she asked, hearing, for the first time, a note of hope in her voice.

"May I sit down, Faith, so we can talk?" Luke was gentle and smiling, not like the doctor, who always wanted her to do something she wasn't quite ready for. It was a nice change.

As he spoke, he pulled a chair in front of her and settled into it. "These are for you." He thrust a sheath of yellow roses toward her. She hadn't even noticed them till now.

Lifting them to her nose, she tentatively inhaled their scent. At Timmy's service there had been so many roses the scent had overpowered her, making her ill. That was the last time she had seen her sister: there in the chapel with the tiny white coffin covered by dozens of roses. Strangers had taken Heidi away, and then David had brought her back here.

David shouldn't have let Heidi go away. She'd depended on him! It was David's fault, and she'd let him know she was still angry. She needed Heidi; she had always depended on her. Now there was Luke, Peter's brother.

"Where is Peter?" she asked quietly. "Does he know about Timmy?"

Luke's strong face softened with emotion, making him look younger, more like his brother. "No, he doesn't know about his son." He leaned forward, speaking very softly. "When he returns would you like to see him so the two of you can talk about Timmy?"

"No!" Leaping to her feet, Faith again wrapped her arms tightly around her waist, holding herself together. Her feelings about Peter ripped her in two. He was the cause of all her pain, when once he'd been all her delight. "Heidi and I both decided Peter had no rights. He left. Said Timmy wasn't his." Her harsh laugh burned her throat. "He knew better."

Luke had risen when she did, and now looked down at her upturned face. "I know my brother. But we aren't alike. I... Peter's family would have accepted responsibility for Timmy. I wish I could have known my nephew."

There was pain in his blue eyes. She recognized it from the look she'd seen in Timmy's eyes when they put him on dialysis. She didn't have the strength to face that again.

Stepping past him, she went to her window. She felt safe here looking out at the world, not being part of it. She could rest here. She wasn't ready to put everything back together, after all.

"I'm tired. You'll have to leave."

"I understand, Faith. Can I come again and visit you? I'd like to get to know you better. I'd like to talk to you about Peter, and Timmy... and Heidi."

Grateful that he hadn't tried to urge her back to his world, the way David always did, Faith nodded. "Yes, you can come back."

"Thank you." She didn't turn to say goodbye, just waited at the window to watch him cross the parking lot to a dark green Buick. His walk was less confident than it had been when she had seen him arrive. Had she caused the change? She'd ask him the next time he visited.

HE WOULD MAKE it up to Faith, Luke assured himself. And next time he'd be better prepared. He closed his eyes and rested his head on the back of the seat. He would help take away the pain in her eyes. She was very much like her letter—soft and vulnerable. Not like her sister, who had been hard enough to end a child's life.

Then he remembered the fear in Heidi's eyes the last time he'd seen her. Being locked away from everything and everyone you loved would be hell.

Had DeVries done anything about the trouble obviously brewing in that place for Heidi?

Stop it, you fool! he chided himself, impatiently starting the car engine. *You did what you could. More than you should have. Forget it!*

All the way back to Chicago his hands gripped the steering wheel so tightly that his arms cramped to the shoulder as he tried to concentrate on the road and not let his mind wander back to Elmwood and the woman he'd left there with tears in her eyes.

When he was safely in his condo, a Scotch and water in his hand, sitting on his patio gazing out at Lake Michigan, he didn't have to fight it anymore. He could let his feelings flow; all the disbelief, anger, pain, even horror that in one moment Heidi had robbed him of his nephew. What had made her do it?

That was what haunted him. If she hadn't interfered, Timmy might still be alive. *Probably only by a few days. Probably.*

He couldn't seem to think of anything else. He was having a tough time accepting probably. A tough time accepting his own guilt for being halfway around the world solving other people's problems when he'd been needed here by his family.

He was having second thoughts about the priorities in his life. Was Heidi having second thoughts about the decisions she'd made? Is that what haunted her eyes? There was so much he needed to know and understand.

Sliding the dog-eared press clipping from his pocket, he studied it again, rereading it, trying to find the answer in the words. But the answer wasn't there.

As he stared from her photo to the baby picture, fresh pain seared through him. The picture had banished any doubt that Faith's child didn't belong to his brother. It was Peter's baby picture. And his own.

He stared until the two photos blurred into one. Blinking, he focused on Heidi—a woman who had shown loving devotion to a child for months, then was driven to end his suffering.

Surging to his feet, he poured himself another Scotch, neat, and drank it in one gulp. He looked around at his well-ordered house. Everything was right where it should be, the way it always was. The way things should be. He went to his answering machine and played his messages, anxious only for one from the detective he'd hired to find Peter. No results yet, but they were making progress. Good!

On impulse he scribbled a note to Heidi. Two lines. "Saw Faith. She has agreed to see me again." And his name. Nothing else.

He'd do the same for anyone. Fair play was the cornerstone of everything he'd ever done. It certainly didn't mean he forgave her, or even remotely understood her. Sending the note only meant...hell, he didn't know what it meant!

Striding back onto the patio, he stood at the railing and watched the waves breaking slowly and rhythmically on the rocks below. Slow yet constant. Luke would have to move slowly and consistently to help Faith. He could help Heidi, too, if he wanted.

His hands gripped the railing. He wasn't going to think about her! He'd stop reading the newspaper article, stop staring at her picture, stop wondering about the tension he'd sensed between the women in that visiting hall. Stop wondering why, when he'd always been so sure about what was right and what was wrong, he couldn't condemn Heidi for her choice without knowing her reasons.

Maybe this time he was just too involved to think straight. He wouldn't go back to the prison. He had permission to visit Faith; he didn't need anything else from Heidi now. If he didn't see her again, maybe he could let go of it.

Nevertheless, a week later, again face-to-face with Faith, almost the first words out of his mouth were about Heidi.

"Have you heard from your sister?"

She nodded, her thick ponytail bobbing. Faith looked better today. She was dressed in a blue knit top and slacks, and a light makeup gave her some color.

"She writes every day. But I don't write back."

"Why? Are you angry with her for what she did to Timmy?" His heartbeat quickened as he waited for the answer.

Faith's pupils dilated and her smooth forehead crinkled into delicate furrows. "I don't know what to say to her."

"Perhaps you should write your feelings. You must be angry with her."

Her brown eyes looked at him with sudden clarity. "Are you angry with her?"

A hot rush of pain caught at the back of his throat. This girl was so young and so vulnerable. She deserved the truth.

"Yes, I'm angry with her," he answered as gently as possible. "I'm angry she decided it was time for Timmy to die before I had a chance to help him. But most of all I'm angry with myself because I wasn't there to help all of you. I should have been. Then perhaps Peter and Timmy would be here with us, and... your sister wouldn't be where she is."

Faith's frown disappeared and her eyes widened. "If you'd been there to help Heidi, she wouldn't have been so alone, like when Mom and Dad died. Heidi had to make all the decisions." Getting to her feet, Faith paced the floor. "Heidi always takes care of everything. She always helps me. Always!" She turned, her slender fingers clasped tightly in front of her. "I asked her to help Timmy so he wouldn't be in such pain. But... but I didn't want him to..."

The terror in her eyes brought him to her side. "Faith..."

She pulled away before he could touch her. He wanted to somehow comfort her, to take the hurt away.

"I can't talk about Timmy now. Or Heidi," she whispered, her fingers still tangled in front of her, her brown eyes dark and large in her smallface. "But... but I want to talk about Peter. Can we? Can we talk about Peter?"

He nodded slowly and lowered himself into the chair. Slowly, cautiously, she followed suit.

Luke didn't say anything; he simply did as she asked. He listened as she talked about Peter—his young brother whom she had loved. Who in return had betrayed her by deserting her and denying the child she thought they had created in love.

It wasn't easy listening to what Peter had done, and it was equally hard to accept the emerging picture of Heidi. Faith said she couldn't talk about her sister, but Heidi's presence pervaded every thought—her strength, her support, her love. Her love for Timmy.

"Timmy was such a beautiful baby," Faith whispered, tears trickling down her cheeks. "He had my dark hair but Peter's curls and... and your eyes...."

Leaning forward, Luke took her nervously twisting fingers into his hands. "Faith, I want to help you."

She licked one tear away from where it had pooled on her lower lip.

"Let me help you," he repeated, squeezing her fingers gently.

"Will you come again so we can talk? It... it helps because you're Peter's brother."

Drawing a sharp breath of relief, he nodded. "I'm glad it helps you to talk to me. Can I do anything else for you? Bring you anything?"

"David brings me what I need." Faith sat up straighter, pulling her hands away. "You could do one thing. When...when you see Heidi, tell her...tell her, hello from me. I wish she were here with me. I...I need her."

A piercing shaft of pain lodged in his chest, but he ignored it and smiled comfortingly at the young girl, who seemed to be trying so hard. "I'll tell her."

Luke sensed from her silence that she wanted to be alone. In the parking lot he turned to look back at her window. She was standing, staring down at him. He waved, and she responded with a slight movement of her hand.

All the way back to Chicago the pain compounded as he pictured the young innocent, betrayed by his brother; the infant, betrayed by her sister.

He would write to Heidi again. But to help Faith he'd have to do more. Finally admitting to himself what had to be done chilled him to the bone, but he had no choice. Tomorrow he'd make those phone calls.

LUKE WAS WAITING at a corner table of the Union Club dining room when Charles Goodman arrived.

Charlie spotted him and grinned, then made his way through table after table of businessmen.

"Well, here it is!" He dropped a file onto the table and slid into the chair across from Luke. "It's right up your alley, but small potatoes compared to your regular caseload. I don't mind bending the rules a little for a good cause, but I wish you'd tell me what this is all about."

Luke didn't reply. Instead he opened the file and scanned the affidavits. What he read shook him to the core.

He looked up at his colleague. "Given this, why didn't you get her off?" He kept his voice even, noncommittal, so Charlie wouldn't take it personally.

"She didn't want me to. Actually, she convicted herself." He shrugged, taking a drink of water. "If she'd been Timmy's mother, even if she'd pleaded guilty, I think the judge would have given her probation. But she was the kid's aunt. Although, according to the depositions I took from the hospital personnel, she stayed with him night and day for months. Even that cold fish Dawson didn't really want to testify that the kid might have lived a few days longer."

"I know. He wouldn't tell me anything." Luke slowly shut the file and leaned back in his chair, a hard lump expanding in his gut.

"Luke, what have you got in mind? Has she agreed to let you appeal?"

"Not exactly. But I intend to go over the trial transcription, maybe re-question the hospital staff." How could he sound so calm and cool as if he were discussing just any case?

"If you can convince Heidi Allan to go along with you, I don't see any problem. But, if you ask me, she wants to be punished. She couldn't stand to see the kid suffer, so she ended it. God, what a decision!" He shook his head in denial. "How did she ever do it?"

"Out of love, she says," Luke muttered, waving the waiter away.

Charlie's narrow face grew even longer as he leaned across the table. "How did you get interested in this case? God knows if anyone can get her out of jail, it's you, but this is so different from your usual stuff. Are you a friend of Miss Allan?''

His warring emotions brought Luke to his feet. "Let's just say it's personal. *Very personal!*"

Charlie's stunned look brought Luke up short, so he shot him a quick smile. "Thanks, Charlie. I owe you one. Lunch is on me.''

He signed the check brought by the hovering waiter and fled the dining room, wishing he could escape his decision just as easily.

CHAPTER SEVEN

"ALL I'VE HAD ARE two short notes from Luke. Dr. Vogland's reports are encouraging, but how does Faith seem to you?" Heidi leaned across the table toward David.

Placing his large palms over her fists, he gave her his lopsided grin. "I think she's better. I hate to admit it, but Luke Jefferson's visits seem to be helping."

"Has she sent any other messages for me?" Even as she asked, the knot in her stomach tightened. If Faith had said anything to David, he would have told her immediately.

The brief shake of his head didn't surprise her. "Maybe next time, Heidi. I'll see her again this week. She even asked me to bring some magazines."

Falling back in her chair, Heidi fought back her disappointment. "That's great. It's just that Luke's last note came three weeks ago and I keep thinking I'll hear more good news. I mean, she sent me a message, David! Do you know what that means to me?"

"Yeah, yeah, I do." His voice was gentle. "I've got to give Jefferson credit. I wasn't sure at first what his game was."

Uncannily David hit on the one constant fear that had been nagging at her for the past month. Luke had said he would be in touch, yet she had heard so little. She couldn't help wondering what Luke was doing. At

both of their meetings there had been strong undercurrents raging between them, leaving Heidi confused. Yes, he wanted to help Faith, but she also knew
he blamed her for everything.

"David, could you call Luke and tell him I'd like to
see him to talk about Faith?" she asked suddenly.

For an instant she actually thought he would refuse
her. Angel was right: the two men didn't like each
other. Finally, though, David nodded and looked at her
searchingly. "If there was anything wrong here, anything you needed help with, you'd tell me, right?"

"Of course!" Heidi forced a smile. "I'm doing fine
with Angel's help."

"Yeah, well, I admit having that little toughie in
your corner makes me sleep better at night."

"David, all I'm worried about is Faith. Will you talk
to Luke and find out how his visits with her are going?"

"Don't worry about Luke. I'll make sure you see
him. Now let me buy you a drink. You look like you
need one. Diet or regular?"

Laughing, she took his outstretched hand and let
him pull her to her feet. "Diet. But I'll take a candy
bar."

"Want me to buy some for Angel?"

Heidi suddenly stopped dead in her tracks, turning
to look up at him. "David, have you given any more
thought to what I asked about Angel's dancing?"

"Maybe." He shrugged. "Hey, I just offered the kid
a candy bar, not a career. Don't get so excited."

"David, I know you!" She couldn't keep the eagerness out of her voice. "There's so much more to Angel than you see. So much she doesn't even realize. We

can't stand by and let it all go to waste when we're in a position to help."

"Yeah, well it looks like she could use some help now." He looked beyond her left shoulder. "Who's that lowlife she's with?"

Startled, Heidi followed the direction of his eyes.

In the far corner, slumped in a chair, her small face deathly white, Angel sat with Santos. What was he doing here again? Heidi had thought Angel was in the Helpers' room. She'd been so caught up in her own problems, she hadn't even noticed Santos's arrival.

Ignoring David, she pushed past him, heading straight for Angel. She'd seen that look on her face before.

Angel saw her coming. Her eyes widened, and she surreptitiously shook her head, but Heidi refused to be put off. *You do me a favor I do you one.* She could repay Angel by protecting her from Santos. Angel was afraid of him whether she admitted it or not.

Forcing a bright smile, she stopped at Angel's shoulder. "Hi! Sorry, but Officer Connell needs you with the children."

"What the hell!" Santos's swarthy face turned toward her and his eyes narrowed. "If it isn't Doll Face again. Sit down, babe, and join us." His oily voice, his sly, narrowed gaze sliding over her body, made her feel dirty.

"Sorry, can't. Angel and I have our duties in the Howell's Helpers room. C'mon, Angel. Connell is waiting."

Santos maintained his grip on Angel's arm. His mouth curled in a smirk. "Can't let my Angel go just now. Just got here."

"Sorry, buddy, the ladies have another engagement," David's voice boomed from behind her. Santos gazed upward, the smirk disappearing, replaced by a dangerous twist to his thin lips.

"What's it to ya? This here's Angel's visitin' day. Isn't there rules or somethin'?"

"Yeah. I think you're breaking them. Let go of her!"

Santos insolently eyed David's bulk before he released Angel, throwing his shoulders back in a mocking shrug. "Ain't goin' to give no problems to no body builder."

Before Angel could hide her hands, Heidi saw bruises marring the delicate skin.

Angel rose slowly, refusing to meet anyone's eyes. "Sorry, Santos. I'll see you around."

"Better believe it. Yer my girl. Don't ya forget it!"

Her hair fell forward over her cheek so that Heidi couldn't see her expression as she nodded and turned away.

Heidi followed, not concerned about David. He could make mincemeat out of the likes of Santos. It was Angel Heidi was worried about as she dejectedly made her way across the visitors' area with none of her natural grace. In the safety of the Helpers' room, with the door pulled shut, Angel fell into a vacant chair and buried her face in her hands. Heidi saw that she was trembling.

"Is she all right?" David asked quietly, suddenly behind her.

At that Angel flung back her head, her hair cascading down her back, her eyes gleaming black pools. Slowly but surely her chin thrust out with her usual spirit.

"*She's* just fine. Sorry I interrupted your visit."

"David is just leaving."

His stunned expression made him look like a little boy. A wave of affection made Heidi give him a hug. "Woman talk," she whispered into his neck before stepping away.

"All right, I'll see you soon, Heidi." For the first time he gave Angel one of his real smiles. "Take care of yourself, Angel," he said, his green eyes crinkling.

"Don't I always?" she parried, refusing to give ground in their ongoing squabble. She watched until he disappeared through the folding door. "Sometimes I can't figure him." Shaking her head, she looked down at her bruised hands, flexing them tentatively.

"Santos hurt you," Heidi observed quietly.

"Hell, this is nothing! Wait until I get out and he realizes I'm not going back to the gang. That's when he'll really hurt me!"

Heidi leaned closer. "Angel, I don't understand. What does he want from you?"

"He wants me to come back to the business. That's what got me in here. Santos and the gang have their fingers in theft, extortion, protection, you know. He's smarter than he looks. And meaner. I helped him in all his deals. We were stealing cars and selling them for parts when I got busted. He still has a booming chop shop business going." Angel's voice was resigned. "I can't believe I was ever hooked up with him."

Heidi wasn't shocked by Angel's past, but she was stunned by the defeat in her usually defiant voice. "You don't have to settle for that kind of life anymore. You have so much potential, so much to offer. You have to know that." She touched Angel's shoulder.

For once Angel didn't jerk away.

"You don't have to go back to Santos." Heidi insisted, almost desperate to get through to her. "You *shouldn't* go back. There are others ways to survive."

"Yeah, sometimes I dream about other things. I used to dream a lot when I was a kid. You know, about dancing and stuff. I...I just don't know if I've got what it takes to walk away from the old life and find a new one."

"I'll help you. I *want* to help you."

"You have. This is the second time you've helped me out with Santos. I won't forget it."

"That's what friends are for." Meeting Angel's open look, Heidi recognized the truth: she and Angel had a real friendship, based on need but bolstered by respect. "You'd do the same for me. I know if it weren't for you, Maxime would be a real problem for me."

As if mentioning her name had conjured her up, Maxime suddenly loomed over them. The smirk cracking her wide face told Heidi something had happened that made her courageous enough to confront them. It was a mark of Angel's exhaustion that she didn't immediately leap to her feet in confrontation. Instead, she leaned back and almost casually said, "Get lost! Haven't you learned your lesson?"

"What kind of talk is that?" Maxime's ruddy face fell into an exaggerated pout. "Just came in here to congraduate ya. Heard what's comin' down through the grapevine. Honor Cottage! We'll miss ya, but Heidi here can make some new friends. Don't worry, Angel. I'll take care of yer old roomy."

Her crackling laughter echoing against the concrete walls as she swaggered out sent icy fingers of fear through every cell of Heidi's body. She looked questioningly at Angel, who shrugged, her eyes hard.

"Don't worry about that piece... I'll take care of it, Heidi."

SHE'D SAID she would take care of everything. But sitting in the warden's office, Angel still hadn't made up her mind. She was so confused that she couldn't think straight. The Honor Cottage or Heidi Allan?

Tense and hot, she couldn't stop her foot from tapping out her indecision. The warden glanced down at her restless stacatto, then up into her face. "There's no need to be nervous, Angel. I've got good news for you. Even though Coralee isn't back yet, I'm moving you into the Honor Cottage tomorrow. You've earned it."

This was it. No time left. Hell, this was what she'd wanted. What she'd earned. There was only one answer.

"I don't want to move."

What had she said? She was as shocked as Warden Howell. That wasn't what she had planned to say! Where had it come from?

Drawing in too sharp a breath, Angel blinked sudden moisture out of her eyes. What had she done? For the first time Warden Howell's brown eyes reflected understanding rather than impartiality. It was frightening. Howell knew.

Not since Angel was a little girl at St. Bart's wanting to please Miss Juliette with a new step, wanting to make people happy with her dancing, had she put someone else before herself. That realization scared her down deep inside where all those precious, secret memories were stored. Tears burned behind her eyes and way back in her throat so that it was hard to swallow.

She was turning down the Honor Cottage to stay with Heidi, who needed her. Heidi had helped her; now it was her turn. It was that simple.

"Are you quite sure about this, Angel?" the warden asked, leaning across her desk, pinning her with knowing eyes.

"Yeah." Angel shrugged. "I'm real honored and everything, but I'll be getting out in February. I might as well stay with Heidi. We get along good." She was running off at the mouth, talking faster, trying to spill out her energy. "We both like music, you know."

"Yes, I know."

Angel tried to sit quietly while Warden Howell studied her, but heaved a great sigh of relief when, at last, the warden stood and dismissed her.

"I'll want to discuss this with you again at three this afternoon."

Not again! Angel didn't know if she could do this again. "Warden Howell, I'm not going to change my mind."

"Three this afternoon, Angel. I'll see you then." The command was explicit and, of course, Angel would be there.

Angel was relieved to get out of the office. She'd made the right decision. Now she'd just keep telling herself she owed Heidi—for the clothes, the radio, helping her with Santos. She couldn't pay her back in any other way. This would work out. It had to! Hopefully, by the time Angel left Elmwood, Heidi would have learned the ropes better. She'd be on her own then.

HEIDI, although apprehensive, was determined. Angel deserved the Honor Cottage. She'd be on her own for the first time and she'd get a new roommate. The grapevine already knew all about it. Now she was going to get the news officially, or why else would Officer Connell be leading her into Warden Howell's office?

It was the first time Heidi had been here. The wood-paneled room was like a oasis from her past life: green hanging plants at the windows, a faded but still-beautiful rug on the wood floor, the creak of leather as she lowered herself into one of the chairs in front of the massive desk.

"How are you getting along, Heidi?" Warden Howell asked, smiling faintly.

"I'm fine, thank you."

The warden flipped through a file. From the smooth way Elmwood Prison ran, Heidi would bet Warden Howell already knew everything in that file, knew everything there was to know about Heidi Allan.

"It seems you and Angel have developed a strong friendship."

Heidi nodded. "I'd like to think we're friends. We actually have a great deal in common."

"Well, I can assure you of one thing. Angel considers you a friend. She turned down the Honor Cottage to stay with you."

"No! You can't let her do that!" Heidi was on her feet before she remembered who she was talking to. "I'm sorry," she eased back down, her heart still pounding. "It's just that I've heard how nice it is in the Honor Cottage. Angel deserves it! You can't let her give that up for me."

"Yes, Angel deserves it. And I have no intention of letting her give it up." Warden Howell folded her hands firmly on the desk blotter. "But we both know that if

Angel gets stubborn, she could easily stop this transfer. Say, for instance, she had a fight with Maxime.''

Heidi held her breath. She was right. The warden knew everything that went on here. She lifted her head, her eyes locking with the warden's. She held that look, silence stretching between them until a certain unspoken understanding was reached.

"I intervene whenever it is necessary for personal safety. I want you to be quite certain of that,'' the warden stated quietly.

Heidi took a long breath into her aching lungs and sat back in her chair. The warden was assuring her protection if needed. But Heidi wasn't worried about that; she had to make sure Angel didn't lose the Honor Cottage.

"I can take care of myself. Angel's shown me the ropes.'' It gave her confidence to realize the quiet words were really true. Because of Angel, she could make it here on her own. "Now I want to make sure she gets what she's earned!''

The warden's brows lifted. "It seems we do have a strong bond here. Which is why I'm going to make you an offer.'' Slowly turning in her swivel chair, Warden Howell looked out the window into the prison yard.

Heidi looked, too, but beyond the buildings to the high brick wall, the barbed wire curling ominously above. It was all too familiar: lines of women moving across the compound to their appointed destinations with no spontaneity, no self-determination, merely a never-ending routine.

"This is your world now.'' The warden turned back to her. "Even though you're a prisoner here, in this facility we want your time to be productive. For some this is their only chance for an education or job training. We don't want to simply punish you for your crime against society. We want to reeducate you so you don't make the same mistake again." She paused. "The return rate here is over fifty percent. Did you know that, Heidi?"

Stunned, Heidi shook her head. What was the warden leading up to?

"Shocking, isn't it? And sad to contemplate our failure with so many. But when I see a change, as I see in Angel, I encourage it in every way possible. I don't want to see Angel return here, and I think you could help her beat the odds." She stood and walked around to the front of her desk. "That's why I'm moving you into the Honor Cottage with her—but only temporarily. Her roommate, Coralee, will be hospitalized for a while longer. When she returns, you'll be moved."

Heidi's relief was overwhelming. She had never expected any special treatment here, nor had she received it. "I don't know what to say."

"You don't need to say anything. Just continue to do whatever you've been doing. It's working for both of you. And the social worker informs me even little Joyce is making outstanding progress because of you. It was wonderful how you knew the piano was the key to helping her. Have you ever given any thought to music therapy if you don't go back to entertaining?"

"Actually, I have." Heidi finally gave voice to the idea that had been forming at the back of her mind.

"It shouldn't be too difficult. You already have a masters in music. I'll set up an appointment with the Watkins State College counselor to see if there are any classes available to take here."

Warden Howell moved toward the door in dismissal. "Officers Needham and Connell will assist with your move after dinner. Angel will be informed of this decision. Good luck."

As she crossed the compound, Heidi still couldn't quite believe it. Nothing she'd seen or heard of prison life had prepared her for Warden Howell, who seemed more concerned about individuals than about the system. Her afternoon at the shirt works flew by. The excitement even kept her usual worries about Faith and Luke at bay. She couldn't wait to see Angel's reaction.

For the first time Angel voluntarily touched her, grabbing her hands, dancing around their small room.

"I can't believe it! We're both going! Heidi, the Honor Cottage! Do you know what this means?"

They came to a laughing, breathless halt, and Heidi sagged against the bunk bed. "No locks, you said. And a kitchen with a microwave."

"And a TV room. We can sit up all night if we want. And on weekends our visitors can come right to the cottage." She peered questioningly at Heidi. "That Luke guy, the one who looks like Redford, where's he been? Haven't seen him for a while. He can come there to visit you."

Not wanting to spoil Angel's excitement, Heidi forced a smile. "He'll be coming soon, I hope. David's going to talk to him."

A light pink color stained Angel's hollow cheeks. "Oh, yeah, David will be coming to the Cottage, too." Heidi wasn't fooled, even though Angel shrugged dismissively and began to plait her long hair. "I forgot all about him. I'm not sure the Honor Cottage TV room is big enough for both of them."

"You might be right." Heidi laughed, determined to concentrate on nothing but Angel's happiness. She wouldn't think about Luke until she had to, yet perversely she longed for him to fulfill his promise to keep in touch about Faith's progress.

What was he doing? And why?

DAVID BARRELED through Luke's door unannounced, the scowl darkening his face proof that he wouldn't be deterred, even by Luke's secretary, who followed a step behind.

With a flick of his hand Luke halted her, and she closed the door discreetly, leaving him staring into David's cold green eyes.

"You saw Charles Goodman! Why?"

"Sit down, DeVries, and I'll explain—even though you don't have an appointment."

Without ceremony David eased into a chair and unfastened the gold button on his navy blue blazer. "Just what are you doing sticking your nose into Heidi's business now?" he asked gruffly.

Luke gripped the arms of his chair as he decided how to answer that question. Instead, he countered with a question of his own. "Did you work out that little problem I mentioned?"

"That's not what I want to talk about and you know it! I've understood from the beginning that you blame Heidi for Timmy's death. *That's* what we need to talk about. Your continuing problem with Heidi! Look, Luke, you've said your obligation begins and ends with Faith. But you won't, ultimately, be able to help Faith without involving her sister. You must know that or you wouldn't have met with her lawyer. I'm asking you again—why?"

Luke stared at David, blue eyes meeting green. "I'm not prepared to discuss this with you right now."

"Are you going to help her get out of prison? That is your specialty, isn't it? She can't be punished any more than she's punishing herself," David said softly, his eyes riveted on Luke's face.

Luke surged to his feet, abruptly turning away to the window, depriving David of any inadvertent revelation.

"Let go of it, Luke," David continued relentlessly. "It's eating you up. You know Heidi loved Timmy more than anything. She had the courage to end his pointless suffering with loving dignity. I'm not sure I possess such courage."

Luke didn't know how to respond to David's words. Hadn't he tried to make sense of it all time and again?

"Don't you have the courage to try to understand even if you can't condone her choice? Damn it, you know Heidi is no monster! She needs your help, too!"

Luke spun around. David's last salvo hit home. The truth was, much as he wished it otherwise, Heidi *wasn't* a monster; she was a loving, compassionate, tender woman.

Taking a deep breath, Luke faced David squarely, his decision made. "I've recognized that Heidi's presence would greatly enhance Faith's chance for complete recovery, so I've gone over her case. It's quite clear from a legal standpoint that there were mitigating circumstances which, if presented correctly, should convince the governor to commute her sentence. I can't get a pardon."

"Then you're going to help her?"

Luke nodded. It was some slight victory to see stunned relief on David's face.

"Can we appeal without her knowing about it? She won't even discuss it with me." For once David looked uncertain.

"No, it's unethical to proceed without her consent. I'll have to convince her. I'll use Faith's well-being to bring her around."

"I've got just the place to start. Heidi's birthday is this Saturday. Bring Faith to the prison. I've spoken to Dr. Vogland, and he thinks she's ready." David's voice was even, controlled again. "She's still angry with me, and I can't convince her to do anything, but I think she would go with you. Believe me, you and Heidi, working together, might be able to pull Faith out of herself." He looked at Luke hopefully. "What do you think?"

For an instant Luke was back at school on the football field with an enormous linebacker ready to annihilate him. He sidestepped quickly. "I'll talk to Faith about it." But even as he said the words he knew he'd convince Faith to go. The key to helping both sisters was their need and love for each other.

He was relieved when David left, so he could mull over his decision alone. He looked down at the case files on his desk. "Crusader Lawyer," indeed. Until this moment he'd never realized the full extent of his need to see injustice righted. It even went beyond his personal feelings.

After all, what had Heidi done but end a baby's suffering. Given what he'd learned, he could almost understand how she could be brought to that point of despair. Almost, and if it hadn't been his nephew, he wasn't sure if his feelings might be different. That was his personal demon, and he had to face it.

He dropped into his chair and buzzed for his secretary. If he sent a note by messenger, Faith would have time to think about it before his regular visit on Wednesday.

"YES, I...I think I'm ready to see Heidi." Faith twisted her fingers nervously.

"Faith, it isn't necessary to be there for her birthday. You could send her a gift or a card with David."

What was the matter with him? He'd already decided what had to be done, what path to take.

Faith twisted the end of her ponytail between her fingers. "I hate to ask, but I need another favor. I think I have to see Heidi, and I should take a present. She's never forgotten my birthday even when she was on tour in Europe. Can you get something nice for me to take her?"

He quelled the hot rush of panic at the thought of making so intimate a selection for Heidi. He needed to put emotional distance between them not choose gifts for her!

Nevertheless, he nodded. "What do you want me to get?"

"I...I don't know." Slumping into a chair, she gazed at him with wide, questioning eyes. "What can she have in...in that place? When you visit, does she ever ask for anything?"

Luke thought of the last time he'd seen her, of the emotions that had exploded between them. He remembered how, even in the midst of his rage, her light floral fragrance had drifted across the table to tug at his senses.

"I don't really know," he said, slowly. "What about perfume?"

Straightening up, Faith smiled confidently. "Oscar. It's her favorite. Could you get a bottle for her?"

"I'll take care of it." Springing up, he paced the floor like a nervous cat. "I'll fill out all the papers in Dr. Vogland's office today so there will be no delays on Saturday."

He halted in front of her and studied her upturned face. God, she was so young to have suffered so much pain. "Are you sure you're ready for this, Faith?"

"No. I . . . I don't know what I'm going to say to my sister, but I know I have to face this or I'll never be well."

Her words haunted him for the next two days. He was no different from Faith: he was afraid how he really felt. He would help Heidi only to support Faith's progress and because her case merited it. If there were other reasons stirring inside him, he wouldn't accept them; he'd simply lock them away as if they didn't exist.

If Faith could find the courage to conquer her fears, surely he could overcome his demon.

But his uncertainty lingered, gaining strength when Faith insisted they stop at a florist to get flowers on their way to Elmwood the next Saturday morning. Not roses, but gardenias, she insisted. Heidi had always had gardenias on the piano when she performed. It helped soften the scent of smoke and wine in some of the clubs she played.

In contrast Faith appeared quietly resigned to this meeting with her sister, even as they stood in line in the prison waiting room. To his surprise, when the officer learned their names, he motioned them to one side, where a female guard waited.

"If you'll follow me, I'll show you to the Honor Cottage."

Instead of going through the double glass doors, Connell led them out a side entrance into the very heart of the prison yard—a grassy field crisscrossed with paths leading to surrounding buildings. If you kept your eyes level, it could have been a college campus.

Luke noticed Faith's eyes widen as she looked beyond the buildings to the high stone walls and the menacing barbed wire. Her steps faltered, and she came to a halt.

"Oh," she murmured.

Placing an arm around her shoulders, he urged her on. "It's all right. I'm here with you," he said with more assurance than he felt.

They were led to a stone bungalow set slightly apart from the longer, lower buildings. With a jangle of keys Connell unlocked a large wooden door and shoved it open, motioning them through.

They could hear low voices and snatches of laughter coming from huddles of people in a room off the front hall.

"Heidi Allan is probably in the TV room back there." The officer gestured to the left before stepping back and shutting the door.

A shiver ran down Luke's spine. This wasn't quite what he had envisioned when he lay awake nights thinking about Heidi, trying to untangle everything in his mind. But the snap of the lock put it all back into perspective.

She was sitting on a stiff brown couch at the back of the room, smiling and talking to the petite dark-haired girl called Angel.

Angel saw them first and nudged Heidi's shoulder.

Heidi's eyes took them both in at the same instant, and something sharp and piercing ripped low in his gut at the look of stunned joy in her face.

"Faith?" she gasped, standing utterly still before stepping toward them, her slender arms outstretched. "Faith, honey, it *is* you!"

In response Faith shrank back into Luke's embrace, turning her face away and burying it in his chest.

Once, a lifetime ago, he had wanted Heidi to experience pain, to know what he'd felt when he learned about Timmy, but now it tore him apart to see her beautiful face crumble, her eyes filling with tears as her arms dropped limply to her sides.

He looked away, to Angel. Never before had he noticed her resemblance to Faith—the same petite body, the same long, thick, dark hair falling about a piquant face. But something in Angel's eyes as she stared at Faith made him tighten his protective grip.

"You must be Faith, Heidi's sister," she said, shoving herself forward between Heidi and Faith. "I just found out it's her birthday. Is that present for her?"

Since Angel was nearly shouting right into Faith's ear, she couldn't ignore it. Shifting in his arms, she timidly glanced up. "Yes, it's for Heidi's birthday."

"Good!" Angel removed the cream-and-gold gift bag from Faith's unresisting hand and placed it on the coffee table.

"Luke brought her something, too," Faith whispered.

Luke forced himself to look again at Heidi. Her face was devoid of all color as her dark, anguished eyes hungrily watched her sister.

"Here, these are for you." He thrust the florist box forward, and like an automaton she took it from him.

"Great!" Angel laughed with forced cheerfulness, whisking the box away. "Now we can have a birthday party."

"You can't have a party without a cake!"

They all stared at David as he strode into the room. He gave Luke the barest flicker of a grin before striding up to Heidi.

"Hey, birthday girl, feast your eyes on this!" With great ceremony he lifted the top of the bakery box, revealing a chocolate frosted cake that had already been cut into narrow slices. "This is what took me so long. The guards had to be sure I wasn't sneaking in a nail file," David quipped, placing the cake beside the two gifts. "Got any plates and forks in your new digs, Angel?"

"Yeah, I'll get them from the kitchenette. Got some soda in the fridge, too. C'mon, Luke, you can help me carry."

Startled, he stared at her, and she gave him a frank grin. "Yeah, you. I can't carry everything myself."

"I'll help you, Angel," Heidi said softly, shaking off the effects of Faith's rejection.

"No, you stay and visit. It's your birthday! C'mon, Luke," Angel insisted, refusing to take no for an answer.

Glancing down at Faith, he lifted his brows. "Are you all right now?"

"Sure she's all right." David moved closer. "Faith and I are old friends, even if she is still mad at me."

"Don't be a smart aleck, David," Faith snapped with more spirit than Luke had heard before.

Laughing, David jerked his head toward where Angel waited, impatiently tapping her foot. "See, what did I tell you? Go on. Everything's fine."

Reluctantly Luke took his arm away. Faith didn't cling to him, but she refused to look in her sister's direction. She'd wanted to see Heidi, and for a moment he found himself wishing she'd face her.

From the hallway he glanced back. Somehow David had maneuvered Faith and Heidi to the couch, and he was carrying on a one-sided conversation, the sisters silent on either side of him.

When Luke stepped into the tiny galley kitchen, Angel was already removing plates and forks from the cabinets.

"What can I do to help?"

"Tell me what's going on with that sister of Heidi's," she demanded, glaring at him. "Why the hell did she come if she was going to be such a brat?"

His back stiffened. He of all people understood Faith's ambivalence. "Faith has had a difficult time of it. This is her first trip outside. She's still in a sanatorium."

"Oh, yeah, and this is summer camp! Heidi isn't exactly having the time of her life, either, you know!" She shoved two cans in his hands. "The diet pop's for Heidi. Do what you can with the kid, will you? It's Heidi's birthday, for God's sake!"

Following her graceful lead back into the TV room, Luke couldn't help smiling. *The kid.* Angel and Faith could barely be a year apart. Heidi seemed so much older. He noticed that David had finally coaxed her to smile.

Serving the first slice of cake, she cast a tentative glance at her sister's averted face. "Would you like a piece, Faith?"

"Yes, please." She barely glanced up long enough to take the plate from Heidi's hands.

"Here! This is for you!" Angel plopped a cold can in front of her.

"Thanks," Faith muttered, nibbling at the cake without enthusiasm.

By now Luke was ready to break the awkward silence himself, but David and Angel beat him to it. They kept up a barrage of repartee that, once, even got a flicker of a smile from Faith. But not from Heidi. She couldn't seem to keep her eyes from feasting on her sister's face any more than he could keep his own from watching her.

"Open your presents," Angel demanded when they finished their cake. "If I'd known sooner, I'd have ordered you something out of a mail-order catalog."

Heidi's face softened, her lips curving with genuine emotion. "You've already given me my present."

No one could miss the understanding that flashed between the two women. Even Faith glanced up and frowned at Angel.

"Go on, open your presents," Angel laughed, moving them closer.

Heidi's hands were graceful as they carefully removed the tissue paper. "Oscar! Oh, thank you, Faith! I love it."

Faith merely nodded, and Angel flashed Luke another exasperated look.

The girl was right. He was standing around like a stick, letting the situation degenerate around him instead of taking charge. From David's inquiring look, Luke knew that he, too, was waiting for him to act. He'd said he would convince her to let them help her. So far he wasn't doing a great job of it.

"I picked up the other present at Faith's suggestion. She said they were your favorites," he said in near desperation. It must have been the right thing to say, though, because Heidi's face softened as she opened the box.

"Gardenias." Heidi breathed, lifting the two entwined blossoms to her face. "I love them! I always have gardenias on the piano when I play."

"I remembered," Faith said softly, her fingers twisting together in her lap.

David flicked him another knowing grin and, absurdly, he was relieved.

Angel held the flowers next to Heidi's hair. "They smell great! Here, let me pin them in. There! Don't they look pretty, Faith?"

The force of Angel's inquiry brought Faith's head up. Finally she looked at her sister. "Yes...very pretty."

"Well, birthday girl, now that you've opened your presents, how about showing us your new place?" David suggested.

Luke was grateful that no one was paying any attention to his own inner struggle. Faith was pale and quiet, Angel looked ready to slap her, and Heidi...well, he just wasn't going to think about Heidi except as his potential client. And probably a reluctant one at that!

Her long fingers carefully settled the flowers more securely into the heavy, honey-colored curl behind her ear. "The TV room, kitchen and laundry room on this floor are all there is to see. Our bedroom is upstairs and off-limits."

"No, it's not," Angel said with determined cheerfulness. "One of us can take a visitor up, as long as it's less than five minutes. Hey, I can give you a present after all! Go ahead, you take someone first."

They all watched anxiously as Heidi rose slowly to her feet and took one step toward her sister. "Faith, would you like to see where I'm staying?"

Shaking her head, Faith sank deeper into the couch. I'm ... I'm a little tired. Maybe ... maybe next time."

Luke saw color come and go in Heidi's cheeks as she sucked in a deep, shuddering breath. "All right, then. Maybe next time." Swinging around, she caught him staring at her. "Luke, would you like to see our room?"

Stunned by her request, he nodded, then instantly realized it was the break he needed. He had to plant the seed soon, and he could feel that this was the right time.

Side by side they climbed the narrow tiled stairs, the clicking of their heels the only sound. The upper hall had four open doors on each side, and at the end a large opening indicated shower stalls. Heidi stepped into the second doorway on the right.

The room was neat and compact. Two beds jutted out from one wall, built-in shelving lined the other, and in a corner was a toilet and small stainless-steel sink. There was no window. The bars of this cell were invisible but invincible. He could feel them pressing down on him. Especially when he finally turned to confront her.

They stood at the center of her world now and the scent of gardenias surrounded them. For a few moments they searched each other's eyes.

"Why did you ask me up here?" His voice was rough. He still needed anger as a barrier, he realized.

"I want to thank you. For your notes. For your visits to Faith. You've helped her so much. David thinks so, and Dr. Vogland's reports have been encouraging.

But most of all I want to thank you for bringing her here today.''

He stood his ground, determined to do what he planned—to help her despite herself, despite himself. So he didn't step back from the open look on her beautiful face; he didn't step back from the softly appealing body so close to his. He never backed down once his decision was made.

"How long have you been here, Heidi?" he asked abruptly.

Surprise widened her eyes. "Since early summer," she answered quietly.

"It must be...hard...being locked away. How much longer do you have?"

The soft brown eyes studied him cautiously, her nervousness betrayed by the rise and fall of her breasts beneath the cream sweater.

"You know how long my sentence is, don't you, Luke?"

He shrugged, his insides coiled in a tight ball of apprehension. "With good behavior you could get released early. Or you could appeal to the governor. I could do that—for Faith's sake."

Stunned confusion parted her lips. "I'm surprised you feel that way. I thought..."

He shook his head as if to deny all his feelings. He needed to keep talking. "My family owes its help to Faith. David pointed out that you're vital to her recovery. Certainly you would be more effective at helping her if you were out of here." He paused, ordering his thoughts. "This isn't turning out very well, is it? It's not the breakthrough visit for Faith we hoped for."

"But it's a beginning!"

For the first time he experienced her warmth and joy. It reached out to him, drawing him to her.

"It's a beginning," she repeated, stepping forward, closer to him. "It's more than I'd hoped for. It's the most wonderful birthday gift anyone could have given me. I don't know why you did it, but thank you so much."

Before he could move away to safety she touched him. She took his hand between her long, graceful fingers. Survival depended on pulling away, but he couldn't—it was no use denying the torrent of raging heat that threatened to consume him. He had to get Heidi out of prison. The reasons why made it impossible to move, to do anything but stare into Heidi's eyes.

CHAPTER EIGHT

HEIDI WAS SUFFOCATING. Her heart pounded, trying to draw oxygen from blood that had stopped flowing, her lungs refusing to expand for life-giving air.

Life, her life, was frozen in one unendurable frame. Just like the picture, forever fixed in her subconscious, of Timmy closing his eyes and growing still in her arms. Now this could be added to her torment; this instant she had touched Luke—the man who had made her admit to herself what she had done. Yet she continued to hold his hand within her fingers, for he, too, seemed caught up in this terrifying immobility.

Finally she tore her fingers away, fighting a hot rush of fear. His kindnesses to Faith had blinded her to his danger. This man broke through all her fragile fortifications, exposing her darkest fears. She mustn't forget who he was.

She pulled her trembling hands away and hid them behind her back. "I'm sorry...I shouldn't...have done that, knowing how you feel. It's...it's just that I don't understand why you're being so kind to me."

"*You* don't understand!" He laughed mirthlessly.

Heidi leaned back against the bed frame for support. "I don't expect anything for myself. But I hope you'll live up to your promise to help Faith."

"I always do what I promise," he insisted, then quickly whirled away from her, putting as much space between them as the tiny room would allow. "We must all live up to our responsibilities to Faith. And that includes you! Don't you understand that none of this should have happened at all?"

Mentally she pulled back into herself as he turned and stepped closer—so close that their bodies were separated only by a hairbreadth.

"Peter should have lived up to his responsibilities to Faith. I should have been close enough to Peter that he could come to me for help. If I had really been there for him, none of this would have happened. I'm trying to understand and deal with the wrong choices I've made." His voice was softer now yet somehow more frightening. "What I still can't deal with or understand is your choice!"

She closed her eyes, trying to gather what was left of her courage. "I told you...I loved Timmy," she whispered through her tear-choked throat.

"I believe that now."

Dizzy with relief, she opened her eyes.

"Yes...I believe you loved him," he whispered, "but that makes the rest impossible to understand. Loving him, how could you give up? Explain so I can try to make sense of it. I need to make sense of 'probably'— Dr. Dawson's judgment that 'probably' Timmy would have lived a few more days. What if he was wrong? What if Timmy suddenly went into remission? What if they found a cure? How could you, who loved him so much, settle for 'probably'?"

There was no defense. His questions were her nightmares brought in all their grotesqueness to the clear light of reason. All her pain, all her doubt rose up and destroyed the last of her facade. She fought back sobs.

"Don't you think I've asked myself those same questions a thousand times?"

The air simmered with tension as each of them tried to deal with the pain. Then, at the point of total despair, some feeble spark of courage enabled her to meet his eyes.

"God help me, if I could give you your answers I would." Tears flowed down her cheeks and echoed in her voice. "I need them to go on myself."

Rubbing sweaty palms over her wet cheeks, she took a deep breath to quiet her pounding pulse. She was caught off guard when Luke swiveled around, locking his hands to the bed frame on either side of her.

She was trapped, his body intimidating, although he still didn't touch her.

"Listen to me, Heidi. I want you to think about something. Nothing can change what happened. I've got to accept that and so do you. The only thing we can change is the here and now. Now Faith needs you. Everyone agrees that if you could see Faith regularly, you might be able to break through to her. By continuing to punish yourself you're also hampering Faith's recovery. You don't need to be locked in here to punish yourself. I can see in your eyes that you will do that wherever you are."

Heidi drew a ragged breath, stunned that he saw so much. She would never again touch him to offer any form of solace, but she knew she had to do something. "I want to help Faith more than anything," she whispered, her insides knotted so tightly she could hardly breathe.

"Then let me come back and talk to you about your options."

Something in his eyes prompted her to nod slowly.

Relieved, Luke dropped his arms and stepped away, enabling Heidi to escape. She started down the narrow stairs and forced herself to look natural. Her face ached from forcing a fake smile. She settled beside David on the hard couch and asked, "Would anyone like some more cake? It's quite delicious."

Angel looked at her suspiciously, but Heidi turned to her sister. "Faith, can I get you anything else?"

"I'm tired. I should leave now if...if it's all right with Luke."

"Of course it's all right with me. It's been a long day for you." Leaning over, Luke helped Faith up from the couch. His smile was gentle and so was his voice.

Heidi was relieved to see how careful he was with her sister, not allowing any of the undercurrents to reach her. Unable to stop herself, Heidi stood for one last try. "It was good to see you, Faith. Thank you for my presents. I hope you'll come again soon." She couldn't keep the pleading tone out of her voice.

For just an instant Faith's downcast eyes rose to meet hers, then quickly she looked to Luke. Angel shot Heidi a look that spoke volumes, but suddenly Faith surprised them all. "I'll come...if Luke will bring me."

If Heidi's gaze hadn't been locked with Luke's, she would have missed the flash of something...new.

"Yes, Faith and I will be back," he promised, his voice soft and a flicker of confusion in his eyes.

Heidi watched them longingly while an officer unlocked the door and they disappeared into the yard.

"Heidi." The pressure of David's hand made her turn to face him. "Are you all right? Did you and Jefferson come to any understanding?"

She'd seen this calculating look before. "What kind of plan are you concocting for my benefit, David?"

He had the good grace to give her his silly, lopsided grin, which she knew was reserved only for those he cared about and trusted. "We're all in this together. He's helping Faith, and I think you and he can help each other, too. In fact, I'm betting on it."

She hoped David was right. Luke had said she must think about how they could help Faith. For now she'd focus on that, not the tension that had sprung to life between them in her tiny room.

Throwing her arms around David's broad frame, she gave him a quick, tight hug. "You're a good friend, David. Luke and I talked. He said something tonight that made me think. If I could see Faith more often, maybe I could break through to her."

He gripped her shoulders, his face incredulous. "Does this mean you're considering an appeal?"

Tilting her head back, she forced a smile. "I don't know, David. But I am going to think about what might be best for Faith."

"Well, hallelujah! Birthday girl, you've made me very happy." He laughed, playfully cuffing her chin. "There's something else I want to talk about. Your guardian angel." He stopped abruptly as Angel came back from carrying dirty dishes to the kitchen.

"Hey, Heidi, want me to share this cake with the other girls? Or do you want it, David?" she asked, giving his body a slow once-over. "Nah, I forgot. You body-builder types probably don't eat cake. Especially at your age." Grinning, her face glowingly beautiful, she twirled away to flit around the room offering cake to the other visitors and inmates.

"As you were saying?" Heidi tried to prompt him. But David wasn't paying attention. He was following

Angel's laughing progress around the room. "Da-vid?"

Blinking, he turned back to her. "What?"

"You wanted to talk about Angel," she reminded him gently.

"Oh, yeah. I just wanted you to know I'm thinking about what you asked. We'll see what happens." He engulfed her in another bear hug. "First things first. Think about what Luke said."

Heidi shivered as the door opened for David and a cold blast of air cut through her thin clothes. Angel glided past her with a long look at the closing door.

Still shivering, Heidi wrapped her arms around her shoulders. What would the next few weeks hold for all of them? If she got released early, she would be thrown together with Luke in their efforts to help Faith. That thought kept her awake long after everyone else had gone to sleep. She tried to be careful so her restlessness wouldn't wake Angel. But sometime after midnight, she heard the faint strains of an old love ballad. Angel must have fallen asleep with the radio on.

Or was she awake, too? Did thoughts of freedom taunt her? Her sentence would end in February; after the time she'd spent here, that would seem very close. Maybe she thought about David; Heidi hadn't missed the brief look of longing on her face as he left.

Were they both restless for the same reasons? She had told Warden Howell they had a lot in common, and they grew closer every day. Whatever happened, she could never simply walk away from Angel, their bond was too strong. Strong, like her bond with Timmy had been . . .

Heidi sat on the glider, cradling Timmy in her arms. He was so tiny, so fragile . . . as if any sharp movement would shatter him. Out of nowhere Luke appeared, grabbed her hand and pulled her up.... Timmy was gone and she was a murderer. Murderer. Murderer. She could see the word reflected in Luke's eyes and in the eyes of the spectators who packed the courtroom. She lifted pleading hands, begging for understanding. But one by one the judge, Luke, Faith and even David turned their backs to her. No one would listen. Desperately she pirouetted around and through them. If she could say the right words, do the right thing...

Then she saw Angel standing at the back of the courtroom, watching her urgent, ineffectual spinning. Angel would understand. Angel would help her. She ran toward her—but when she reached the spot, Angel was gone. An uncontrollable shivering seized her.

The shivering wasn't from the cold outside; it came from inside her. She woke to the familiar pain, which slowly dissolved as she became aware of the radio, still playing softly across the room. It was just another dream. Not real. But the shivering wouldn't stop, even though she pulled the blanket tightly beneath her chin. Luke was right—the icy pain would always be with her, in prison or out.

The chill in the air grew sharper, more biting. Winter settled in suddenly, blowing across the prison yard, swirling dead yellow leaves before light flakes of snow. The high walls didn't keep the wind from sending drafts up pant legs and through light jackets.

In a matter of a few weeks their clothes were boxed, labeled and stored. David sent warmer slacks and sweaters for both of them, without being asked. She hadn't heard from Luke. Had that first step with Faith been a dead end? No. According to Dr. Vogland, her

progress was promising. In fact, he hoped she could
visit for the holidays.

The holidays were going to be particularly difficult
to deal with. She and Faith had always begun their
Christmas preparations the Monday before Thanksgiving. It was strange to discover it was the same here
in prison.

The Thanksgiving turkeys on the bulletin boards
suddenly sported wreaths of holly around their necks.
Gifts from outside began appearing regularly, so there
were new sweaters and gloves and colorful barrettes in
the inmates' hair.

There was a feeling of cheerfulness in the shirt works
where, during their break, she and Doreen made doll
clothes for her daughters out of the scraps. Even Letty
took an interest, making surprisingly neat stitches in
the tiny garments. Maxime was still always there,
watching with her colorless cold eyes; but, since dis-
covering that first flicker of courage, Heidi knew she
could handle her.

Now the visitors' hall was nearly always packed with
friends and relatives, but on this particular day there
were wall-to-wall people.

Since she hadn't heard from Luke, and David was
scheduled to be away on business, Heidi happily volunteered for the playroom. There were more children
milling around than she'd ever seen before. Nevertheless, Angel had them quickly organized. Some played
games, a few girls danced in a corner, some sat round
the piano for a sing-along. The festive air intensified
with all the laughter and innocent chatter.

Heidi, with Joyce on the bench beside her, sang holiday songs with five eager little girls and two reluctant
boys. A new spirit of hope was gaining power from

reaching out and touching these children with some
little joy for however brief a time.

Only by chance did she see Angel leaving. A visitor?
That could only be Santos, and that meant trouble.
Her fingers kept playing by habit while her mind de-
bated how she could get out to the visitors' hall.

But Joyce needed her, too. All the other children
rushed across the room as Officer Needham wheeled in
a cart of cookies and juice.

"Don't you want a treat, Joyce?" Stroking her long
blond hair, Heidi smiled into the tiny upturned face.

She shook her head, but her brown eyes gazed longingly at the red and green sugar sprinkled on the cookies.

"Well, I'd like a treat. Would you get some for me?"

Grinning, Joyce instantly slid from the bench, ran
across the room and eagerly pushed into line. A few
months ago she would have been too timid or too
afraid to interact like this with the other children.

The more Heidi worked with these children, the
more she was certain her music training would take her
down another path when she got out. Entertaining was
no longer enough—the thought of it didn't contain the
sense of fulfillment it once had. If music was her special gift, she would use it to help others. The awareness of this decision enabled her to begin fanning the
embers of her spirit, which had seemed to die with
Timmy. Knowing what she would do with her music
gave her new energy and a purpose to not only survive
this prison life, but to learn and grow from the in-
sights it could teach her.

A prickle of awareness made her swivel around—
only to stare straight into Luke's eyes. He stood in the

doorway and suddenly she found it hard to breathe normally.

Luke's pulse rate rose when his eyes met Heidi's. He willed the ache in his gut to go away. He would simply ignore her beauty and the gentle smile she had given that little girl. He would ignore the unacceptable thoughts and feelings that had tormented him since those few moments of privacy in her room. If only that was possible!

With a nod the guard at the door let him past, but Luke had to step carefully to avoid children of all sizes, ages and colors sitting on the tile floor crumbling their cookies and spilling their juice. The high-pitched chattering and laughter was jarring, but Heidi remained sitting quietly at her piano, waiting for Joyce to present her with a napkin full of cookies.

She acknowledged him with a cautious nod. "Hello, Luke. I'm sorry I couldn't come out to see you, but Joyce just brought me a treat."

A red rim of sugar around her mouth, Joyce looked at him measuringly before thrusting one thin arm out to offer a cookie.

He began to shake his head but found he wasn't proof against her crooked-tooth smile. "Well, if you're sure you don't want it yourself."

In response she pushed the cookie closer, so he took it. Avoiding Heidi's eyes, he bit into it. He'd forgotten how good decorated sugar cookies could be.

"Thanks, Joyce. It's good."

The red rim of sugar expanding, she offered her plastic cup of juice.

"No, no thanks." Now unable to avoid Heidi's gaze, he found her studying him with frank bemusement. Damn it! Did she do this on purpose? She looked so beautiful and possessed such an underlying sweetness that her smile could melt an iceberg. He was drawn to her in ways he just couldn't accept.

"Joyce, I think Sissy and Dottie want you to play dolls." Heidi urged her off the bench as two little girls with rows of pigtails beckoned. Only after Heidi nodded encouragingly did Joyce allow the other girls to draw her away.

"I think you've made a friend there," he laughed, leaning against the piano. He watched her fingers lightly brush across the keys. Did he make her nervous? Somehow the thought displeased him.

"Don't be nervous, Heidi. I came to talk about Faith. She'll be able to visit you for the holiday." His other reason for coming he wouldn't even admit to himself. "Have you given any more thought to that petition to the governor?"

Her fingers continued stroking the ivory keys. "I'm happy about Faith. Christmas is a time when families should be together." She stared up at him with those dark, unfathomable eyes. "Why do you want to help secure my release, Luke? I know you want to help Faith, but it's obvious that you can't accept what I did."

Her question stirred the ache in his gut to a painful throb. "Once I took an honest look at your case, I saw the mitigating circumstances. If you hadn't pleaded guilty, if you'd given any defense at all, the judge might not have sentenced you to prison. If you'd been Timmy's mother, the sentence would have been lighter. But, except for the birth pangs, you were Timmy's mother in all the ways that counted, weren't you, Heidi? You gave him a mother's love when Faith couldn't. Nothing will ever diminish that."

Her full lips quivered, and tears glistened in her eyes as she continued to search his face.

Recoiling from a fierce wave of attraction, he ran impatient fingers through his hair. "You're not a threat to society. No good purpose will be served by your continued incarceration. On the other hand, your release would benefit your sister."

For the first time she didn't retreat. She faced him, laying her palms firmly on the piano top. "But regardless of the mitigating circumstances, my decision concerning Timmy...our nephew...isn't something you'll ever understand, is it?"

"It would never have been my decision," he admitted grimly. "But the issue at hand is justice and helping your sister so we can all put this behind us, not what I would or wouldn't have done under the same circumstances."

"Oh, but I think that particular issue has a great deal to do with everything." Her mouth curved in a gentle smile. "I'll let you know my decision. Goodbye, Luke."

"Goodbye, Luke," Joyce echoed, running back to cuddle into Heidi's side.

Her parting words still ringing in his ears, his last image of her as he made his escape was Heidi running her long, slim fingers over Joyce's straight blond hair. He could still feel the soft warmth of those fingers gently squeezing his cold hands. If she hadn't pulled away, what would he have done? That was the torment—once he would have known. But nothing in his life had prepared him for feeling so totally inappropriate.

Angel couldn't quite figure the look on Luke's face as he stepped out of the playroom. He was so preoccupied that he nearly tripped over her chair.

She spoke to him, anyway. "How you doing, Luke?"

Startled, he stopped to stare blankly at her. "Sorry, I didn't see you. Hello, Angel. Happy holidays."

Now it was her turn to be surprised. "Yeah, same to you."

Nodding absently, he continued past her, not even noticing Santos.

"Hey, Angel, ya gettin' to know some uptown guys. What's he drive?"

Shrugging, she gazed toward the playroom, unable to keep from worrying about Heidi. After her last encounter with Luke, Heidi had had nightmares for a week.

"Hey, babe, what's the deal!"

His heavy boot nudging her foot brought her swiftly to the present. Santos didn't like to be ignored.

"Nothing, Santos. I just don't know what he drives."

"Don't matter. Me and the gang have a sweet deal cookin'. We're drivin' six Beamers down to Miami after the first. Stayin' till February. How's about that? *Me* winterin' in Miami Beach!"

Angel didn't have to fake her enthusiastic nod. If Santos was in Florida, he might not be around when she got out.

"But I'll be back for your comin' out. Me and the gang got big plans for ya."

His implication made her so nervous that she could hardly sit still. "I don't know exactly when I'll be released."

Suddenly Santos trapped her tapping foot between his two steel-tipped boots. Her nervousness was replaced by cold dread. She knew this cruel twist to his full lips.

The steel tip bit a little deeper into the toe of her gym shoe. "You ain't tryin' anythin' funny, are ya, Angel? Yer my girl. Ain't nothin' goin' to change that."

"No, Santos. I just don't know what's going to happen."

A sharp stab of pain jolted up her calf as the steel tip pressed harder.

"I do," he mocked. "Dancers ain't so good with broken legs. Be too bad if my Angel couldn't dance no more, wouldn't it?"

Swallowing a cry of pain, she forced her mouth into a faint smile. "I just didn't want to spoil your trip. I'm being released on February second."

Slowly the pressure lessened, and she carefully eased her foot back to safety beneath her chair.

"I'll be here for ya. It'll be just like old times. Me and the gang, we'll have a welcome home party for ya."

"Is someone having a party?" Heidi's question was matched by a guileless smile as she sat down at the table.

She didn't need this! Heidi didn't know what she was in for, tangling with Santos. Angel couldn't believe it—Heidi wasn't even flinching as Santos, leering, stripped her clothes off with his eyes.

"Heidi—" Angel began, only to be interrupted.

"Santos, I could use a soda. Would you mind?" Heidi almost purred, batting her long, dark lashes. "I have money if..."

"Hey, for a classy babe like you, only the best! I'll buy. Be right back, Doll Face." Swaggering across the room, Santos became lost in the crowd around the concession stand.

Angel turned on Heidi. "Get the hell out of here! He's in a mean mood. You can't help me!"

"I'm not leaving without you." Jumping up, Heidi grabbed Angel's arm. "Let's get out while we can."

Wanting nothing more than to escape Santos's cruelty, Angel stood but stumbled as her foot cramped, sending her reeling against the table edge.

Heidi caught her. "Did he hurt you again?"

"Yes," she bit out between clenched teeth. "Let's get the hell out of here."

Officer Connell locked the bolt behind them at the door of the Honor Cottage. It had never sounded so good!

Heidi helped Angel limp up the stairs to their room, where she fell onto the bed. She tore off her gym shoe and sock, examining her foot. Her toes were already black and blue.

"My God, Angel!" Heidi gasped, her eyes wide in her pale face. She soaked a towel in cold water and wrapped it around Angel's burning foot.

The coolness helped. Sighing, Angel closed her eyes.

"What are you going to do about Santos?"

"I've already done it. I told him I'm out on February second. It's really the first. When he gets here, I'll be long gone, although I can't imagine where. I'll never go back to the old neighborhood."

"Angel, I have somewhere for you to go. I want you to move into my condo in Chicago."

Unable to believe her ears, Angel slowly opened her eyes. Even staring into Heidi's calm face, she still couldn't believe it. "You're serious? You want *me* to move in with *you?* You trust me in your condo?"

"Besides David and Faith, I've never trusted anyone more than I trust you," Heidi answered simply
with the sweetness that had confused Angel from the
beginning. In the beginning, when she set out to befriend Heidi for her purposes. What she'd got, though,
was something she'd never known before—couldn't
label. Friendship? A bond of affection? Something she
hadn't felt since Miss Juliette and her mom.

"I don't deserve it, Heidi. I'm not a damn goody-
goody." The words came harshly through her tight
throat. "I became your friend for what I could get.
You gotta know that."

"I know it started out that way." Heidi shrugged.
"Why wouldn't you? We didn't know each other. But
then it changed for both of us. I know you would have
given up the Honor Cottage to protect me. I want to
repay the favor. Please let me." She used her last ar-
gument. "Remember I told you Luke wants to appeal
my case to the governor? I don't know what will happen to me. If the appeal doesn't go through, it will help
when you're gone to know you're safe from Santos."

Angel turned her face into the sheet and let it soak
up tears which, somehow, had escaped her control. She
was so lucky! She'd never let Heidi down. She raised
her head and licked the remaining tears from her lips.

Whipping strands of hair off her face, she twisted
around. "Do you like Christmas, Heidi?" The ache in
her chest made it hard to talk, so her words came out
a whisper.

"I love it. It's always been my favorite time of year."

"Then this year we'll have the best Christmas ever,
because soon we'll both be out of here." For the first
time since she was ten years old, Angel reached out for
someone.

Heidi took her hand, curling their fingers together. "I know it will be a great Christmas for all of us."

Heidi remembered her words in the days ahead. It was curiously exciting to see how the women created their own unique holiday spirit without the benefit of stores stocked with glittery decorations and merchandise; without the benefit of a Santa Claus ringing bells on every other corner and lights strung on buildings or twinkling in trees.

At least there was a tree, a real one, with the faint tangy scent of evergreen, placed in the corner of the visitors' hall. The officers strung it with white twinkling lights, and each inmate was allowed, if she chose, to place an ornament on it.

The playroom rang with high-pitched renditions of "Jingle Bells" and "Frosty the Snowman." For those few weeks everyone had the same goal—to bring in as much of the outside world as possible, to make believe the holiday would be like it was on the outside.

Caught up in the excitement, Heidi found her spirit lightened for the first time since those dark, dark hospital days. There was something good to think about: she would help Angel make a better life. If she gave Luke permission to appeal and got out sooner than expected, she could help her sister rebuild her life. And she could help children like Joyce through her music. Positive thoughts like those helped to push the darker moments away. Slowly she was building enough confidence to face anything, even Luke and the forbidden feelings swelling between them, with a shadow of her former spirit.

Her thoughts strayed to him so often lately. Especially since she'd received the card from Faith saying she would visit on Christmas Eve.

Something wonderful was going to happen at the party in the visitors' hall on Christmas Eve. She could feel it—the hope, the joy, the anticipation around her, all were gathered inside, fanning to life feelings she once thought dead and gone forever.

As Heidi's barely contained excitement grew, Angel became quieter. Heidi could hardly begin to guess the changes that were going on inside her.

But when a package arrived from David, her dark eyes filled her narrow little face with wonder. She held the card out.

"What's he up to?" she demanded as she lifted bright new unitards from the box.

David's bold black handwritten note was short and concise: "Keep practicing! See you Christmas Eve. David."

"It seems pretty clear, Angel."

"I can't get him anything." She seemed near to tears again—so unlike her old self-sufficient persona. Huddled on the floor in the midst of the colorful clothes, she looked very young.

"He doesn't expect anything," Heidi consoled her. "He sent me gifts, too, but I can't give them in return. Angel, David may not look it to you, but he's a very generous person. You'll see that when we're together in the condo."

Angel went very still. "David will be staying at the condo? You guys don't live together, do you?"

"No, he'll just spend a lot of time with us. We're like family."

Angel shook her head. "David and me under the same roof! What a sight that will be!" As if suddenly realizing Heidi might not be there, too, Angel struggled to her feet, clutching the dance clothes protectively to her. "I know you'll probably be there before me. Give Luke permission to send that petition to the governor. It's the right thing to do. I know it!"

"Angel, don't worry. It's Christmas. Wonderful things happen. Let's concentrate on that."

Christmas Eve promised to live up to her expectations. It was snowing, light large flakes that quickly covered the hard brown grass with a glistening white blanket as they walked across to the visitors' hall. The aroma of hot mulled cider perfumed the room. In honor of the holidays the concession stand had added the drink to its limited menu.

Angel grabbed a table near the tree. They didn't have a clear view of the entrance, so she stood to watch. Suddenly her face changed, her full lower lip curving up in a smile and her heavy-lashed lids widening. Heidi assumed David had arrived. An instant later Angel confirmed it.

"David's here, with Luke and your sister right behind him."

As Angel waved them over, Heidi slowly rose to meet them. To Heidi's delight Faith sat down next to her. Her stomach muscles tightened as Luke eased down on her other side and their legs brushed together.

His blue eyes were unflinchingly wide but unreadable as they met hers. He wanted her answer, and she was still afraid to give it. She'd made so many decisions that haunted her, and she no longer trusted her own judgment.

An hour later she still didn't know what to do. She only knew her hopes and dreams were all rolled in a tight, hot ball low in her stomach. They sat over the cider as if they were sitting around a table in a noisy restaurant, reminiscing over holidays. When Faith broke in, they all grew utterly still.

"Heidi, remember the year I was eight and we went to Florida? I was so sad there wasn't any snow, so you and Dad bought canned stuff and sprayed all the bushes in our little courtyard. It must have taken a dozen cans."

"Sixteen to be exact. And we had to get up at four to get it done before you woke at dawn to see what Santa had left." Heidi gave a tentative smile, afraid to move, to shatter the fragile bond of memories. If Faith wanted to concentrate on the happy memories—the times before their parents' deaths, before Peter, before Timmy—she would help her. Remembering the good times made it easier to face the bad.

Luke shifted restlessly, their legs again coming into brief, tingling contact, and the ball of emotion inside her pushed up into her chest.

When David poured another round of cider, Luke leaned so close to her that she caught the crisp freshness of his lime after-shave.

"Let me petition, Heidi. This is the right time. For all of us."

Caught in the power of his gaze, the decision she'd already made subconsciously came swiftly to her lips. "Yes. Do it."

The blaze of emotion in his eyes burned into her. Childish shrieks shattered the moment, and she trembled with relief, her insides a knot of pain.

"Angel! Angel! Look what we've got!" screamed two high-pitched voices. Doreen's daughters, Sissy and Dottie, rushed up, each holding a small spray of mistletoe. Her pinched face widened in a smile, Joyce followed. A quick glance across the room showed Doreen laughingly urging them on.

"Angel, Mom says give the football player a kiss!" the girls screamed in unison. Jumping up, Sissy and Dottie dangled mistletoe as they clung to David's and Angel's chairs. Their excitement was contagious; even Luke laughed beside her.

Shrugging, Angel slid her fingers around David's sport coat lapels, pulling him toward her. She hadn't quite reached his cheek before he shifted slightly so that their lips met in a brief kiss.

Did anyone else notice the flush creep up Angel's slim throat, or the slight narrowing of David's eyes as they pulled slowly apart? Heidi's mind leaped with speculation. There was no way she could have anticipated what happened next.

Clapping, the girls jumped down. In that instant Joyce grabbed Sissy's mistletoe and ran to Heidi. Standing on the chair rung, she dangled the mistletoe over Heidi's head.

"Kiss Luke now, Heidi!"

Her squeaky voice echoed in Heidi's ear. How could she disappoint this child who was just finding her way out of fear and pain? Yet how could she reach out to Luke again?

The blue of his eyes darkened with startling emotion as he stared at her.

Giggling, Joyce waved the mistletoe toward Luke. "Kiss Heidi, Luke!" she squealed.

Luke leaned toward her, and Heidi closed her eyes for a moment before their lips touched. His mouth brushed her lips and, for a heartbeat, lingered.

The hot ball of emotion inside her burst as waves of feelings too powerful to resist crashed over her, and allowed them to carry her with their power. Finally she struggled through the pounding surf and pulled herself away, gasping for air.

Luke slowly eased back into his chair, his eyes a blue blaze, scorching her.

Everyone but Joyce fell victim to the same paralyzing silence. Squealing with delight, Joyce jumped down and ran over to Sissy and Dottie. "See! Luke kissed Heidi." Giggling, the three held hands, skipping merrily back to Doreen's table.

"Hey, all this Christmas cheer is making me hungry." Angel broke the spell and grabbed Heidi's hand. "Help me get more cake for everyone."

Heidi glanced back at the table. David's eyes were narrowed thoughtfully; Faith was tugging nervously at her ponytail. But she didn't need to look at Luke—she felt his eyes boring into her back as she followed Angel.

Did he know?

Long ago he had toppled the walls of protection she'd built around her after Timmy's death. Could he now see into her mind and heart, as well? Had all of her secrets been revealed?

Heidi kept her face averted, even from Angel. The feelings surging through her were too new, too unfathomable, to be shared. She needed time to accept them herself, to understand them. How had the emotional tidal wave of their previous confrontations led her to this?

How could she be falling in love with a man who would never understand her?

CHAPTER NINE

LUKE SHOCKED the night watchman so much that he nearly dropped the fruitcake he was eating as he scanned the security screens.

"Golly, Mr. Jefferson! It's nearly Christmas morning!" He sat up straighter, eyeing Luke with concern. "Something wrong?"

"No, Joe. I need to finish some work in my office. I just wanted you to know I was here. Merry Christmas."

"Same to you, Mr. Jefferson." The guard nodded, relaxing back into his chair, although he still seemed perplexed.

When Luke got off the elevator, the utter silence settled eerily around him. He flipped on the light switch in the outer office and then in his own before going to the window and opening the blinds. The lights of the city blazed all around him as far as the eye could see. Tonight families were together, children tucked snugly in bed, eagerly awaiting Santa. Tonight was a time for goodwill, for the sharing of joy. Tonight was a time to reach out to those you loved.

But his brother was gone and his mother was on a cruise with friends. So he had reached out to Faith, who needed him and, because of a child, he'd reached out to Heidi in a way that haunted his thoughts.

He flung back his head, drawing a deep breath. Everything he felt for Heidi—all the contradictions, the attraction, the anger, the concern, the confusion—were held in check so tightly that he almost ached. The path to understanding, to untangling these feelings, wasn't clear, but the path to securing her release was.

He was still at his desk when the sun slanted through the blinds, patterning the carpet with warm strips of light. He read the petition again. It ranked among his best work. Fired with an eagerness that burned away his fatigue, he couldn't wait for his secretary or the regular red tape. His fingers banged away at the word processor until it was done, then, satisfied, he headed home for a cold shower.

Tomorrow he would be on the road to Springfield to personally present his case to the governor. He knew that Heidi's sentence would be commuted to time served because it was just, given the circumstances. That was a fact, just as her choice with Timmy was a fact. A fact that stood between them.

LUKE HAD the governor's letter in his hand on New Year's Eve and started the process with the State Prison Board the morning of January second. By that afternoon he had a call into David and was waiting in his office. Before David could even sit down, Luke was on his feet to hand him the letter.

"You got it already!" David gasped, staring at the document.

"Yes. She's already served more than half her sentence and her behavior in prison has been exemplary. Even Warden Howell spoke on her behalf."

"Then there's nothing stopping us from taking this to her right now!" David's face looked younger and more relaxed than Luke had ever seen it.

"I've already got the ball rolling with the state penal system. But I think it would be better if you went alone to tell Heidi. It will mean more coming from you."

David's eyes narrowed, studying him intently. "I'm not so sure about that." David's voice held a slight edge. "I think it would mean more coming from you, considering you're the one who pulled it off."

Luke met David's stare and held it. "This isn't something I'm prepared to discuss with you, David."

David looked away first, nodding. "I know. But you're both going to have to deal with it eventually." Folding the document, he placed it carefully in his inside jacket pocket. "I don't know how to thank—"

"Then don't!" Luke bit out, unable to maintain the calm facade another instant. "I did what was in the best interest of justice and for Faith's well-being. I don't want any thanks."

"I know." David squared his shoulders. "I'll talk to you soon."

"I'm going out of town." Luke straightened the papers on his desk. "The detective agency has a lead on Peter. I won't be able to take Faith to visit Elmwood until I get back. By then Heidi should be home."

"Running away isn't going to change anything, Luke."

David didn't expect a reply, and Luke simply stood watching until David closed the door behind him. Only then did he lower himself into his chair and shut his eyes.

David was right; he couldn't run away. His feelings haunted his every waking moment, and even his dreams, when he slept. There was no conceivable path that could lead him where he wanted to go. There were too many barriers. But he'd spent a lifetime breaking down barriers. Why did he feel so helpless now?

FROM THE MOMENT of that shattering kiss Heidi couldn't stop thinking about Luke, about the feelings that had no place in any relationship that might grow from their mutual desire to help Faith. She drifted through the days after Christmas and on into the New Year in a daze, not even noticing Angel's persistent cough until one night the violent hacking became all too apparent.

Heidi knelt beside Angel's bed. "Are you all right?"

"Sure, I'm—" A fit of rasping coughs shook the small body under the covers.

Disgusted that she'd been so tied up in knots over Luke that she hadn't noticed sooner, Heidi pressed a hand to Angel's forehead. It was too warm and too moist.

"Angel, I'm going to call a guard!" Alarm sharpened her voice.

"Hey, it's just a bad cold," Angel whispered hoarsely. "Let me get some sleep. I'll get some aspirin from the nurse tomorrow. Go back to bed."

The strength in Angel's voice lulled her into believing, so she crawled back into her bed. Angel definitely didn't like to be fussed over.

But when Officer Connell informed Heidi the next afternoon that Angel had been taken to the infirmary with bronchitis, she was overcome with guilt.

"Stop worrying. Angel will be fine," Connell told her matter-of-factly. "She's on antibiotics and bed rest for the next three days. She'll be back before you know it."

Despite her reassurance, Heidi fretted alone in her room. How could she have been so wrapped up in herself that she had ignored Angel's health?

Logically she knew Angel's illness wasn't really her fault, yet she had always accepted responsibility for the people around her, but now she could no longer care for them. She'd let Angel get this sick. She'd let Faith get sick. She'd let Timmy die.

How could she have allowed all those things to happen?

Finally she turned the radio on, but that just made Angel's absence more pronounced. How had she ever thought this room too small for two people? It felt cavernous and cold without Angel's vibrant warmth. She pulled the covers over her head and gave in to a bout of angry weeping, but it didn't help much. After a while she got up and washed her face and brushed her hair. She couldn't decide if she cried for the others or for herself, but she knew that self-pity wasn't the answer. All night she paced the small room, searching herself for answers. They had to be here, somewhere deep down inside her. Sometimes she could almost sense them, pushing toward the surface, especially when she was with Luke.

Bleary-eyed from fatigue, she could barely go through the motions at the shirt works the next day. After the third time she caught herself falling asleep at her machine, she went into the bathroom to splash cold water on her face. Never had she been so glad to go back to her room for her hour of free time. She was stretched out on her bunk resting, trying not to worry about Angel or think about Luke, when Officer Connell brought an elderly woman into her room. Her skin was like cracked parchment and her white hair so thin that Heidi could see glimpses of scalp.

"Heidi, this is Coralee Johnson. She's just come back to us from the hospital and is being transferred to the infirmary until she gets her medical okay. She wanted to take a look at her old room."

Coralee was so weak and fragile-looking that Heidi scrambled to her feet. "Here, why don't you sit on the bed?"

"Now that's right nice of you, child. Do you suppose I could rest a moment, Officer?"

Pushing her glasses back onto her nose, Connell flashed Coralee a rare smile. "Welcome back."

"Thank ye, Marilyn. It's right good to be home."

Chuckling, Coralee winked at Heidi as the officer closed the door. "Marilyn's not as uppity as she seems."

"I didn't know her first name." Heidi couldn't help smiling as Coralee rose and walked around the little room, running her fingers over the bed railing.

"Of course you wouldn't know. New, aren't you? I've known Marilyn since her first day. My, she was a green one!" Coralee sighed. "It's good to be home. But I've got to go see the gals. It's been a while. Have to catch up on the gossip afore they stick me out in the 'firmary. Want to come along?"

"No thanks. I'm not expecting any visitors, so I volunteered to work in the helpers' room."

"My, that's a grand idea of Warden Howell's, isn't it? She's the best of the lot, and I've seen my share of wardens. Six since I came here."

"Six! How long have you been here?" Heidi asked, curious despite herself.

"Probably since before you were born. How old are you? Twenty-five? Thirty? I've been here thirty-one years come May."

Shocked into silence, Heidi stared at her.

"It's all right, dearie. Don't look so sad. This is home. All my friends are here. Speaking of which, I'm busting to see them!"

With a cheery wave she bustled into the hall with more energy than Heidi would have thought possible from her delicate appearance. Heidi could hear her lilting voice call to people as she descended the stairs.

Still reeling from her meeting with Coralee Johnson, Heidi crossed the yard to the visitors' hall. Wending her way through the tables, still bemused by the unexpected encounter, she was startled to hear David's voice call her name.

Swinging around, she saw him rush toward her. He wasn't supposed to be here!

The accelerated beat of her pulse drove her toward him. Had something happened to Faith?

David grabbed her shoulders as she swayed to a halt in front of him.

"I've got a letter from the governor."

She was thankful David's hands were gripping her shoulders, or she would have crumpled where she stood. Relief that her fears were unfounded was quickly replaced by anxiety.

"What does it mean, David?"

"Sit down and I'll tell you!"

Urging her down, he pulled another chair closer, placing an arm along the steel back, creating an oasis of calm in the visiting hall's activity.

"It's not a pardon," he said. "The governor can't do that. It's an election year and the right to die is a hot political topic. But considering the supporting medical data and the depositions of the nursing staff at Timmy's hospital about your obvious love and care for him, the governor is commuting your sentence. Warden Howell praised your active participation in Howell's Helpers, and your exceptional behavior, and the long and the short of it is that in less than a week you'll be free!" he ended triumphantly.

Free. The word itself was so simple. One she'd once taken for granted—but never again. Free.

Free to leave the prison and go back to her old life. Yet she knew with sudden clarity that she could never really go back, because she was no longer the same person.

Happiness, fear, shock, even sadness warred within her. She stared into David's flushed face unable to believe Luke had moved ahead with this so quickly. She really didn't have time to think about whether it was the right thing to do.

"Heidi, you're coming home," he breathed, his hand patting her shoulder. "You're coming back where you belong. In a few weeks I'll line up some small club dates and—"

"No." Heidi folded her hands in her lap. "David, I'm not going back to entertaining. It's not right for me anymore."

Covering her fingers with his other hand, he nodded. "It's the kids, isn't it? Using your music to help them. I could see it coming. Some kind of therapy program?"

"Music therapy. I've already talked to a college counselor here. I'll need to do an intern program, but I have all the other credentials."

He squinted his eyes, squeezing her fingers. "I see why you want to do it, but don't throw away your career. I didn't want to mention this before, but Timmy's and Faith's medical bills used up a lot of your savings. The sale of your cars and your parents' house helped, but a few club dates would tide you over while you're doing the intern program."

To pick up the threads of her life, to go out in front of the public again, made her feel uneasy, vulnerable. "What club did you have in mind?" The hesitation in her voice wasn't lost on David.

He gave her a measuring look. "I know you're scared. But I've given this a lot of thought. You love Yvonne's. It's small, has a select clientele, and Georges adores you. A few weeks there should ease you back into the swing of things. Can I arrange it?"

"Yes. Thank you," she whispered, her throat cracking with so many emotions that she'd never be able to explain to him. "For everything."

Embarrassed, he shrugged. "Luke did all the work. Thanks to him, you'll be home before you know it."

Home. Her condo overlooking Lake Michigan. She'd tried not to think about it, not to miss its comforts and privacy. Soon she'd be with Faith, rebuilding their closeness and strengthening her ability to face the world again.

Soon she'd face Luke. Why hadn't he come himself to tell her the news?

"Have you told Faith?" she asked.

"Luke is with her now," he said quickly, looking away. "That's why you're hearing the news from me."

"When will he be coming? I want to thank him." She tried to keep the eagerness out of her voice, but she must have failed, because David's face stiffened slightly.

"He's going out of town to check into some leads from the detective agency about Peter. He won't be able to bring Faith here until next week. By then you'll be home."

"Does he think he'll find Peter?"

"Well, the kid's got to show up someday." David straightened, thrusting his massive shoulders back against the chair. "When he does show his face, Faith will have to deal with it. The whole thing will be dredged up again for everyone. I hope we can *all* deal with it!"

Thinking about the future, about coping with it, no matter what it held, occupied her thoughts as she entered the playroom. Even the kids noticed her preoccupation. Finally she came back to the present and banged out a series of lively songs on the piano, making the children whirl about until they were exhausted.

But walking back across the compound, Heidi couldn't deny her thoughts any longer. Despite his feelings, which were too painful for Heidi to think about, Luke had secured her release. She'd have to stop trying to guess what he'd do next and concentrate on the future. She couldn't wait to tell Angel the news! Imminent freedom, for both of them!

The old, familiar pain tugged at her senses, reminding her there were some things from which she would never be free.

A soft knock on her door startled her. Before she could open it Coralee peeked in.

"Hi, again. Want some company to walk over to the dining hall? I know you miss Angel and all. I'll bet she'll be pleased to hear you'll be leaving us soon. My, your friends did a right good job for you."

"But ... how did you find out?"

"Haven't you learned there's nothing like the prison grapevine?" Coralee settled onto the side of the bed. "I found out all about you today, Heidi. Talked to Angel in the infirmary. I decided I needed to see you again." The faded brown eyes were kind as she patted the covers. "Sit down beside me so we can chat."

Perching next to her, Heidi could see the ravages of Coralee's illness. Her skin was pulled tight and dry across the hollows of her face, and the flesh hung loosely on her throat and arms. This woman had lived here, in prison, for thirty-one years and, perhaps, she would die here. It seemed a sad life, a waste; even though she hadn't known Coralee beyond the brief moments they had spent together.

Her thin hand patted Heidi's knee. "I heard what you did with your nephew Timmy. And I heard what you've been doing since you came here. Some of the gals are right big fans of yours. Want you to know that up front! Isn't easy to fool these gals, so I figure what you did with Timmy was the best for him. I hear you're that kind of person. You'd turn yourself inside out to do the right thing."

Drawing in a quick breath, Heidi could feel her heart pounding, the too-familiar pain squeezing her insides into a tight ball. She must simply learn to live with the constant ache of regret and sadness.

"Oh, my, just as I thought!" Coralee sighed, shaking her head. "I can see it in your eyes—you haven't accepted it yet, have you? Still got doubts. Got to rid yourself of those. It won't matter if you get out of here if you don't accept what you did. Accepting you did what you had to will give you true freedom.''

Battling back a wave of tears, Heidi tried to smile. "How did you get so wise, Coralee?''

"Because I took a life once." The faded brown eyes hardened, and along with them, her voice. "Except I didn't do it in love. I did it in fear and pain and desperation. I'm paying the price for taking that life by spending most of mine in here. And I'll die in here. But in my heart I'm free because I've accepted what I did. I'm not a victim anymore.''

"I'm so sorry, Coralee.'' Heidi's heart constricted again—this time for Coralee.

"Oh, my, I had no intentions of making you sad!'' Struggling to her feet, Coralee bustled to the mirror and patted her wispy curls. "There, look, my eyes are a mite watery, too.'' Turning, she shrugged. "Have to try to help. All of you in here are my family. Oh, good, there's the bell!'' She winked. "Hope the food's as good as ever.''

The food was exactly as it had been day after day, but nothing else was the same. Everyone knew the message David had brought. No doubt word had already reached Angel at the infirmary.

Letty and Doreen saved her a place at their table, urging her down beside them.

"Hey, those fellas really came through for you,'' Letty crowed. "Hell, I'm going to miss you. Paint old Chi-town red for me, will you?'' she asked wistfully, her thin eyebrows disappearing into her bangs.

"I'll miss you, too,'' Doreen sighed. "But I bet Prince Charming will be happy.''

Heidi drew in a deep breath. "Doreen, I told you, Luke isn't..."

"I know, I know." She smiled, shaking her head. "But I've got an eye for romance. Bet I'm right. Will you write and tell me?"

Studying their eager faces, Heidi was struck by a truth. These women had become more than casual friends—they had helped her through the worst time of her life. In the normal course of things she would never have considered their joys and sorrows; might even have thought that, being in prison, they were different somehow.

"I'll write both of you," she promised, but she was determined to do more. "You have been good friends. I won't forget it."

Letty hunched her shoulders, bending over her dessert, but Heidi glimpsed a pleased smile.

"We're all going to miss you, Heidi," Doreen sobbed, her soft cheeks glistening with running tears. "My little Sissy and Dottie will miss you in the playroom. But poor little Joyce! She's so much better since you've been helping her. That poor baby will be lost without you!"

In the midst of her excitement about leaving she'd almost forgotten Joyce. The little girl had made great strides both in her music and in her ability to play with other children. Heidi had to do something to ensure her progress would continue. Luke, and her life outside, were pushed to the back of her mind in an effort to decide how best to tell Joyce. Tomorrow was her day to visit; that might be Heidi's only chance.

She waited nervously on the piano bench, watching Joyce run across the room to her, still torn with indecision. Joyce didn't give her trust easily, and she'd broken out of her silent prison so recently that Heidi knew she had to proceed carefully.

"Hi, sweetie. I have a new book for you." She smiled as Joyce climbed up beside her. Instead of their dog-eared beginning book, Heidi placed a red-and-white intermediate playbook on the piano. "We're going to learn lots of new songs today."

Joyce eagerly followed her instructions, staring intently at each measure. If she could just give Joyce a good start in this book, maybe she'd be able to finish it on her own. It might keep her busy enough not to be devastated by Heidi's absence.

"My, my, what a pretty little girl. And making such pretty music!"

Heidi looked up to find Coralee standing at the end of the piano. When she glanced down and saw Joyce's pleased smile, Heidi instanteously came up with a plan.

"Joyce, this is Coralee. She likes your music."

"I love your music, honey. I always wanted to play the piano. Never had the chance. My, I'm impressed a little thing like you can play so good." The thin hand stroked the smooth blond hair.

Although Joyce looked at Coralee with some reservation, she didn't jerk away. Encouraged, Heidi slowly rose from the bench.

"Why don't we let Coralee sit next to you. Maybe you could teach her the way I taught you."

Joyce tilted her face upward. "I could teach her 'Happy Birthday.'"

Heidi nodded, her pulse racing as she waited.

Carefully setting aside the new book, Joyce replaced it with the old. "Sit, Coralee, and I'll teach you," she commanded in her squeaky little voice.

Dutifully Coralee settled down on the bench. She laughed. "These old hands are mighty clumsy."

In answer Joyce took Coralee's bony index finger and very slowly punched out "Happy Birthday."

The old face, near the end of its days, and the new face, just beginning, both broke into glowing smiles.

A huge lump formed in Heidi's throat, and she looked away. This was right! It was the music that was the important thing—the music that would draw these two, so different, souls together. She wouldn't give in to tears. She had too much to do to strengthen this beginning so that, when she left, neither Joyce nor Coralee would be alone.

THE END OF HER STAY at Elmwood was the same as the beginning: Heidi was alone. Officer Needham brought news that Angel had to stay in the infirmary a few days more than anticipated. Heidi had said her goodbyes to everyone and set in motion the tentative friendship between Joyce and Coralee, but she couldn't leave without seeing Angel. Angel had changed everything here by showing her how to survive and make a life for herself within these walls, just as Heidi would help her to rebuild her life on the outside. Heidi wanted to reaffirm her promises, to let Angel know she intended to keep every one of them. It seemed so long since she'd had the chance to talk to her.

Inexplicably Heidi felt a sense of separation from everyone. They knew she was leaving and would no longer be a part of their lives. They let go quickly, not wanting to have much to do with her. It wasn't like anything Heidi had ever seen inside before. There had always been so much sharing, so much joy on each other's behalf. This wasn't the same.

She refused to believe that Angel would be this way.

By the morning of her release day she was almost sick with anticipation and frustration. She'd begged Connell to get permission to visit the infirmary but had had no luck. It was against the rules, and the rules here couldn't be broken. The fact that Coralee seemed able to come and go as she pleased was an exception Heidi never even considered.

Waiting alone in the small holding cell with all her belongings around her, Heidi paced, torn between the pull of freedom and the need to see Angel before she left. She spun around as the door opened, expecting David. Instead, Officer Connell beckoned to her.

"Heidi, there's someone to see you in the visitors' hall." A rare smile lit Connell's face, and relief surged through Heidi. It could only mean one thing.

Nearly stumbling over her suitcase in her eagerness, Heidi rushed to the visitors' hall. As she had hoped, Angel was there waiting. She was pale and weak, but she still wore her cocky grin.

"Never say I didn't get out of my sick bed to say goodbye," she quipped, rising slowly to her feet.

Heidi gave her a fierce, tight hug, but stepped back quickly, respecting Angel's reserve.

"Oh, Angel, I'm so glad to see you! I couldn't leave without saying—"

"Hey! Don't worry! I got a real rest in the infirmary. People waited on me. It was great." She laughed, a slight pink coloring her cheeks. "I kinda worried about you out here alone, but I see you made it okay." The graceful legs did a little shuffle step, and she shrugged. "Well, I guess this is it, roomy. Maybe I'll see you around sometime."

The look in her dark eyes tore at Heidi's heart. "You can't get rid of me that easily. This isn't goodbye. We'll be together again before you know it. Less than a month, Angel. Don't forget you promised to move in with me."

The delicate shoulders lifted again, and suddenly Heidi was reminded of how Angel had looked facing Maxime that first night. "You don't have to do anything more for me. We're even."

"No, we're not! You still owe me—you promised you'd move in. I'm going to hold you to that promise. Just because we haven't seen each other for a few days, it doesn't change anything, Angel. I won't forget."

Although tears burned suddenly behind her lids at Angel's tentative nod, Heidi refused to give into them. When Needham arrived to lead Angel away, she felt a moment of panic. Suddenly there was a monumental chasm between them.

"Angel, I promise I'll be back for you."

Perhaps some of her fierce determination got through, because Angel shot her a sudden grin.

"Yeah, I know you will."

Heidi stood helplessly watching as Angel's small back, ramrod stiff, disappeared through the door that led to the compound. Taking deep breaths of air, she forced herself back into the waiting room. She knew all of Angel's old distrust had returned, and she had been able to do very little to reassure her. But she'd be back to visit soon.

By the time David arrived she was numb from fighting her memories. It was almost unbelievable to walk out through the door—*free*—and leave the prison behind. Just as if she'd been a visitor.

She looked back at the high stone walls looming overhead in the bright January afternoon. All that had happened to her within was a part of her now and always would be. Still, she had to fight to keep the tears at bay.

LUKE COULDN'T STAY away from the homecoming, even though part of him wanted to. Deep down he wanted to see Heidi with something close to aching desperation.

He'd had to stop fooling himself after he kissed her on Christmas Eve. He'd only meant to touch her lips briefly to appease the child. He'd been totally unprepared for the rush of desire that had swept him away on a sensual tide. It was as if that brief touch had opened a floodgate, and there was no turning back. He'd tried to channel those feelings into his relentless fight for her release, even as he forced himself to stay away from her. He tried to concentrate on anything and everything except the one thing foremost in his thoughts. If he gave in, he knew where it would lead, and it scared the hell out of him! It was terrifying to realize everything was subordinate to his sudden admission that he wanted her.

He had stayed away from the prison, but he wasn't strong enough to stay away now.

David's booming voice could be heard in the hallway a moment before the door opened. From a far corner of the living room he observed Heidi's entrance as he tried to keep a rein on his emotions.

"I'm home," she whispered, walking into the living room of the condo. Slowly she moved around the room, touching each piece of furniture, as if to reassure herself it was real.

Then Faith burst through from the kitchen, and Heidi stopped still. As she turned, he saw tears streaming down her cheeks. "Faith." As if she were in a trance, she moved slowly toward her sister.

He recognized the tension in David's stance, probably from trying to guess what he would do. For David had known he was here, had asked him to bring Faith as a surprise for Heidi.

"It's good to see Heidi at home, isn't it, Faith?" David's deep laugh as he engulfed Heidi in a one-arm squeeze brought her eyes up and around straight to where Luke waited. He had the advantage this time of taking her by surprise, so she didn't have the opportunity to conceal her feelings.

The stunned pleasure on her beautiful face astounded him, left him defenseless.

"Welcome home, Heidi." Striding forward, he took her fingers, holding them. Stunned by his own action, he couldn't break the contact of their hands.

Hers trembled with cold. Or was it the feelings swelling between them? Was she as confused as he by conflicting feelings? Did she wonder, too, how anything good could come out of the tragedy which had brought them together?

If she had been what he'd first thought her, he wouldn't be here now. But now he couldn't walk away, even though he would never condone her choices. What kind of relationship could grow from such a dichotomy of feelings?

"Welcome home, Heidi," he repeated, squeezing her fingers before stepping away.

He found himself automatically reaching to help her out of her heavy jacket before David could offer. Over her shoulder she slid him an almost shy smile of thanks. He hadn't been this close to her since he'd kissed her; then, as now, her perfume surrounded them with an alluring fragrance. Her hair, soft and silky, swung against her cheek and brushed his hand.

Glancing up, he found David watching him carefully. David had told him he couldn't run away. That was why he was here. To see if, somehow, the urgency, the tight coil of tension he always associated with being near her, had more to do with the prison environment than the woman herself. But, now that she was here, free again, he realized his feelings were just as powerful, and he was at a loss as to his next move.

"I'll get drinks for everyone." Smiling, David urged them all to settle in the living room. "The three of you relax. I'll be right back."

Faith wandered to the glass doors facing the lake, looking out into the darkness. Suddenly she turned back.

"I've always loved this place from the first moment you brought me here. Remember, Heidi? Could I see my old room?"

"Of course. It's just as you left it." Heidi watched carefully as she wandered down the short hallway and disappeared through her door.

Now no one was left to break the silence encompassing them. He could, if he dared, reach out and touch her.

"Luke, I want to thank you for—"

"Don't!" Seeing the flash of hurt in her eyes, he softened his tone. "Please. It's done. Over. Now we all have to get on with the rest of our lives."

"All right." She finally nodded, a vein throbbing at the base of her throat above the blue V-neck sweater.

"David said you've been out of town looking for Peter. Any luck?"

He glanced toward the bedroom before answering. "Not yet, but I'm close. He knows I'm looking for him. I thought I had him in Kansas City, but he'd already moved on. He did this once before when he was in high school. Just picked up and left when he couldn't handle a problem." Not wanting Faith to hear, he glanced around again. "I'm not sure what will happen when I finally find him and tell him about his son."

He hadn't meant to hurt her with his words, but he could see pain again in her eyes and her breasts rose in a ragged breath.

"I mean that his son died," he added quickly. But it was no use.

Heidi straightened her shoulders. "Peter may want to see Faith. Do you think she's ready for a confrontation with him? You'd know better than I."

Luke was saved from answering by David's noisy entrance. He banged the tray down upon the coffee table and yelled over his shoulder. "C'mon, Faith! I even got those rich chocolate cookies you like so much."

They were all so polite, so careful not to touch on anything painful. But Luke was glad Faith at least seemed more relaxed. Even so, she sighed as she glanced around. "When I was a senior in high school this was my dream. A condo in the city with a lake view."

Slowly Heidi lowered her coffee cup. Luke could just see the fearful anticipation she tried to hide in her eyes.

"Faith, now that I'm home again, you can move in here with me whenever you're ready. You know that, don't you?" She looked to David for confirmation, then back at Faith, who didn't reply. "Angel will be coming here soon. Wouldn't it be nice to be here with us?"

Fidgeting with the end of her ponytail, Faith nodded, flashing a hard, quick look at Luke. "Maybe we should go now." Jumping up, she made a beeline for the foyer.

"Damn it! What's the matter with her now? Jeez, it's her sister's homecoming," David muttered before going after her.

The stricken look in Heidi's eyes brought a sharp pain to Luke's gut. He'd seen that look before. He'd put it there. Now he wanted to take it away. "I'll talk to her. It will be all right."

She stared up at him in stunned surprise.

"I promised we'd work together to help Faith. I meant it!" His voice was harsh, he knew, but he needed to push away the desire to take her in his arms and kiss her quivering mouth.

"I believe you. I've always known you're a man who accomplishes what he sets out to do."

He moved one step toward her before he realized what he was doing. She didn't retreat, but stood as if waiting, and he stood staring into her hauntingly beautiful eyes, searching for the answers to the questions that were tearing him apart. Slowly he stepped back, away from her.

"I'll talk to Faith tonight on the way back to the sanatorium. Then tomorrow I'll pick you up and take you to visit her if you wish."

"Yes." She nodded, taking a deep breath. There was fresh color in her pale cheeks. "I'll see you tomorrow."

It was more a plea than an insistence, but it stayed with him through the long, silent drive back to the sanatorium. Faith fell asleep, so it wasn't until he had her safely installed in her room that they could finally discuss what had happened.

"I think you should consider your sister's offer. Dr. Vogland could recommend someone in Chicago for your therapy sessions. You'd be in a place you really like, with all your own things. It's time for you to move forward with your life, Faith."

There was complete silence as she stared blankly into his face. Damn! He'd blown it, but he couldn't quit now.

"Heidi loves you, has always loved you. And I'm sure she wants only the best for you. Every time I visited her in prison, her only concern was for you."

Faith stirred, shaking her head. "I know. But I'm not sure it would work out, living with Heidi and Angel." She tugged at her ponytail. "Angel makes me nervous. She's like David. Demanding. Expecting more than I can give."

Jumping up, she paced to the window. "I mean, she's been in prison, too," she whispered, as if trying to justify her feelings. "I know she and Heidi are friends, but I don't know her. I...I don't even know Heidi anymore. Once I had total confidence in everything she did. Now...I'm not sure she hasn't changed."

He thrust up his chin at that, inexplicably angry. "Your sister thinks only of you! Don't you think she deserves a little support in return?"

"Don't pull this with me, Luke!" she snapped back, pointing at him accusingly. "When you first came here, I thought you hated her. Now you're taking her side against me."

Luke didn't try to defend himself. How could he? It was true. But, more important, for the first time something was actually breaking through to Faith. He saw the tears welling up in her eyes as she stepped toward him.

"I'm not crazy anymore. I don't imagine things the way I used to, and I don't wish for things that can't come true. Sometime during my sessions with Dr. Vogland...in the hours I sat staring out this window...talking with you about Peter...sometime during all of that Timmy became a part of the past, a distant pain. But Heidi's right here." She clutched her fist to her heart. "Heidi made choices I don't understand, and that pain won't go away." Her voice broke on a little sob, then she lifted tear-drenched eyes to him. "And I don't think you know what to do about that, either!"

His anger with her was replaced by sadness for all of them. "You're right, but we both have to deal with it, Faith. Maybe if you move in with her again, talk to her, you'd be able to come to terms with it."

Wiping tears from her cheeks, she stared up at him with bright eyes. "When you kissed Heidi on Christmas Eve, the look on your face gave me goose bumps. Are you in love with her?"

He turned away, toward the window, as if looking at the sky could somehow provide the answer. His sadness was replaced by something he couldn't, wouldn't, put a name to. Taking a deep breath, he turned back to Faith and found her eyes burning with questions.

"Let's take it one step at a time. Talk to your sister in the morning. Just talk about moving up there with her. Then we'll see where that might lead all of us."

"Yeah, one step at a time." She trembled, but her voice remained firm. "That's what the doc says. I've been taking little steps till now. I guess it's time I thought about a big one. Bring Heidi to visit me, Luke. I know what I have to do now. Do you?''

Now it was his turn to hesitate, knowing he didn't have the answers she wanted. He waited so long to speak that she finally gave up, shook her head sadly and walked away from him.

CHAPTER TEN

BEING TRULY ALONE and able to do exactly as she pleased kept Heidi awake for hours after Luke took Faith home and she finally convinced David to leave. She roamed the condo, finding everything exactly as she had always kept it. David had obviously had a cleaning crew in and stocked the refrigerator. He was a good friend; if she had taken his advice in the beginning, and perhaps been spared her time in prison, would her life be so different now? She wouldn't know Angel, and that would have been a great loss. And she wouldn't be taking this new direction with her music. But she was really no closer to an answer than she'd been all those months ago.

She stared down at the baby grand piano that had been her parents' last gift to her and tentatively ran her fingers over the keys. To her trained ear it was slightly out of tune after months of sitting unused, but she sat and played, anyway, letting the music flow and fill the room around her. She played it all: classics, show tunes, love ballads, "Happy Birthday." Her tears fell as her fingers moved over the keys, but it didn't matter. She played on.

She was home. But home seemed different now. No matter where she was her pain was with her. Her hands banged the keys as she played through the fight scene from *West Side Story*. She remembered Angel trying to get the children to dance to the Jet song, teaching them to turn tension into control. It was a lesson everyone learned in prison.

She finished playing, and with the last pure note she smiled. Slowly she closed the piano and went to the sliding glass doors, watching until the first streaks of dawn lit the surface of the lake. Letty and Doreen would already be up if they were working in the kitchen. They seemed to like it. She and Angel had done everything they could to avoid it. In two hours Angel and Coralee would also wake to the routine. Here, she didn't have to worry about routine anymore.

Coralee's words came back to haunt her. Would she ever find the peace Coralee had found? Would any of them?

From the beginning she'd sensed Luke's anger and confusion. Somewhere along the line, despite her terrible dreams, she'd been lulled into thinking he'd changed. Was it because of his kindness to Faith? His kindness to her? Or was it because of the new feelings stirring to life between them? Once she'd been the kind of woman with the courage to face those feelings honestly and openly. Now she felt powerless before them.

In a few hours she would see him again. That thought brought both excitement and fear. She wasn't sure which was stronger. Nevertheless she was ready in a soft teal sweater dress when the doorbell rang.

Luke stood in the hallway, his thick wavy hair disordered and fresh color on his face from the cold wind outside.

She had both feared and yearned for this moment. Now that it was here, she still didn't know which feeling was stronger. Suddenly she felt even more unsure of herself as his eyes roamed over the soft dress that clung to her curves. Self-consciously she slid into her coat.

"I'm ready." Quickly she stepped past him and walked to the elevator.

"I'm glad Faith's ready to talk to you," he said, once the doors slid shut. "I can't promise what the results will be, but we had quite a talk last night. I think I see a breakthrough for her."

She stared up at him, willing her heart to beat normally. "I don't know how to thank you for all you've done for Faith. And me."

He shrugged her words away, his jaw tightening as he returned her gaze. "I promised to help Faith recover from my brother's desertion. I owe that to her. And all I did for you is what any competent lawyer would have done once he'd met you."

During the drive they exchanged banalities, but more often there were long stretches of silence. Reaching for change at a tollbooth, their hands touched briefly, and both withdrew as if they'd been burned. For a moment their gazes locked, but the green light flashed and Luke accelerated sharply.

When they neared the outskirts of Bloomington, her pulse raced and her hands were clammy. She hadn't been back since before she'd been taken to Elmwood. By the time they reached the hospital, she was having difficulty breathing normally. Aching regret squeezed her insides with its familiar power. Here, where she'd made the decision that changed all their lives, the memories waited to taunt her.

She had spent hours at this hospital and the one she didn't dare glance at across the street. Even with Luke beside her, once again she was alone.

She slid out of the car and took a step toward the mental health wing. There, in front of her, was the park. She stopped, her heart skipping a beat as she stared at the snow-covered playground, now empty, the swing frame a bleak, forsaken structure of tubing. The park was cold, desolate. Like her heart. Acceptance had never seemed farther away.

"Heidi, what's wrong?" Luke's question seemed to come from a great distance, drawing her back.

She tore her eyes away from the park just in time to see him look at the scene of her torment. Understanding darkened his gaze.

She didn't wait for his reaction; she wasn't sure she would be strong enough to deal with it. Nearly running, she pushed the glass doors open and made her way to the desk. She forced herself to inquire about Faith, to walk casually through the hospital corridors. He didn't catch up with her until Faith opened the door to her room.

For the first time Faith met her eyes squarely. "Hello, Heidi. I've been waiting for you. Come in."

Heidi stepped into the sterile room which, in its own way, had been Faith's prison. A jolt of relief almost made her smile when she saw the stack of fashion magazines next to a reclining chair. Maybe Faith was getting better, after all.

"Take off your coat. You, too, Luke." Faith's voice was as close to normal as Heidi had heard it in a long time.

Studiously avoiding Luke's eyes, Heidi placed her coat over the end of the bed and then stood waiting.

Faith sat at the edge of her bed. "Luke has made me understand that I have to get on with my life. I have to face my feelings about what happened. I have to face you, Heidi. And I want to talk about it.''

Over Faith's shoulder she saw Luke back up two steps and turn away to the window. Afraid of what was coming, Heidi practically collapsed into the chair. She gripped her hands together, prepared to sacrifice whatever was necessary to help her sister.

''Can you talk about your feelings now, Faith?''

Closing her eyes, Faith drew in a deep, shuddering breath. ''There's no easy way to say this. So...so I'm just going to say it. I've got to talk to you about Timmy.'' Her lids opened, revealing eyes awash with tears.

Old, protective feelings rose up, forcing Heidi closer. ''Faith, you—''

Faith raised her palm, stopping her. ''Let...let me talk while...while I have the courage. I made a lot of wrong choices. The biggest was my relationship with Peter. Then I let myself go to pieces when he left and I was pregnant. You...tried to put the pieces back together, but by then I couldn't deal with much. When Timmy got sick I couldn't handle it. I dumped it all in your lap, as always.''

''It wasn't your fault. You weren't well enough yourself to cope with his illness,'' Heidi said automatically, her lifelong habits impossible to abandon.

''You shouldn't have had to cope alone. You loved him as much as I did. You were in as much pain as I. When I asked you to help him...to stop his pain...''

The hesitations grew longer as Faith struggled to find the right words. Heidi wanted to reach out to her, but she knew Faith must do this on her own. Luke was right. It was a real breakthrough.

"Did I ask too much? Did I force you into a choice you would never have made otherwise?"

Looking into the young face ravaged by tears, Heidi knew what Faith needed to hear. For the first time she forced herself to accept the truth.

"You know how much I loved Timmy. I would have done anything to help him." Swallowing the lump in her throat, Heidi dashed away her own tears. "I did what I thought best for him. Even if you hadn't asked me to help end his pain, I would have made the same choice."

Weeping, Faith bent her head, burying her face in her hands.

Lifting her eyes, Heidi found Luke staring at her. He had heard the answer she had given her sister, the answer Faith needed to hear in order to heal. But she still didn't have the answer Luke wanted and, God help her, she wasn't sure she ever would.

Faith reached for her hand and brought it to her cheek. "I've felt so guilty. As if it was all my fault you were in that place. I was afraid to face you."

Heidi tried to protest, but Faith stopped her. "I know everything's going to be all right now. And Heidi . . . I love you."

"I love you, too, Faith," she whispered, tears rolling down her cheeks.

Stepping toward them, Luke offered Faith a handkerchief but she refused it, shaking her head. "I'm going to see Dr. Vogland," she whispered, tears choking her voice. "I'll be right back."

Luke remained by the window, staring at her, even after Faith hurried away. Heidi rose to confront him. "I'm sorry I can't help you understand as easily."

His jaw tightened. "I've recently discovered I can only find the answers myself. I should have known that from the beginning."

"I know you don't want my thanks, Luke. But I have to give it. Without your help Faith never would have come this far."

"It's not over yet. We have to get her settled in Chicago and back to some semblance of normalcy. On our next visit we can talk to Dr. Vogland about some kind of trial period at home."

Heidi nodded. "Next week I can swing by the prison to see Angel and then drive on down here."

"Fine. But I'll bring you. You'll need my help." He bit the words out crisply.

"Luke, you don't have to do that."

"You know I do," he stated grimly, as if the words were torn from him against his will. He turned away, only to twist back and grip her shoulders. Just like the first time, his touch burned deep into her soul, but she didn't flinch away. She didn't want to.

"I want you to know I heard what you said to Faith. I *really* heard it. But I don't know how I feel about anything. Hell, that's a lie!"

The look in his eyes made her heart beat painfully against her ribs.

Restlessly his hands roamed over her shoulders, up her throat, until his fingers were splayed across her cheeks, holding her as he stared into her eyes.

His facade of control was stripped away, and what she saw beneath made her tremble.

"What's back there, Heidi?" he asked with wonder. "What haunts your eyes so that I can't think of anything but them? Your lips. You. Nothing about you is what I thought it would be, most of all my feelings for you. I don't know what this is between us, but I know you feel it, too."

She didn't need to answer; she knew he could see it in her face, feel it in the air around them.

He swayed closer, then suddenly moved away. "I'll go see what happened to Faith." He stalked from the room as if fleeing from this force building between them.

Her body shook with the feelings his words evoked. She lifted her trembling hands to wipe her tear-soaked cheeks.

Acceptance. When she looked at the park, it had seemed far out of reach. Now it was here, nearly at her fingertips.

Luke's silence on the return trip and his abrupt farewell was almost easier to deal with than any words he could have said. They both needed time to sort through their feelings before they could understand and accept what they might mean. There was so much she had to learn to accept!

In the next few days she learned to adjust to the simple pleasures she had once taken for granted: getting up when she wished, retiring at will, talking on the telephone. She made inquiries into her music therapy internship and filled out the forms, sending a copy of her transcripts so that she could start in the spring semester. It was a new beginning.

A walk along the frozen lakeshore with the wind whipping into her face held new joy. And in her thoughts, always, Luke. With piercing clarity, like the penetrating lake breeze, she knew what haunted him—his desire for the woman who he could never accept had made choices for his nephew. Her own torment was in recognizing that she loved him, anyway. She wished he could understand everything that occurred during those long lonely months of watching Timmy suffer, but how could she ever reveal herself so completely to a man who was determined not to care?

She glanced at her watch. David would be back at the condo, waiting for her. He already had her opening date arranged with Georges, the owner of Yvonne's. Heidi wasn't sure she was ready to face an audience who probably knew of her past, but she realized she really had no choice. She had relied on David long enough. Now it was time to be strong, to establish her independence by taking charge of herself, and Faith, and soon Angel.

She smiled, lifting her face into the fresh, free wind, remembering how David had grudgingly accompanied her to three dance schools and several job interviews until they found exactly what Heidi was looking for.

"Well, I hope you're happy now. Your guardian Angel is going to get her chance."

The glint in his eyes had reminded her of what she sensed between him and Angel on Christmas Eve.

Her plans for Angel made it possible to assume a semblance of normalcy on the morning Luke picked her up for the long-awaited visit.

The tension-filled hour alone in the car with him was nearly unendurable. Since those shattering moments in Faith's room, Luke had stayed away physically, although he called briefly each day to see how she was doing. She always told him the truth; she was picking up the pieces of her life slowly and carefully. What they were both struggling to understand was where, or if, he could ever fit into it.

She knew where Elmwood fitted, recognized the changes it had wrought. She entered the building with what she hoped was an air of confidence, but at the crowd and noise of the waiting room she halted in confusion. She'd never approached the visiting hall from this end. Luke took her arm and led her through the proper steps. He stayed by her side, offering unquestioning support all the way. Then he stepped back.

"Take your time. I'll wait here."

Walking into the high-ceilinged room gave her a strange feeling. Had she looked as fearfully eager on the other side, waiting for David to visit? Had her eyes been as full of yearning when Luke appeared? Now she was an outsider. The life she'd led here seemed so far behind her, so alien. How had she managed to survive?

The answer was surprisingly easy. The routine, the confinement, the lack of privacy had only been endurable because of the women she had shared it with.

She searched the tables, finding a familiar face or two. Finally she saw Angel through the crowd, and an instant later she saw Santos beside her. Her heart pounded in her chest as she walked toward them. Nothing would stop her from helping Angel. Nothing and no one.

Angel, white-faced, her eyes dark pools of misery, her arm captured by Santos's meaty fist, was shocked to see her.

"What a pleasant surprise, Santos!" Heidi flattered him smoothly. "I thought you were in Florida for the winter."

Her loud greeting had the desired effect. He dropped Angel's arm and swung around to face her.

"Well! If it isn't Doll Face!" His eyes slid over her body, and he whistled appreciatively. "What ya doin' here?"

In that instant she slipped between him and Angel.

"Babe, yer lookin' hot. Ain't she, Angel?"

"It's good to see you, Heidi," Angel answered quietly, more subdued than Heidi could remember. Always when she thought of Angel, she remembered her dancing or with the kids or standing up to Maxime. Did she remember wrong, or had her perspective changed so radically? Maybe Angel had been sicker than she'd thought—her huge eyes filled her face, which seemed paler and narrower. The dull tone of Angel's voice called for desperate action.

"Santos, you wouldn't mind if Angel and I talked alone for a while, would you?" she cajoled, flashing what she hoped was a coy smile. "Girl talk, you know."

It seemed he might refuse. He gave her a calculating look that sent shivers up her spine and laughed, the loud, obnoxious laugh that had first drawn him to her attention.

"Gotta go, anyway. Got a big deal cookin' tonight." Pushing himself to his feet, he flexed his shoulders. "So long, Angel. Don't forget I'll be picking ya up on yer big day." He flicked Heidi a glance and winked. "See ya soon, Doll Face."

The minute he was out the door Angel let out a loud sigh of relief.

"What's happened?" Heidi asked.

"He came back early so he'd be here when I get out. What if he knows I'm lying? I'll never get away from him. What if he's waiting when I get out?"

The fear in her usually defiant gaze made Heidi forget Angel's reserve and clutch her nervously moving hands.

"If he's here, he'll have to deal with me!"

Angel jerked away, surprise widening her dark eyes. "Don't be stupid, Heidi. You can't take on Santos. He's dangerous. Real dangerous. If he's here, I'll have to go with him or we'll both pay."

Folding her arms across her breasts, Heidi fell into the chair Santos had vacated and met Angel's eyes. They had come so far together that a bully like Santos certainly wasn't going to stop them now.

"I understand. I'll bring David with me. He's more than a match for someone like Santos. Remember, Santos backed down from David once before."

Angel nodded. "Yeah, I remember. Do you think David would do that for you?"

Heidi smiled, leaning closer, remembering David's not-so-subtle reference to Angel. "I think David will do it for *you*. Don't worry, Angel. Nothing and no one can stop us from getting on with our lives."

NOTHING WAS MAKING sense with these papers! Luke swore, slamming his briefcase shut. Who was he kidding? He couldn't concentrate on business or anything else. All he seemed capable of doing was thinking about Heidi. He was so tense around her he broke out in a cold sweat, but desperation drove him to torment himself again and again. His cool, controlled calculations had flown out the window, obviously with his survival instincts. He wanted her. He wanted what he couldn't have and remain true to himself. But still he couldn't let go of it.

He could sense the guard watching him carefully as he restlessly prowled the waiting room. He got himself another cup of the foul coffee from the machine. Leaning against the wall, sipping from the plastic cup, he noticed the guy lounging on the next sofa. He looked as if he should be in prison rather than visiting it. There was something vaguely familiar about him. Then Luke remembered seeing him with Angel. If she was severing all ties with her former life and moving in with Heidi, what was this lowlife doing here?

He didn't have long to wonder, because Heidi soon appeared across the crowded room. Pushing through the turnstile, she didn't notice the guy until he grabbed her arm, pulling her off to one side. When he saw the fear in Heidi's eyes and saw her struggle to get free, something primal propelled him toward them.

"Let go of her!" he spit out between gritted teeth. "I said let go of her," he repeated when he reached them. "She's with me."

"What ya gonna' do, man? Hit me with yer brief-case?" Santos mocked. "Hey, Doll Face, you can do better."

Rage lent power to his fist as he knocked Santos's hand from Heidi. When he staggered back, Luke stepped between them, a warning in his eyes. "Keep your filthy hands off her!" It was all he could do not to smash his fist into Santos's smirking face.

"Is there a problem here?" an approaching guard asked.

"Everything's under control, Officer," Luke said smoothly, his eyes on Santos.

With a nod the guard moved away, and in that second Santos leaned closer. "Next time, man, it'll be just you and me."

Luke found himself welcoming that thought and braced himself as Santos swaggered past Heidi.

"I'll be seein' ya, Doll Face," he sneered.

"What in hell was that all about?" Luke demanded, resisting the nearly overpowering urge to touch Heidi himself. She was trembling, her cheeks drained of all color.

"Not here. Let's go," she pleaded.

His gaze never left her face all the way across the parking lot. But as he got into the car he noticed a red Porsche idling in the next row. It pulled out right behind him and turned toward the highway.

"I think that guy is following us." He looked into her stricken eyes and wanted nothing more than to keep her from harm. "Don't worry. I won't let him hurt you. But who the hell is he?"

"Santos is Angel's old boyfriend. He wants to drag her back into his gang when she gets out of prison. But I'm not going to let that happen."

The tone of her voice drew his eyes from the rear-view mirror to her set face. "What does that mean?"

"When I pick Angel up next week, I'm going to ask David to come along in case Santos tries to make trouble." Her chin jutted out in defiance.

It was mildly reassuring to know David would be handy, but the idea of Santos being anywhere near Heidi made him clench his hands on the wheel.

"I'd rather you didn't see that guy again," he told her, trying to regain control. "I'll go instead." A quick glance at the mirror showed nothing but empty highway behind them. "He must have given up when he saw me heading away from the city."

"Good." She nodded and gave him a tentative smile. "I didn't mean to involve you in this, Luke. It isn't your problem. Anyway, David has...a particular interest in Angel."

He shrugged. "All right, if that's the way you want it. But guys like Santos run in packs. If David goes to pick up Angel, I think I should stay at the condo with you just in case there's a problem.''

She tilted her head, studying him. ''Maybe you're right. If I'm not there, David can concentrate on getting Angel out of there.''

''Good, that's the plan then.''

Their momentary accord lightened the atmosphere in the car. He glanced at her, noting that she seemed more relaxed than he had ever seen her. She seemed to trust him—not only with Faith, or this simple decision about Angel's homecoming, but with herself.

From deep inside him came another, stronger feeling. What would it be like if they could be like any other couple out for a drive in the country, forgetting everything that kept them apart?

He pulled into the hospital parking lot, locked the door and walked around to Heidi's side of the car. She stood, the wind whipping honey strands of hair across her face. The sweetness of her smile captivated him, and he did forget everything between them as he cupped her chin with his fingers. He couldn't keep his eyes from her parted lips. He swayed closer, until they were separated only by a whisper.

A shout jerked him away. Over Heidi's shoulder he saw Faith waving from the doorway. He stepped back, releasing her.

She took a deep breath, her eyes meeting his for a split second before she turned, hurrying to where her sister waited.

New beginnings—for Faith and Angel and Heidi. He didn't want to see any one of them hurt. He would do everything in his power to make sure they got what they wanted. And perhaps then he could find the path to his own new beginning.

THE LAST FEW DAYS of Angel's four-year stay at Elmwood flew by. She'd always thought they would drag, but now, almost without warning, she stood in the prison yard for the last time. In her hand was the cheap brown suitcase they gave her for her things and in her pocket was the hundred dollars cash allotted every inmate upon their release.

She was really getting out. She would finally have what every woman at Elmwood longed for—freedom. Freedom to do anything she wanted, anytime she wanted. Four years ago this moment had seemed impossibly far away. But here it was and now, strangely, she was hesitating.

At a signal from Connell the gate swung open, and slowly Angel stepped outside into the real world for the first time in four years, two months and one day. It was scary until she saw David waiting for her in the parking lot.

Who would have ever thought when Angel Ramon left here she'd go with someone like David? Hard to believe that big lug with the lopsided grin was a show biz hotshot and her friend. Maybe that was why sometimes looking at David made her feel strange inside—like right now.

With a squeal of tires a red Porsche shrieked to a halt in front of her. Angel's insides lurched as Santos stepped out. He'd known all along she was lying about the date, she suddenly realized, sick fear rising in her throat.

"Hey, Angel, babe, surprised to see me?" A detestable smile twisted his mouth as he strolled toward her. "Told ya I'd pick ya up in a Porsche. I always keep my promises!"

A firm grip on her shoulder pulled her tightly against David's side as Santos's hand reached for her suitcase.

"Sorry, buddy. I'm here to pick up Angel."

"Don't get in my face, man!" Santos snarled. "Angel's goin' with me!"

David laughed. "You came for nothing. Have a safe trip home."

"Don't provoke him," Angel hissed, adrenaline pounding in readiness to launch herself between them as Santos reached into his pocket. She knew what he kept there.

Before she could move David thrust her behind him.

"Listen, you punk, get the hell out of here! Even you aren't stupid enough to try something with two officers watching through those gates."

Glancing over his shoulder, Santos slowly slid his hand out of his pocket. Angel had seen that look on his face before. Even in the old days it had stirred fear, but now she was terrified of the rage in his eyes.

"Remember, Angel, I warned ya. I'll be back to get ya. You and your new friends can count on it," he growled, smirking as he slowly strutted to his car.

With a grinding of gears he roared out of the parking lot. Angel leaned weakly against David's broad back.

"Get in the car," he commanded.

She complied instantly, regretting her weakness at allowing him to protect her, but determined not to let him see it. She always took care of herself. Always had, always would. She slid a furtive glance at David's pug-nosed profile. Why didn't he say anything? He'd just risked his life to keep her safe from Santos, to keep her from having to go back to her old life. Didn't he realize what that meant to her? Maybe he did know and he just didn't care.

Forcing her eyes away from David, she watched the outside mirror. Whenever she saw a flash of red, she held her breath until she was sure it wasn't a Porsche. Santos would never let her go easily.

"We've got to talk, Angel," David finally bit out. "I assume you didn't really want to leave with that guy."

"Yeah, you assume right. In fact, I—"

"Fine! Since we have that straight, let's lay down the ground rules!" he said brusquely in what she now recognized as his professional voice. "Starting next week I have five job interviews set up for you. They are entry-level positions, but you have to start somewhere. Also, next week your classes at the Fine Arts Dance Studio begin."

She'd just had four long years of someone else running her life, so why was she taking this? Instead of anger, warm sensations reached all the way down to the toes curled under her on the seat.

"I don't expect this stuff from you, David," she found herself saying.

"You've got it, anyway."

She looked up at him, tilting her head all the way back so that it rested on the seat back. "Why are you doing all this for me?"

"Because Heidi asked me to a long time ago. Back when you only saw her as a main chance." He narrowed his eyes. "If things hadn't changed between the two of you, I wouldn't be doing this. I'm glad for both your sakes it did."

There was no fooling this guy. Angel had recognized that from the beginning, so she didn't even try to answer; she just watched him, his strong hands on the wheel, taking her somewhere safe for the first time in her life.

One thought kept whirling crazily through her mind. Because Heidi had gone to prison, she, Angel, had a chance for a different life. It didn't seem fair on the one hand, but then on the other it was kind of like a balance—something positive coming out of a tragedy. Angel had always known life wasn't fair or equal for everyone, but if she was getting this break, then she'd make sure she didn't screw it up! And somehow, someday, she'd pay Heidi back.

Paying Heidi back seemed nearly impossible when she saw the condo overlooking Lake Michigan. Angel had never seen anything like it except in the movies. She didn't give herself away by oohing and aahing like some nut, but it was hard, especially when Heidi flung open the door to a beautiful blue-and-white bedroom where everything matched perfectly.

"This is your room, Angel." Heidi smiled.

Twirling around, Angel hugged herself. "Hey, it's nice, really nice!"

"I'm glad you like it."

How could Angel ever repay the goodness shining out of Heidi's eyes? She was doing all this and she didn't expect anything in return. Angel was just beginning to understand stuff like this. But when she returned to the living room and Luke and David stopped talking about Santos as if they didn't want to upset her, she was shocked into silence. Nobody had ever treated her like this before.

Heidi had made all this possible. How could you repay someone who gave you a second chance at life?

It got harder and harder to sit still. Finally she could take it no longer and jumped up from the table. "Well, I hate to break up the party, but I'm kind of tired."

Heidi understood. "Of course you are. I'll see you in the morning."

Angel threw a "Good night" over her shoulder and fled down the hall.

She was able to hold back her tears until she was soaking in a rose-scented bubble bath. For a full hour she wept. She couldn't believe her luck. She knew she didn't deserve all of this. Freedom. It would take some getting used to.

CHAPTER ELEVEN

"ANGEL, I hate to leave you alone tonight." Heidi fretted with her hair for the hundredth time and sprayed a bit more perfume on the cleavage revealed by the cobalt-blue evening gown. She was stalling, and when she met Angel's eyes in the mirror, she saw Angel knew it, too.

"You've gotta go, Heidi. You'll be great! Play that classical stuff you were practicing today. I like it."

"But what are you going to do here alone?" Turning to face her, Heidi smiled. "I'd call David, but I know he's seeing clients tonight."

Stretching, Angel rose from the bed where she'd been perched while Heidi turned herself into her professional persona. "Hey, don't worry about me. I'm kinda tired from the bookstore and I have dance class tomorrow, so I'll probably turn in early. Unless you want me to wait up for you."

"No, I'll be late. Speaking of which, I will be if I don't get a move on." Turning back to the mirror, she fastened long crystal drops to her ears and stared at her reflection. It had been a very long time since she'd seen this Heidi Allan. But it wasn't quite the same; the eyes that looked back at her were changed forever.

"I've got to go. My cab will be waiting downstairs." Grabbing her coat, she headed toward the door, throwing instructions over her shoulders. "I know you hate locks, but lock up behind me. I'm sure Santos hasn't any idea where you are, but we should be careful." At the front door she turned to find Angel grinning at her.

"Hey, I'm a big girl. I know my way around, remember? It's been a whole week. I feel kinda confident Santos is long gone. And you'd better be, too. Oh, Heidi, if Luke calls tonight, what do you want me to tell him? Or do you think he'll show up at Yvonne's?"

She met Angel's frank gaze as calmly as possible. "I don't know what Luke will do. And I doubt that he does, either."

She nearly flew through the lobby and into her waiting cab. Her heart was racing so fast that she actually felt overheated in the icy February wind. She took long, deep breaths as the cab headed north on Michigan Avenue. She wished Angel hadn't mentioned the possibility of Luke showing up at Yvonne's tonight. She was nervous enough at being in front of an audience after so long, wondering what they knew about her absence from the stage. But to have Luke there... The attraction between them gained power at each meeting; the tension he engendered was so overwhelming that she shivered now, remembering. She had to learn to accept that she couldn't have the man she loved.

When she arrived at Yvonne's, Georges's piercing dark eyes searched her face momentarily, then he shrugged in a typically Gallic gesture.

"Heidi, *petite,* you are as always divine!" Pressing kisses on each cheek, he continued to hold her hands while urging her toward the white baby grand piano placed in a well-lit corner surrounded by green plants and freshly cut flowers. "No one has compared to you. Play Chopin for me tonight, eh?"

"Of course, Georges. It's lovely to be back."

David had chosen well. She had made her first professional appearance at Yvonne's, and even after she was in greater demand she'd still occasionally play at the intimate club for sentimental reasons. She felt safe here, with Georges holding court at the front entrance, and Philippe, the bartender, waving at her through the foliage to her left. She even recognized a few regulars, who smiled at her as she played. Her heart slowed to its accustomed beat as she lost herself in her music. When she finished, the applause was enthusiastic. She stood and bowed before going over to the bar for mineral water.

Luke was sitting there, just where the plants blocked her view from the piano bench.

"I didn't know you were here." Joy exploded through her, and she laughed lightly to cover it, slipping onto the padded stool beside him.

"You play beautifully." His voice sounded raspy tonight, and in the dim light his eyes glistened like gemstones. "I brought you something." He shoved a white box across the bar toward her.

Pulling off the lid, she caught the fragrance a moment before she uncovered two gardenias floating in a crystal bowl. Lifting one into her palm. she stared up at him, an indescribable feeling pulsing between them so powerfully that it seemed to fill the room. She looked away first because she had to; she was beginning to tremble.

"Thank you, Luke." Taking a deep, steadying breath, she met his eyes. "I have to get back. Will you be staying?"

"Yes, I'm having dinner."

His thoughtfulness and the fact that he'd come here to see her after weeks of avoidance confused her. What had changed?

As she played Georges's favorites, Luke was seated at a small table directly beyond the bowl of gardenias, placed at her left side. Every time she glanced up at them she saw him. Warmth and chills played along her skin all at once. She took a sip of the mineral water Philippe brought to the piano, and with the deep breathing Madam Romonov had taught her was able to bring her turbulent emotions under control.

She began a medley, interspersing classical pieces with show tunes. A patron came forward with a request. By the end of the set there were several more notes. Adjusting the microphone, she welcomed all the newcomers and announced she'd sing "Tonight" and "Memories" as part of a show tune set. She asked for other requests, deliberately avoiding Luke's table.

Amazingly her voice was clear and strong. If she concentrated on the audience and her craft, she could almost forget how long she'd been away. She stood again and bowed, moving swiftly away from the piano while the applause still thundered around her. The emotions the music evoked were too powerful, too close to her own feelings. She willed her pulse to quiet, gripping the edge of the bar so hard that her fingers numbed.

"Miss Allan?"

She swung around. A tall man who had been seated with a woman at the table next to Luke's smiled at her.

"I just wanted to tell you how much I enjoyed your playing. My wife and I have been coming here for years. We'd read you'd been ... away. I'm glad ..."

"Bill! I'm ready to go!" The woman who had been sitting with him rushed up, grabbed his arm and turned him abruptly away. "I told you not to do that. I told you what she did...."

Her words were lost as they hurried out, but Heidi had heard enough for the pain to pierce her heart. She hadn't been able to let go of that pain, and now it seemed no one else would, either. Timmy's death would haunt her for the rest of her life.

She felt his gentle hands on her shoulders an instant before she knew he was there.

"I heard. I'm sorry," Luke whispered, bending his head close to her cheek. "Let me take you home."

For an instant she let her feelings out and swayed back against his protective warmth. "I can't go yet. I have another set."

"*Petite,* of course you must go now in your moment of triumph!" Georges rushed over from the end of the bar where he'd been quietly speaking to Philippe. "My patrons will be disappointed, but always we must leave them wanting more."

Luke dropped his hands away, and although she felt suddenly bereaved, she smiled, stepping toward Georges to place a kiss on each cheek.

"Thank you, Georges. I'll see you this weekend."

With his usual efficiency of movement Luke helped her on with her coat and had the valet bring his car. He was silent as he concentrated on driving, but his jaw was locked and his hands gripped the wheel with iron fingers.

Wanting to defuse the tension, Heidi laughed lightly. "I haven't played or sung professionally for so long that I hope I wasn't too awful."

He threw her a glance from eyes shimmering with something she couldn't guess how to interpret. "You were wonderful and you know it. Heidi, we have to talk."

"I know." She resigned herself to the inevitable. "Come up for coffee. The underground parking entrance is on the north side of the building. I have an empty space there since David sold my car."

He nodded, following her directions until they stopped in the low-ceilinged garage. She got out of the car swiftly, her heels clicking along the concrete as she hurried toward the elevator. Thank goodness another couple got into the elevator with them, preventing the need to make small talk.

Her hand trembled ever so slightly as she tried the key, only to find the condo door was unlocked. Angel couldn't yet bring herself to lock anything. Heidi understood, but it still made her nervous.

Uncharacteristically she flung her coat over the back of a chair and said, "Sit down. I'll make coffee."

"Heidi, we've got to talk about what happened tonight."

His voice stopped her halfway across the living room. Knowing she must confront this once and for all, she turned to face him.

"I'm sorry about what happened tonight," Luke said softly. "I'm afraid you're going to have to learn to deal with how people feel about Timmy and what...happened." He moved closer. His face was stamped with confusion.

"I think what I really have to deal with is how I feel about my choice. And how you feel." Her voice was low as she fought for control.

"I thought I knew how I felt."

Something in his voice made her stand utterly still, waiting for what her instincts screamed would happen.

He took another step closer and lifted his hands to her shoulders, tracing a slow pattern with his fingers on her bare flesh.

"This is the gown you wore for your press photo, isn't it? The one that was splashed all over the papers." His eyes traveled the length of her, taking in her slim body wrapped in clinging cobalt-blue, the bodice straining with her breathing.

She couldn't speak, didn't want to break the spell between them.

"I studied that picture a thousand times. Reread the story. It didn't fit. I felt such rage, such hate when I realized what had happened to Timmy. But nothing I discovered about you fit. You're right. We have to deal with how we feel about everything. Neither one of us can pretend this isn't happening or ignore the feelings we have."

Laying his forehead gently against hers, he brought one hand to her cheek, caressing it with the back of his fingers. She tilted her head under his touch, stunned by the heat that surged through her.

"Let me help you find your answers, Heidi. Then, together, we can find mine," he murmured. Then he added softly, "Please."

Suddenly she was caught in his arms, his kiss consuming her with fiery pleasure. His lips glided over the skin of her cheek, smoothed the curls at her throat and nibbled there at the delicate skin above her gown. She gasped, and his mouth found hers again. She stepped closer, holding him, reaching for all the things she needed.

A loud, persistent ringing echoed in her mind, as if someone were leaning against the doorbell. They sprang apart, almost guiltily. Did her eyes reveal the same dazed, frustrated longing she saw in Luke's? She stumbled back, trembling. "I've got to answer before it wakes Angel," she gasped, turning toward the door.

She was too late. Angel, yawning, strolled into the living room as David walked through the door.

"What's going on here? I just came from Yvonne's..." Then his eyes fell on Luke, and he reddened. Squaring his shoulders, he turned back to Heidi. "I went to Yvonne's after I found a call from Dr. Vogland on my recorder. Georges told me what happened. Are you all right?"

"Yes," Heidi said quickly, new fear burning through her. "Has something happened to Faith?"

"Something good. Dr. Vogland is releasing Faith next week. She's ready to come home."

"Yeah, he called here, too. I left a note on your pillow." Angel's knowing eyes brushed over Luke's set face and rested on Heidi's. "Guess it's been quite a night, hasn't it?"

Talk about understatements! Heidi lifted her chin and stared directly into the blue blaze of Luke's eyes. "Yes," she said. "It's been quite a night. Thank you for bringing me home, Luke. I'll see you soon?"

"I have a case in California, but I'll be back for Faith's homecoming. I promise."

With both Angel and David watching them, there was really nothing else to do but smile and nod, letting him walk away.

HAPPINESS QUICKENED Angel's stride as she swung through the Fine Arts Building door and made her way up Michigan Avenue. She still couldn't believe it! A real dance class! Nobody there knew anything about her past; they just accepted her as one of them. She wanted to hug Heidi for all she'd done for her. And David, too.

Tightening her dance bag strap more securely on her shoulder, Angel darted across Michigan Avenue to grab her bus. She looked around, as she always did, not quite able to suppress the need to know who was near her or how to make a quick getaway. The bus squealed to a stop and she got off. A stiff wind numbed her cheeks. She squinted into the sun as she crossed the last street to the condo. Right in the middle of the crossing she did a pirouette. Freedom was great! And tonight was Faith's welcome-home party. She hoped the kid had finally gotten her act together.

The wind had really chilled her, whipping right through the wool coat Heidi had insisted on buying. Angel was eager to reach the warmth of the building just ahead, but some instinct made her stop and glance back. A black Cadillac was inching down the block toward her. Quickening her steps, she ran the last few yards and ducked through the glass doors. Her lungs ached as she breathed in dry, warm air, her breath a light film on the ice-cold windowpane. Through it she saw the Cadillac cruise slowly by. Santos sat behind the steering wheel.

He didn't see me. He didn't see which building I went into, she told herself over and over. She was still repeating it when she walked into the condo.

Faith was reading a college catalog in the living room. She looked the way Heidi had first described her, with her rich brown hair shining and healthy around her face, her sloppy clothes replaced by rust suede pants and a matching sweater.

"Welcome home, Faith," Angel said, hoping the change in appearance meant she was on the road to recovery.

David suddenly appeared in the kitchen doorway. He'd obviously come straight from his office and made himself at home. He'd loosened his tie, and a mug of coffee steamed in his hands.

"You look frozen, Angel. Here drink this." Not waiting for an answer, he thrust the coffee into her numb fingers.

It was hot and bitter going down, but it stopped her insides from shivering. She was home now. Santos couldn't touch her here.

"Are you all right?" he asked, narrowing his eyes.

It was tempting to tell him the truth. She knew he wasn't afraid of Santos, but he hadn't seen the vicious cruelty firsthand. She had. So she wasn't going to tell him. She would handle it herself, if the time came. As always.

"You know me. I'm always okay." Throwing her head back, she gave him a quick once-over. "What have you been up to?"

"Working much too hard for his clients, as always," Heidi answered from behind him in the kitchen. "David is starving for dinner. Faith, do you want to help with the lasagna?"

"Sure." Throwing down her magazine, Faith jumped up.

Faith seemed almost normal. If Angel didn't look carefully into her eyes, she'd never see the hidden pain; the same sort of pain mirrored in Heidi's eyes.

Angel was determined to help Heidi lose that pain. She deserved happiness, because she worked so hard for it for everyone around her. Angel knew there was definitely something going on between her and Luke. It was written all over Heidi's face every time they were together. And even though he tried not to show it, Luke was all tied up in knots, too. They might be fighting it, but what they felt was powerful stuff. He just might be her chance at happiness.

Maybe she could recognize those feelings in Heidi because of what she was feeling herself. She looked at David, sitting with his eyes closed and his head flung back. She would concentrate on her new life, her new feelings. The past couldn't touch her. It couldn't touch any of them. If Santos had seen her, he would have acted immediately. She had to believe that.

Suddenly the doorbell rang. "There's our Prince Charming. On cue as always." Angel laughed. David opened one eye, giving a lopsided grin of approval as Angel whisked away, and she found her fingers trembling as she opened the door to Luke.

Luke smiled but looked past her, searching for Heidi. He'd thought of nothing else since he'd left for the West Coast. It might be wrong, yet something about her made him feel so damnably right! Trying not to stare at her, he watched Faith instead as she set food on the table. This smiling young woman was a far cry from the unkempt girl of a few months ago.

The past months had brought a lot of changes; even David had relaxed, teasing Angel beside him at the table. The only one who appeared unaltered was Heidi. The depths of her eyes were still sad, and that meant everything to him now. He looked at her face, animated now as she talked with the others.

"Oh, Angel, I nearly forgot!" she exclaimed, and her laugh sent pleasure through him. "Something came for you in the mail today. It's from Doreen at Elmwood."

"For me?" Angel's face sharpened with anticipation.

David appeared mesmerized as he studied the play of emotions across Angel's face.

"Where is it?"

"I'll get it for you." Uncurling from the chair, Heidi stepped over Luke's outstretched legs and moved toward the hall.

The phone rang on the small desk in the corner as she passed. "I've got it," she called over her shoulder. "Allan residence. Just a minute." She held out the receiver, her smooth brow wrinkled in puzzlement. "Faith, it's for you."

Faith shook her head. "Who could it be?" she wondered aloud.

Heidi put the receiver to her ear. "May I ask who's calling, please?"

Luke watched Heidi from his place at the table. Suddenly he saw all the color drain from her face, and she leaned limply against the desk. He jumped to his feet and reached her at the same moment she turned to look at him.

"It's your brother," she said flatly.

Suddenly cold, as if someone had thrown ice water over him, Luke removed the receiver from her fingers.

"Damn it to hell!" David swore under his breath, turning back to Faith, but he was too late.

Trembling, she stood transfixed in the middle of the room. The newly confident young woman had once again regressed to the frightened girl.

"Peter?" She gasped, shaking her head, retreating when Heidi tried to embrace her. "I can't see him! Not tonight! Not on my first day home!"

As always when things got out of control, Angel, hands balled into fists at her sides, looked ready to slug someone. "Of course you can't see him now! Do something, Luke. He's your brother!" she commanded.

All eyes turned to him now. Carefully, watching Faith's reaction, he said into the receiver. "Peter, it's Luke."

On the other end of the line there was stunned silence, then a barrage of questions. Why had he been trying to contact him? What was Luke doing at Heidi Allan's? Where was Faith? What in hell was this all about?

"Peter, this isn't the time or the place!" Luke cut in. "Meet me at my place. I've sold the old building and started rehabbing another one since you left. The address is 4230 Marine Drive. Be there in half an hour!" He put down the receiver and turned to face the others.

"Do you want me to go with you?" Heidi asked, her eyes meeting his.

"No. I'll take care of it. I think Faith needs you here," he said quietly, stepping toward Faith.

Faith wanted no part of him. "No, Luke! Don't make me! I'm not ready! Not this soon!" She twisted away, running down the hall and slamming her bedroom door behind her.

"I'll try to talk to her." Heidi looked as stricken as Faith. The only color on her face was in her dark eyes. They pleaded with him, as they had in the prison when he first promised to help. "Try to explain to him about

Faith. She needs more time to heal before the wounds are reopened.''

''We all do, damn it!''

She nodded. He wanted to reach out with his fingertips and smooth the worry from her face. He wanted to enfold her in his arms, to protect her. Instead he retrieved his coat from the closet and shrugged into it.

Heidi followed him to the door. ''I'm sorry you have to do this alone, Luke.''

''It's okay. I just wish he had gotten to know you. It would be so much easier to explain.'' Unable to resist, he rubbed his knuckles over her petal-soft skin. ''If he'd met you, talked to you, he'd understand. But that can come later. When we're all ready. For now I'll make him understand.''

He didn't want to leave her this way, but he forced himself to drop his hand and close the door between them. He needed a clear head to handle Peter, and that wasn't possible around Heidi. He needed to work out exactly how to handle Peter's questions. How to explain that he was in love with the woman the world held responsible for the death of Peter's son.

FAITH, curled up in a tight ball on her bed, caught the delicate scent of her sister's perfume an instant before she felt Heidi's hand on her shoulder. She was torn. Part of her wanted to shrug the hand away and burrow deeper into the quilted spread, away from reality. But she had so recently fought her way back to life. Did she really desire to retreat again? The part of her that cried out no forced her to turn to Heidi.

''I'm all right. I'm just not ready to see Peter yet. Not on my first day home.'' Faith's voice rasped through her dry, aching throat. ''I know I'll have to see him eventually, but it has to be when I'm ready. Can you understand?''

Nodding, Heidi slipped down beside her and patted her comfortingly. "Of course I understand. No one expects you to see Peter until you're ready."

They were the right words, but they didn't ease the painful knot in Faith's chest.

"It all started with Peter, didn't it? If I hadn't fallen in love with him, Timmy would never have been born. If he hadn't left me alone, I might not have fallen apart. If I hadn't ... you wouldn't have had to care for Timmy alone." The beat of her heart jolted painfully against her ribs as she stared up into her sister's face. "Maybe ... maybe you could have been spared ... the time ... away." She couldn't say the words yet, her guilt was still too heavy, despite Heidi's reassurances.

"How can I pick up the pieces, Heidi?" She felt like a child again, entwining her fingers with her sister's longer, more slender ones.

"Someone I met recently told me something I've been thinking about ever since. And I want you to think about it, too." Heidi tilted her head and smiled at the memory. "She said, 'Only by accepting your past can you really be free of it.'"

"Have you done that, Heidi? Accepted your past?"

Faith could see the answer lurking in the depth of Heidi's eyes. She wasn't strong enough to face that, either.

"Well, I need more time!" Jumping off the bed, she scrubbed the tears from her hot cheeks. "Luke will be able to make Peter understand. He has to!"

A frown marring her smooth forehead, Heidi rose from the bed. "I'm sorry Luke has to face Peter alone. I feel as if I should be there, the way he was there for you. And, really, I'm the only one who has the answers Peter will need.''

"Then maybe you should go to him. I don't want to hurt Peter. I just want this to end. Maybe if you went over there to help explain, it would get through to him.''

"Faith, I promise I'll take care of it. We'll all work this out together." She turned away quickly, her hair swinging across her cheek, hiding her face.

After Heidi left, Faith threw herself back onto the bed, burrowing into the pillows, willing the painful jolting in her chest to subside to its normal rhythm. It was different this time, she convinced herself. This time she wasn't asking too much of her sister. Going to talk to Peter couldn't do any harm.

Angel blocked Heidi's path to the doorway.

"What do you mean, you've got to go out!" She knew she was overreacting, but she couldn't help herself. It was dark outside. She didn't like Heidi being out by herself when Santos might be hanging around. It was all right for her—she could handle it, but not Heidi.

"Talk to her, David! Why does she need to help Luke with Peter right now? The kid's been gone for months. Why should he waltz back in here and mess up everyone's lives?"

But David only shrugged his massive shoulders. "If Heidi feels she can help, then she should go. I always trust her judgment. Here are the keys to my car—it's in your space in the garage. You know how to get to Luke's?" His words were rewarded by a quick, fierce hug from Heidi. "Yes, I heard him telling Peter the address. Thanks, David." Stepping away from him, she smiled, and nudged Angel's shoulder. "Trust me, okay? I'll be fine."

"I'm not so sure about that, but I guess you've got to do what you want. I'll walk you down to the parking garage, anyway."

She saw David flash her a calculating look, but he didn't try to stop her. Good thing, because she wouldn't have listened to him. Heidi might think she didn't need Angel to watch out for her now that they were out of prison, but she didn't see it that way. Since seeing Santos earlier, she knew she had to be on guard again for all of them.

In the elevator Heidi smiled at her. "It means a lot to me having you here. You don't need to feel you're indebted to me for anything."

For the first time Heidi had read her wrong. "You mean by being your watchdog, like at Elmwood?" She laughed. "I'm just naturally bossy, I guess. So I don't mind telling you to be very careful."

"I promise. But the real problem won't begin until I get to Luke's. I don't want to deal with Peter any more than Faith or Luke do. But it *is* my battle to fight."

"Forget this Peter! What about you and Luke? And don't pretend you don't know what I'm talking about."

"Angel, when I know the answer to Luke and me, I think I'll have the answer to everything else." With a faint smile and a wave she ran to David's black Jaguar.

Angel looked around the garage. Although it wasn't dark, there were still shadowy corners, and the rows of cars could easily hide anyone who didn't want to be seen. She waited until Heidi pulled out, the car roaring to life and speeding up the short incline to the exit. Her breath caught in a gasp of fear when she spied a black Cadillac parked two rows beyond the Jag's empty space.

It couldn't be, she told herself, but she had to make sure. Slowly she walked toward the car, her muscles bunched in readiness to bolt. When she got close enough to see an infant seat in the back, she relaxed immediately. She was imagining things. Santos hadn't seen her, or he would have taken action by now. She was safe from him here. They all were.

The hand on her shoulder tore a piercing scream from her throat. Fear fed her strength to escape. Blood beating in her ears, she was halfway to the elevator when she realized it was David's voice.

"Angel, it's me!"

Anger replaced terror as she whirled around to confront him.

"I didn't mean to scare you," he said, his concern written plainly on his face. "I got worried because you were gone so long."

"I can take care of myself, and don't you forget it!" she declared, trying to conceal her relief with a sneer. Pushing past him, she marched to the elevator and jabbed the button repeatedly. "Anyone would scream if they were alone down here and they found you looming over them! C'mon, you shouldn't have left Faith in the condo by herself."

That stupid lopsided grin of his made her even madder, particularly when it remained plastered to his face all the way up to their floor. Even back in the safety of the condo he still seemed pleased with himself.

"Why are you grinning? You let Heidi go off alone and you scared me half to death! Is this the way you get your kicks?"

"Calm down, Angel. Just think about it. Heidi is trying to regain control of her life. That's positive."

He was always so damn logical! It made her want to hit him. No, she admitted, curling up in the chair opposite where he sprawled on the couch, that wasn't really what she wanted to do to him. But she wasn't going to think about that!

"So what's positive about scaring me?"

"The old Angel wouldn't have let me see that. You aren't really as tough as you put on, and I like what I'm seeing now, Angel. I like it a lot."

For some reason David's words made her feel safe and warm. His smile did funny things to her stomach, but she refused to move. She didn't want to break the rapport building between them. If she could just get past her fear of Santos, she could really start building this new life Heidi had made possible. She only wished David could be a part of it.

LUKE FOUND his brother leaning against the wall outside the front door. He appeared annoyed. Straightening his lanky frame, a frown twisting his mouth, he began, "Luke, what the hell is...?"

"And hello to you, too!" Luke cut him off. "Come inside first." He didn't utter another word as he unlocked the door, flipped on the lights and shrugged out of his coat. Then, at last, he turned to confront Peter, who was standing much as he had on their last encounter, his legs spread apart, his slim shoulders hunched, his face stiff with self-defense. But over the past months Peter had filled out. He looked older, his blue eyes harder. Had he grown up enough to comprehend what Luke needed to tell him?

Before he could open his mouth, Peter held up his palm. "I know what's coming, so let me fill you in to save time. I know I was immature, irresponsible, unprincipled and stupidly thoughtless not to let anyone know where I've been. I've already called Mom in Florida and spent two hours soothing her ruffled feathers. My next step is Faith. Her old number is disconnected, so I called her sister's. Obviously you already know I left some unfinished business there. Well, I'm ready to deal with it now."

"Unfinished business?" Luke echoed, appalled by Peter's belief he could simply walk back into Faith's life and coolly pick up where he left off.

"Don't play games with me, Luke!" The familiar angry redness brightened Peter's cheeks and neck. "You obviously know about Faith and the baby."

"So do you now admit the child was yours?" Luke heard the anger in his voice, but he couldn't stop himself. "How could you just walk out on that poor girl and your own child?"

"Because I'm not *perfect* like you!" Peter jammed his hands into his jean pockets as he paced the carpet. "I was confused and scared. How could I take care of a wife and child?"

"You could have come to me for help. Why didn't you, Peter?" Luke had to know where he'd failed, even if the truth hurt.

Peter shrugged. "You were always too busy solving the problems of the world to deal with mine. Anyway, I'm tired of being the screw-up brother. I didn't want to disappoint everyone again. Do you think I don't care what your opinion of me is? You think I don't know I'm always compared to you and come up short?"

"Peter, no one ever expected you to be perfect. All we ever asked was for you to be responsible. Responsible enough to buckle down and stay in school. Responsible enough to admit your mistakes."

Peter's eyes were no longer hard; they were wide and vulnerable, very much like his son's had been in the picture Luke had carried for so long.

"Well, I'm back now to give responsibility a try. I told Mom I'm enrolling at U of I Circle Campus here in Chicago. About Faith and the baby...well, we'll work something out. I want to be part of my child's life, even if Faith and I aren't together." His restless pacing halted in front of Luke. "How did you find Faith, anyway?"

"I found a letter she wrote you right before Timmy was born."

"I have a son?" Peter asked. A smile flickered across his face, but just as swiftly vanished. "Luke, why are you looking at me like that?"

Now that the moment had come, Luke found he had to turn away. It wasn't easy to say the words, to cause Peter pain.

"What is it, Luke? Is there something wrong with Faith or my son?" Peter demanded, coming around to confront him. "What the hell's going on?"

Pushing past him, Luke went to his desk and removed the manila folder from the top drawer. "This will answer all your questions." He dropped the file on the couch and fell into the armchair opposite it.

"What is this?" Cautiously Peter picked up the folder.

"Read it." Luke heard the weariness in his voice. "Read it first. Then we'll talk."

Peter flipped the file open almost defiantly. Luke knew the contents by heart: the letter from Faith; the copy of Timmy's birth certificate; and the letter Luke had drawn up to receive permission to visit Faith at the sanatorium.

Peter glanced at him, his face pale, but Luke offered no information. He wouldn't soften the blow. Peter would find out exactly the way he had. The remaining documents, the newspaper clippings and the transcript from the trial struck tremors of disbelief and horror across Peter's face.

"My son is dead?"

Luke ached for his brother. Peter's anguish was real, but there was no comfort he could offer. "Yes . . . I'm sorry," he said sadly.

The pictures of Heidi and Timmy clutched in his fist, Peter ran across the room and wrenched open the front door.

Stunned into action, Luke jumped to his feet. "Peter, where are you going?"

His eyes wild, Peter twisted around. "I've got to see Faith! My God, she let her sister kill our baby!"

Luke didn't even realize he'd lunged for Peter until his hands were grasping his shoulders, pulling him back into the room. The door stood half open, but Luke ignored it. Peter struggled to keep his balance.

"Have you gone crazy, Luke? What are you doing!"

"Stay away from Heidi and Faith! Faith isn't well enough to see you yet. And Heidi's suffered enough because of you!"

"*Me!*" Peter's face was chalky white, his voice raw. "I don't even know her. Timmy was your nephew! Doesn't that mean anything to you?"

"Mean anything to me? It nearly destroyed me to think I wasn't there to help him." He squared his shoulders and took a deep breath. "Other lives were almost destroyed, too. Before you go off half-cocked, you'd better listen to what I have to say."

"Nothing you can say will ever explain this. My son is dead and it's her fault!"

"Don't throw stones, Peter. Where were you when your son lay dying? Because you ran away and Faith collapsed, the only person Timmy had was Heidi. She loved him."

"Yeah, she loved him to death, didn't she?" Peter spit back.

Luke clenched his fist as if to hit him, and Peter took a step backward.

"My God, Luke, why are you defending her? Didn't you read this stuff? You can tell what kind of person she must be!"

"It tells you nothing, you idiot! She's not what you think. She's . . . warm and loving and giving . . . and courageous. She's . . ." He stopped. Yes, she was all those things and more. Defending her to Peter broke the dam. All his confused emotions poured out as he argued aloud everything that had haunted his thoughts for months.

"Listen to yourself," Peter whispered hoarsely. "You're obsessed with the woman!"

The stunning indictment paralyzed him. He didn't try to stop Peter from shoving past him and racing out the door. Only one thought raged through Luke's mind: *It's not obsession. It's love.*

"Luke . . ."

He spun around. Blinking, he shook his head in disbelief. Was Peter right? Was his obsession with Heidi so complete that he was imagining her standing there? He fervently hoped she was real.

CHAPTER TWELVE

HEIDI DIDN'T MEAN to eavesdrop, but the door was half open. Luke's and Peter's voices were clearly audible, their angry words echoing into the night. She hesitated, fearful of what she might hear next but found she couldn't turn and run. The anguish and confusion in Luke's voice pierced her heart. He was defending her, defending her to Peter, defending her even though he didn't understand or condone her choices. She knew that. Just as suddenly she realized why he was doing it.

Listen to yourself. You're obsessed with the woman!

With those words Heidi straightened flat against the brick wall just as Peter rushed past, unseeing.

She knew what she had to do. What she wanted to do. For both herself and Luke. Stepping through the open door, she spoke his name.

"Luke..."

The look on his face shattered all her doubts and ignited to a roaring blaze the flicker of hope she'd thought dimmed forever. Searching his eyes, nearly black with emotion, she felt no fear, only a blinding certainty as he stepped closer. She didn't flinch as his arm swept past her shoulder to slam the door shut. He pushed her against the door, trapping her with his body, capturing her between his outstretched arms. She knew now she had waited a lifetime for this moment.

Tilting her head against the hard wood, she stared up at his rigid face, only inches away. "I heard everything, Luke."

"Peter says I'm obsessed with you. I'm not!" Luke's fingers caressed her throat, stroked her cheek. The pulse at the base of her throat raced at his touch. "I'm confused. No one has ever made me feel like this before. Why do I want you so much? I shouldn't. It's not supposed to happen this way."

Suddenly his eyes blazed bright blue and his fingers tightened around her chin. She closed her lids when his mouth took hers, hot and demanding, then opened her lips, seeking. Entwining her arms around his neck, she arched closer. He crushed her to him, but for her it wasn't close enough. At last her search was over. She'd discover all she'd ever need, here with Luke.

He broke free of the kiss, his searching gaze lending a new vulnerability to his face.

"We can find our answers together," she whispered, slowly brushing the side of his throat with her lips.

He stiffened, shaking his head. "No! As much as I want it, this isn't the way, Heidi," he whispered, his breathing harsh, as uneven as her own.

She was urged on by what his eyes told her, urged on by her own heart. She would fight for what she wanted, what she needed. Every inch of her was sensitized to his touch. Her lips burned as she brushed them against his.

"Yes, it is the way. For both of us."

Iron arms suddenly swept her high against his chest, and her teasing mouth was hostage to his stronger lips. He drew her tighter, demanding her response as he carried her to his bedroom.

Joyfully she gave in to her need, meeting his urgency with her own. Lost in her own haze of desire, she felt disoriented when he lowered her to the edge of a large bed and slid to his knees beside her.

For a heartbeat she feared he would leave her, but he didn't. Without words his gentle fingers undressed her, and she lifted her trembling hands to do the same until there was nothing between them. Nothing to stop her from running her palms slowly over his hair-roughened chest. Nothing to still her trembling as his eyes feasted on her body.

The dim light from the hallway cast a golden glow across his broad shoulders, down his narrow hips and strong thighs as he leaned over her, urging her back onto the cool sheets. "You're even more beautiful than I imagined." His voice was hoarse with longing as his hands cupped her breasts. His lips teased her until her hips arched and she pressed against his hard body. He moaned softly against the sensitive skin at her neck as he clasped her tightly to him, and she threw her head back in abandon as his hot, searching lips explored the curve of her throat. Unthinking now, she urged his mouth back to hers, and their lips clung in a deep, searching kiss as they rolled over and over across the width of the bed.

His whispered words of need, his caressing fingers, his searching lips fueled her senses. Even as his lips sought the place her body ached for his touch, her own mouth moved down his body, tasting the hard, muscular chest, the flat stomach, the corded muscles of his thighs.

Desperation infiltrated the eager straining of their bodies as if these moments of ecstasy could be, at any second, snatched away. Their mouths clung with a sweet, piercing anticipation, and she arced upward, eagerly welcoming his entry. His name burst from her parched, gasping throat as she pressed her swollen breasts against his damp chest. Capturing her breath with his mouth, he answered her pleas, moving deeper, stronger, accelerating to meet the hot, pounding needs of their bodies.

They were so close, so very close, sharing the same air, the same thought, the same powerful force driving them on and on until in one magnificent instant her demands were met. The center of all pain opened, soaking her body with soothing release, and she moaned her pleasure against his searching lips. She tightened convulsively around him, their breath interwoven in dual delight as he filled her with his own release.

They held each other, trembling, the world reduced to nothing more than this moment and these feelings. Breathless, she cradled him in weak tenderness.

"Heidi . . ." he whispered against her throat, his lips pressing a kiss over the quieting pulse.

"I'm here . . . rest now . . ." Stroking a caressing palm down his back, she felt his deep sigh as he buried himself in her softness. She pressed her cheek against his soft, wavy hair, closing her eyes. Nothing else mattered now but this. There was no doubt left. She loved him and she was no longer afraid. She would overcome all that stood between them. For Luke, for her, this was right.

The peacefulness was so profound she sank gratefully into its depth, letting it surround and heal her battered soul—all the old hurts and doubts. She must be dreaming, but it didn't feel like the old dreams.

Timmy wasn't in her arms. Instead she was in Luke's arms, and he held her with tenderness.

"I wish I'd been here to help you, Heidi. Together we would have eased Timmy's suffering."

The understanding in his voice and the gentle touch of his fingers tilting her face toward him brought tears of joy to her eyes. "You do understand, don't you? I did the right thing for Timmy, the only thing a loving parent could do. I accept that now. Do you, Luke? Do you really accept that I did the right thing for Timmy?"

"Heidi . . . Heidi, open your eyes. . . ."

She wasn't dreaming. Luke's face was soft with understanding, and his eyes were open to her for the first time.

"Why did you do this, Heidi?" His voice was the voice of her dream, full of tenderness and longing. His hands cupped her face, his thumbs stroking her cheeks with the same gentleness.

"To sort out our feelings." Taking a deep breath, she gained courage from her newfound peace. "We both wanted each other so much . . . we needed each other regardless of everything else between us."

"Yes," he breathed, dragging his lips across her mouth, his fingers threading through her hair. "God, you're right!" he groaned, pressing her even closer. "I need you so much," he whispered, stirring the curls covering her ear.

But there had been more than need between them. Much more for both of them.

"Luke, I want to tell you about Timmy." Resting her palms flat against his chest, she separated their bodies so that she could watch his face. "I want to tell you how he died."

His gaze bore into her as if he were trying to see into her heart. "Heidi..."

She placed two trembling fingers over his lips. "Please, let me tell you. It's important that you know how it really was. He was so beautiful—with your eyes. At first I refused to believe he was sick. I refused to believe there was no hope, even when the specialist confirmed it. Even during the months I sat by his bedside when he became weaker and weaker. I could see he was in pain. They put him on dialysis, the doctors did everything they could, yet he continued to slip away. And his pain grew worse. I still believed in miracles. I prayed for a miracle. A cure. Remission." Remembering drove her to deep, shuddering breaths.

"When I finally realized there would be no miracle, that the only thing I could give Timmy was a few moments away from the hospital, the sterile, pain-racked world that had been all he'd ever known, I followed procedures. I petitioned the hospital board to allow me to take him home. But they couldn't or wouldn't come to a decision, and Timmy continued to suffer."

Luke lay perfectly still beneath her hands, and she fought the darkness of her own memories to finish the story.

"That last night they were going to put him on dialysis again, even though Dr. Dawson said it probably wouldn't help. Nothing could help anymore. Timmy was beyond miracles. Timmy was going to die." She shook her head as if to deny the reality.

"I couldn't let it happen there. I had promised Timmy one moment of beauty. I had promised Faith I'd do my best for him." Refusing to stop, she pushed on, her voice a low whisper.

"So I gave him what beauty I could. I took him to the park. I sat on the swing, cradling him in my arms." Silent tears coursed down her cheeks. "And I sang lullabies to him until he died."

Drowning in Luke's tortured gaze, she sobbed once as, wordlessly, he leaned closer to her.

Suddenly the room was flooded with light. Her gasp of shock was masked by Peter's voice.

"Oh, my God, Luke, I'm sorry."

"Get out, Peter!" Luke said with icy anger bending over her protectively. But Peter didn't seem to hear.

He stared down at the paper clutched in his hand and then took a step closer to stare at her face.

"Peter, get out!" Luke shouted, his muscles iron-rigid, trying to shield her from Peter's eyes.

"It's her!" Peter thrust the newspaper clipping in Luke's face. "It's her, isn't it? What are you doing with that murderer!"

Peter's voice shattered their intimacy into a million splinters, each one piercing her heart, paralyzing her body. She curled into a tight ball, vainly trying to shield her nakedness as she felt Luke lunge away from her. Twisting the bedspread to cover her, she sat up just as Luke struck Peter full in the face.

"Don't ever call her that again!" Luke's bare chest heaved, glistening with perspiration. "Get the hell out of here, Peter! Now!"

Blood streaming from his nose, Peter backed up, his blue eyes uncomprehending. Numb with horror, Heidi watched him stagger from the room and heard the sharp, ragged intake of Luke's breath.

Grabbing his pants from the floor, Luke yanked them over his narrow hips. When he swung around, she was on her knees, the bedspread gathered around her.

"I've got to go after him. I'm sorry..." His eyes, his body sent a silent plea.

She nodded. "Go. He needs you."

Alone in the room that only a moment ago had been their haven, she buried her face in the spread, the scent of their bodies surrounding her. She'd done the right thing tonight. For herself. For Luke. No matter what happened now, nothing could take away what they'd shared.

She gathered up her clothes and dressed swiftly. Quietly letting herself out of the bedroom, she paused, uncertain which way she'd come. She headed toward the light in what she assumed would be the living room. She found Peter huddled in an armchair. He had an ice bag pressed to his nose, but when he saw her, he let it fall to the floor.

"It's your fault!" he rasped through tight lips. "It's all because of *you!*"

Even though her heart ached for the pain he felt, she would never again allow anyone to destroy her spirit. "I'm sorry, Peter, but very little of this is anyone's fault but your own." To her surprise her voice echoed her conviction.

"What happened tonight between you and Luke isn't my fault, any more than Timmy's death is my fault. There was nothing I, or anyone else, could do to keep Timmy alive for you. All I could do was stop his pointless suffering and give him something besides pain. I know I did the right thing for him. I accept that my choice was right for Timmy. Can you say the same thing about all your decisions?"

His young face paled.

"I haven't the right to judge you, Peter. No more than you have the right to judge me. But until you come to grips with your own choices, you won't be able to understand mine or anyone else's."

How long had Luke stood in the kitchen doorway, another bag of ice in his hands? Heidi realized her words were as much for him as they were for Peter.

"Our past is always with us. We can't escape it or change it. Our only peace is in accepting it." Her body trembled, remembering the bliss of the last hour and her eyes locked with Luke's. "I did that tonight."

She left them, each to find his own peace. She could do no more. By finding her answer she had found herself again. Now she was truly free. Free of guilt. Free of doubt.

But not free of Luke.

The journey home was automatic. After she turned down the ramp into the parking garage of her building, she stared unseeing at the wall in front of her, the car engine idling as she gripped the steering wheel tightly.

For the first time since Dr. Dawson had diagnosed Timmy's condition, Heidi was at peace. The devastating pain in her life was gone. Timmy's brief time had been as full of love as she could make it. She'd done all she could. She'd done what she had to. What she would do again.

One by one all the people who had touched her life since the night she had held Timmy in her arms under that star-filled sky passed through her thoughts. People she would never have met had her destiny not taken such a dramatic turn: Warden Howell...Officers Connell and Needham...Maxime...Letty and Doreen. Tears threatened as she pictured Joyce and Coralee bent over the piano together. Joyce, who had shown her she still had something worthwhile to give, and Coralee, who with poignant simplicity had taught her the most invaluable lesson of all.

Among those whose influence had brought her this far, Angel was a precious gift. If Heidi hadn't made the right choice with Timmy, her life would never have crossed Angel's. That meeting had changed both of them for the better. Heidi firmly believed in the power of their extraordinary friendship deep in her heart.

But also, deep, deep in her heart, pervading everything, was the thought of Luke. Luke, who against all odds, against all logic, she loved. That tiny bud, so closely held, had bloomed this night. She was filled with a new strength of purpose, determined to overcome whatever obstacles lay in her path to Luke, to achieve the full flowering of their relationship. Now she was unafraid to deal honestly and openly with her feelings, and his.

Realizing her fingers were numb from the tension of her grip, she turned off the engine. She locked the door behind her and glanced around at the rows of cars. The silence in the dim, low-ceilinged garage was almost eerie. Walking rapidly, she headed toward the bright light over the elevator door. A loud crash behind her spun her around sharply.

Nothing moved. She searched the dim recesses of the garage apprehensively. There was nothing but silence and her own harsh intake of air. She'd been alone in this garage hundreds of times. She must be on edge because of all she'd been through tonight. There was no one here, nothing to fear.

Forcing herself to remain calm, she continued walking to the elevator and pushed the button. The doors opened immediately; she was oddly relieved when they closed behind her.

She let herself into the condo, wishing Angel would get over her phobia about locking doors. Then she saw her curled up, nearly buried among the pillows and cushions of the overstuffed couch, and decided the lecture could wait.

Angel started when Heidi touched her shoulder. Blinking sleepily, she sat up and stretched. "Hi. I must have fallen asleep after David left. He took a cab. Says he'll be by to get the Jag later in the week. He doesn't need it for the next few days."

"How's Faith?" Heidi dropped down at the end of the couch, stuffing a needlepoint pillow behind her suddenly weary head. "Is she resting?"

"Out like a light." Yawning, Angel curled her legs beneath her and, as always, wasted no time with trivialities. "Well, what happened? Did you help settle things between Luke and his brother?"

The memory of holding Luke tenderly caused a rush of emotion. Closing her eyes to imprint that memory, Heidi nodded. "Yes, I talked to them both."

"It's none of my business, but from the look on your face I'd guess you did more than talk to Luke."

Stunned, Heidi opened her eyes, and turning her head, met Angel's questioning gaze. Was she that easy to read?

"Did it help?" Angel asked with her usual frankness.

"Yes, it helped make everything clear." Heidi pulled the pillow from behind her head and hugged it to her breast. "I know how I feel about Luke. About everything. I have no regrets about anything I've done. Loving Timmy, I couldn't have done anything differently."

Angel smiled, a wide, sunny smile. "Hey, I figured that one out a long time ago. What took you so long?"

Her calm acceptance deepened Heidi's newfound peace. "Thanks, Angel. It means a lot."

"Hey, I'm a quick study!" Angel shrugged her slim shoulders. "Now what happens? You guys live happily ever after or what?"

"I think or what." Heidi looked straight into Angel's eyes. "I know what I want to do with my life now. I'm not going to waste any more time."

"Me, neither!" Jumping up, Angel circled around the room, taking intricate dance steps, holding a pillow gracefully overhead. "We're going to meet all our problems and kick 'em in the knees! Right, roomy?" Laughing, she tossed the fat pillow to Heidi.

Heidi's quiet confidence was fed by Angel's contagious enthusiasm. "That's right! Nothing will stop us from getting what we want. Nothing, I promise you."

"WHAT IN THE HELL do you want from me, Luke?"

Blearily opening one eye, Luke saw Peter silhouetted against the sunrise streaming in through the glass doors.

He'd actually slept here on the couch all night! Peter had obviously showered; his hair was curly and dark with moisture. His swollen nose left Luke cold with shocked remembrance. He'd never laid a hand on his brother in his entire life, not even when they were kids. How could his feelings for Heidi be strong enough to override the habits of a lifetime?

Pushing himself to his feet, he stretched, aching from his cramped position. "How do you feel this morning?"

"How do you think? Like hell!" Peter barked out. "I repeat, Luke, what do you want from me?"

Taking a deep breath, Luke called upon his pragmatic nature to sort calmly through the facts and come up with the proper way to handle this situation. His usual good sense didn't kick in. The master planner had no blueprint.

"Peter, before we talk, let me fix us some coffee and—"

"I've already had three cups," Peter interrupted. "Here's a mug for you!" Thrusting a blue mug into Luke's hands, Peter stepped back, easing down into the deep chair facing him. "Are you awake enough to talk, or do you want to shower first? If you're as hot as you were last night, it better be a cold one!"

The mug burned his palms, but he held on to it tightly. After a moment he said, "Peter, I shouldn't have hit you. But you had no right to barge into my bedroom like that."

"How was I supposed to know you were...?" Peter had the good sense to stop. He hadn't missed the sudden tensing of Luke's jaw. "Occupied with someone," Peter finished at last. "How in hell are we supposed to talk about this if I can't even mention her without you getting hostile?"

"Be very careful, Peter," Luke warned. Taking a deep drink, he let the hot coffee warm him inside. Over the rim of the cup he studied his brother. "I'll talk about whatever you want. But I won't tolerate you mouthing off about something you don't understand."

"You're right. I *don't* understand. Dr. Dawson said Heidi Allan's actions brought about the death of my son, but *probably* only by days. Probably. I didn't think that word was in your vocabulary." Growing bolder, Peter leaned forward. "The Luke I knew would never be able to accept that."

"I didn't, damn it!" Luke banged his mug down on an end table, sloshing coffee over the rim. "I felt the same way when I found out what had happened. God, I felt so responsible, so guilty because I hadn't been there to help! To decide the right course of action! To decide what was right and wrong!" Even saying the words he felt a wave of shame that he could ever have been so arrogant. He stood and paced restlessly back and forth.

"I was going to find you and bring you back to face your responsibility. I would help Faith get well so I could unload my guilt for your part in her breakdown. But most of all I wanted to confront the woman responsible. She'd chosen not to let us know of Timmy's existence, then she'd made the decision to end his life. I wanted to see if justice was being served."

"That sounds exactly like you." Peter said it so matter-of-factly that Luke jerked to a halt.

"Why look so shocked? Anyone who knows you could predict exactly how you would react. I was the guilty party, so I would be returned to pay my debt to Faith. Faith was the wronged party and as such needed your help and compassion. And now I'm back, ready to accept responsibility, right? And no doubt Faith is better, although how the hell could I know, since I can't see her?" Telltale redness crept up his lean cheeks. "But what happened to Heidi? Was justice served?"

Luke turned away from Peter's mocking voice.

Outside his window, far below, Lake Michigan swirled and swelled in the February wind. Gazing out at that same prospect six months ago, Luke had tried to answer that question and been drawn deeper and deeper into Heidi's life. As he watched the lake, the waves crashed against the rocks and then fell back, only to gather strength anew for the timeless battle against the unyielding granite. Yet in the end the waves would win, smoothing and wearing the rock away under their persistent pressure.

"What happened, Luke?" Peter repeated.

"The first time I met her she wasn't at all what I had pictured. She wasn't the person I'd created from the facts I had. So I tried to learn more about her. I discovered Faith's progress might be enhanced if Heidi was able to visit her more often. Then I studied her case and talked to people until I saw there were mitigating circumstances that merited an appeal to the governor. I got her sentence commuted to time served."

"Why? Because from a legal point of view it constituted justice? Or because you discovered you wanted her?"

Luke closed his eyes as he thought of Heidi...her gentleness with the children...her bond with Angel...her strength in the absence of freedom. When had he realized he wanted her? Had it been at their first meeting? When she touched him for the first time? After their unexpected kiss?

"Both," he admitted at last. "She had more than paid her debt to society. The other—it was just *there* somehow. I don't even know when it began, but suddenly it was there. I just didn't act on my feelings until last night."

"Did you think possessing her would cure you? Did it?"

Finally Luke turned to confront his brother. "No."

Peter's eyes bored into Luke. "Then you understand and agree with her choices."

"No." His voice caught on the word this time; his insides cramped in pain. "It would never have been my choice. I know she did it out of love, but I still can't agree with it."

"Then how are you ever going to reconcile the two?"

"I don't know."

His answer brought a change over Peter. "At last we have something in common," he said slowly. "Neither of us has the answer. While you were passed out on the couch I stayed awake thinking about what... she... said last night about my choices. If I hadn't decided to run away, my son might still be alive. How do I reconcile myself to that? How do I face Faith knowing I'm to blame for all her pain?"

"You're not to blame, Peter, any more than Heidi is. It's fate—life—whatever you want to call it. All we can do is pick up the pieces and go on."

"But you said you didn't know how to do that," Peter said.

"I don't. But I know I want to."

A rueful smile curved his brother's mouth. "Since we're both in the same boat, let's pull together for a change. I need to talk to Faith about our child. I need to pick up my own life. Will you talk to her? Ask if she'll agree to see me? You probably need to see Heidi, anyway, after last night."

He'd never realized how clearly Peter understood him. "I'll do my best for both of us," Luke told him.

Leaving his brother staring at the lake, Luke set out to keep that promise. The steaming hot shower, followed by a cold-water rinse, banished the last of his aches. Luke felt vital, more alive with excitement and drive than he'd ever experienced. He'd waited long enough. It seemed like forever since he'd seen her, but when he glanced at his watch, he discovered it had been less than eight hours.

Anticipation shifted to aching need as Heidi opened the door to her condo.

As she stared up at the man she loved, she recognized the passion in his eyes, but passion wasn't enough. She needed understanding. Only hours before she had given herself completely and joyously. She had opened her heart and soul to him, reliving the old pain for his sake, and still it hadn't been enough. Now she couldn't be sure of his feelings.

She noticed the ice crystals frosting his hair and stepped aside. "Come in. You look frozen."

She'd built a fire earlier while fixing breakfast for Faith. She led him to its warmth, and he stretched his hands out to the flames.

Suddenly self-conscious about her appearance, she pulled the satin lapels of her black velvet robe tightly together. Realizing how foolish that gesture was considering all that had passed between them last night, she dropped her hands and asked simply, "Can I get you some coffee?"

Instead of answering, he reached out to stroke one long finger down her cheek. "I'm sorry about last night. About Peter. We need to talk. I know I don't have all the answers yet, but there's one thing I did learn." His fingers slid down, curling around the back of her neck, gently drawing her closer. Lowering his head, he brushed his lips slowly across her mouth.

His touch was so startlingly cold, she drew his shivering body into her warmth. Then she outlined his chilled lips with the tip of her tongue.

With the softest of sighs Luke crushed her to him, his mouth trailing kisses across her cheek and down the sensitive skin of her throat. Cupping her face in his hands, he stared down at her. "Last night was important to me," he whispered. "You do know how much, don't you?"

She nodded, holding her breath, waiting for whatever would come. She would deal with it. Now she knew she could handle anything.

"For the first time in my life I'm not sure of anything except that I needed you last night. And I still need to be with you."

Drawing a deep, soundless breath, Heidi laid her palms over his hands. "What happens now, Luke? How do we work through what really stands between us?"

His fingers tightened on her face. "Heidi ... I ..."

"Oh, God, I'm sorry!" Angel gasped.

Instantly Luke's hands fell away.

Angel hesitated in the hallway, a stricken look on her small face. "Listen, I'm out of here! Don't mind me," she insisted, rushing to gather up her dance bag from the corner.

"Angel, you can't leave without breakfast," Heidi said with an apologetic glance at Luke. "You've got dance class after work. I know you. You won't take the time to eat all day. I've got breakfast ready for you."

Slowly placing the bag back on the floor, Angel looked at her in surprise. "You've only set two places. Where's Faith?"

"She already left for her out-patient program at the hospital."

Luke frowned, shifting restlessly. "I need to talk to Faith. Peter wants to see her."

"Do you think that's a good idea?" The image of Peter's face when he found them together was frozen in her mind. He'd been furious. She didn't want that fury turned on Faith.

"I really think it's up to Faith and Peter to work out what's between them. He's calmed down a bit now. I'm sure he wouldn't do or say anything to hurt Faith. Timmy was their child—they need to talk about him. It will be good for both of them. I'll call Faith later and talk with her."

"I'll talk with her, too. I just want her to know I'll be here for her, no matter what."

Again he gave her a piercing look, as if he were trying to see into her very soul. In the hallway he paused, turning to place his hand over hers on the door.

"I'll be in touch soon, Heidi. I promise. We're going to find *all* the answers. I want that more than anything."

She didn't try to stop him from leaving. His promise was enough for now. It was the first step down the long road ahead of them.

Hurrying into the kitchen, she found Angel already nibbling on cinnamon coffee cake.

"I'll have the omelets made in a jiffy! I have the cheese all grated and—"

"Heidi, you don't have to do this," Angel interrupted.

"I want to. I haven't been able to fuss around a kitchen in ages!" Furiously whipping eggs and milk into froth, she deliberately kept her voice light. "Wait until you see what I'm making for dinner! Chicken and—"

"Heidi, you don't have to pretend," Angel cut in, slipping off the stool to come to her side. "I interrupted something really important, didn't I? Luke had something to say to you."

Closing her eyes, she took a deep breath before looking into Angel's eyes. "The truth is...the truth is, Angel, he still doesn't know what to say because he hasn't found all his answers yet."

On her way to work Angel couldn't stop thinking about what Heidi had said. She had questions, too—about her feelings for David, her fear of Santos. As much as she appreciated her new beginning, it was full of confusing twists and turns. Every day she got dressed in Faith's clothes and went off to a real job. She kind of liked meeting people and helping them find what they needed in the stationery shop. It was nice to feel productive, safe. The way she felt with David. She kept hoping Santos would forget her and that she wouldn't have to deal with him, but deep down she knew she was fooling herself.

At one o'clock sharp she left the shop and walked four blocks to the Fine Arts Building, where her dance classes were housed. She loved the old building. There was even a real person operating the elevator. Snatches of music, trills of arias drifted from the other floors. And once she got into the studio with its mirrored walls reflecting the practice barres and hardwood floors, all her doubts disappeared. Here she knew exactly what to do.

Just changing into her dance clothes made her feel more vital. At the ballet barre she warmed up, watching herself in the mirror. The girls around her did the same stretches and positions. She straightened her back and was able to reach just a little farther.

Her teacher, an older, sterner version of Miss Juliette, clapped her hands for attention. "Angel, I want you to perform this number alone. Front please."

Surprised at being singled out, Angel hesitated for just an instant, but then took her place. Here she didn't question; she absorbed what they could teach her and pushed herself to her limit.

Head up, arms positioned just so, feet angled correctly, she waited for the pianist to begin. The music flooded into her, flowing with and through her, filling her with inspiration. The magic was truly with her today. Music always inspired, but today the beat seemed stronger, lifting her body in ever higher, wider leaps, directing her feet in quick, precise movements, making her turns sharper, tighter. She became the music—rhythm brought to life.

Applause always shocked her, and she was dazed by it today, hardly realizing she'd finished until the noise roused her from her dreamworld. Blinking, she gazed around, getting her bearings. That was when she saw four strangers dressed in dance clothes surrounding the teacher. It didn't matter. Angel wasn't even aware of people when she danced. She was only aware of the music.

Even though she shrugged away the other students' praise, she wasn't as immune as she appeared. Today the old dream of dancing to make people happy seemed somehow closer, and the rest of class flew by so fast that she could hardly believe it when they were dismissed.

She hesitated a little, seeing the teacher waiting at the exit.

"You did very well today, Angel." The teacher smiled and nodded. "Very well indeed."

A hot rush of pleasure burned her cheeks. "Thank you," she managed. What she felt was beyond words.

A cold blast of wind as she swung out the door couldn't dampen her thrill at those words of praise. She was so caught up in her daydreams that she was nearly in front of the black Cadillac before fear yanked her back to reality.

Through the front window she saw Santos's smug smile. Today he wasn't alone. Four other familiar faces stared out at her. The old gang had finally come for her.

Before the car doors could open she was running down the sidewalk. Where could she go? Where would she be safe? She couldn't lead them to the condo! A bus was just pulling away, and she slid through the doors as they closed. She didn't know where it was going, but it didn't matter.

She tried to glance through a window, but the bus was jammed, every seat filled and people standing shoulder to shoulder, hanging on to the overhead straps. Her heart banged against her ribs. She was trapped. The slow, predictable path of the bus would be easy to follow.

Trying to get her bearings, to come up with a plan, Angel recognized certain landmarks. The bus was heading north on Michigan Avenue. Water Tower Plaza loomed ahead. She'd have a chance there! Mingling with all the shoppers, she could lose Santos and slip unseen out one of the exits.

It was all she could do not to trample the passengers stepping out of the bus before her. Every second counted. Glancing over her shoulder, she realized she'd been right. They knew exactly where she was.

CHAPTER THIRTEEN

FOUR OF THEM SPILLED out of the car, leaving Santos at the wheel, and headed toward her. She pushed through the nearest revolving door, praying they'd be slowed down by the crowds. She ran through Marshall Field's, frantic to get as far away from them as possible.

She jumped on an escalator, elbowing people aside as she ran up the moving steps. She'd head for the second floor, catch the connecting elevator to the lobby of the hotel, then take that elevator down to the entrance. She was sure Santos's guys wouldn't know their way around here.

She felt even more confident when she couldn't see anyone behind her. Spying a phone cubicle, she tucked herself in to dial the condo number. Heidi would know what to do, how to help her. The busy signal coincided with the appearance of Ric's swarthy face on the escalator facing her.

Dropping the receiver, she scooted onto the down escalator. Although they were within touching distance, there was no way he could get to her in the press of moving people. She shrank back against the far wall when he mouthed an obscenity at her.

She'd have to change her plan. Weaving through shoppers on the ground floor of Lord and Taylor's, she finally spied a side door. She hesitated only a second before darting through traffic across the street to a cab stand. There was a queue, and although she was tempted to grab a cab out of turn, she didn't want to draw attention to herself. So she waited, sucking ice-cold air into her strained lungs. Nearly light-headed with relief, she opened the cab door only to glance up and find Ric and Juan staring at her from across the street.

The cabbie waited expectantly for directions. Where to go? Her eyes fell on the ad plastered across the back of the front seat.

"Ambassador East Hotel," she ordered. She'd be safe there. They wouldn't let the likes of Santos in. Hell, they probably wouldn't let her in!

But the doorman welcomed her with a pleasant smile and held open the door as she entered. A receptionist looked up, but Angel was too frightened to stop. She turned into the first hallway. Its dark wood-paneled walls were lined with pictures of famous people. Up a few steps, a room stretched out before her, dimly lit, elegant and quiet. A highly polished bar with heavy padded seats dominated one side. Crystal and brass gleamed in the shadows. The whole place reeked of class. She didn't fit in here at all.

As she turned to leave, a voice stopped her. "Welcome to the Pump Room. May I help you?" a young woman inquired politely.

Angel's eyes went back to the bar. There was a phone there. One of the customers was using it. Mustering all her courage, Angel unconsciously imitated Heidi's quiet voice, saying, "I'm just here for a drink, thank you."

With a nod the lady stepped back, motioning Angel to a stool.

Gratefully placing her dance bag on the floor, Angel flexed her shoulders. She was so tense that her body was unusually stiff and awkward. She dug into her purse and found a few dollars. Shyly she ordered a diet cola.

When the bartender brought her glass, it had a twist of lemon. She'd never seen a diet drink with lemon before. Her questioning look caused him to smile and say in a friendly tone, "Hi, I'm Derrick."

"Hi." Suddenly Angel wasn't so frightened. These were nice people—they wouldn't hurt her. "Can I use the phone?"

"Sure. As soon as that gentleman is finished. Just dial straight out." After placing a small glass bowl of peanuts in front of her, he turned away to help someone else.

One eye on the entrance, Angel sipped at her drink, impatiently tapping her foot. She wanted to yank the receiver away from the guy who was still talking to his wife or girlfriend.

Derrick refilled her glass. "Refills are free." He smiled, dropping in a fresh slice of lemon. That drink was almost all gone, too, by the time the guy finally hung up.

She dialed the condo again. This time it rang through.

"Hello. Allan residence."

"Hey, roomy, it's me!" Angel forced herself to sound normal. "Thought you might be worried about me."

"Where are you? We expected you an hour ago!" Worry was evident in Heidi's voice.

"I'm at the Ambassador East Hotel."

"What are you doing all the way up there?"

"Listen, I think we've got trouble," Angel whispered, still keeping one eye on the door. So far so good. Maybe she'd lost them in the rush-hour traffic. With each passing moment she felt more confident.

"Angel, David's brownstone is just around the corner on Astor. He called earlier asking for you. I'll let him know you're there and he can come and meet you."

"No, don't call him!" She didn't want to put David in the line of fire, either. She glanced up at the door and froze. "Oh, no," she breathed, dropping the receiver.

Santos, his hair neatly combed and wearing a dark suit, swaggered into the room, stopping to talk to the hostess.

He hadn't seen her yet. Grabbing her bag, she sidled along the bar, grateful for the dim lighting, and slipped out behind him.

Pushing through the revolving hotel doors, she carefully checked the street. No black Caddy. No Ric or Juan. They must be inside, searching for her. The doorman asked if he could get her a cab, but she refused. She was broke. Slinging her dance bag over her shoulder, she started east toward the lake.

Halfway down the block, out of the corner of her eye, she glimpsed two men keeping pace with her on the sidewalk across the street. Suddenly her insides twisted in fear, and she squinted toward them. Ric and Juan! Terror shot through her.

It wasn't far back to the hotel, but Santos was there. She looked around wildly, then noticed the street sign—Astor. David lived there. She didn't want to involve him, but he was her only chance at the moment. She broke into a run. Panting in the thin icy air, she rapidly scanned the buildings. Dummy! She didn't know which brownstone was his!

She didn't look back; she didn't need to. She could hear the stomp of Ric's and Juan's boots on the sidewalk behind her. Somewhere up ahead she knew the other two, and Santos, would be waiting.

Fleeing past the antique light posts, she was nearly to the end of the block when a man suddenly ran out in front of her. She gasped in fear.

"Angel, what the hell's going on?" David bellowed, striding up to grip her shoulders. "You'd better get inside and tell me about it. Now!"

The footsteps behind her stopped. She was safe here with David. He practically dragged her through the gate and up the stairs into the warmth of his home. She was so weak with relief and gratitude, for the first time ever she didn't protest.

Curiously she surveyed the room David had brought her to. The high ceiling was crowned with carved molding, and the long, narrow windows had the same heavy wooden detail. The structure was old and stately, but the furniture was pure David—all black leather, chrome-and-glass tables and a huge white wool rug that covered half of the dark wooden floor. Everything was large and masculine, just like him.

She started when he reappeared carrying a tray, which he placed on the table in front of her. "Eat this! You must be frozen. I promised Heidi I'd take care of you," he growled.

"Heidi! You've talked to her?" She should have known Heidi would sense she needed help.

"She called and told me you were at the Ambassador East. I was on my way over there when I found you." He stopped until she took a spoonful of soup. "I just called her back and told her you were thawing out in my living room."

"Thanks," she muttered, taking another spoon of the hearty broth. It was delicious and filled the cold emptiness in her stomach. "This is great. Did you make it?"

"It's the best money can buy," he quipped, standing in front of the fire.

"What's an eligible bachelor to do?" she parried, relieved to be on old familiar ground.

"Eat out a lot," he replied. "Quit stalling, Angel. What's going on? Why are you running around town at night in thirty below zero temperatures? It sure as hell isn't to see the sights."

Buying time, she lifted a mug of steaming coffee, letting it warm her tingling fingers. She couldn't tell him. It wasn't his fight. She wanted to forget Santos, put the fear out of her mind for these few minutes. Fear had no place here.

"I've been away a long time, David. After class I was so keyed up that I just started walking. I saw an ad for the Pump Room and decided to go there." Set on her story, she met his skepticism serenely. "You're always telling me I'm not on the street anymore, so I just wanted to see if it showed. The old Angel Ramon wouldn't have gotten into that place."

He didn't quite believe her. She could see it in the set of his massive shoulders. "We'll play it your way for now, Angel. Finish your soup. Then we need to talk."

Grateful for the reprieve, Angel finished every drop of soup and drained the coffee mug.

"There! I belong to the clean-plate club." Tilting her head, she curled her mouth into a large, mocking smile. "Now can I have my dessert?"

"Very funny!" Surprisingly, he grinned. "Actually I have something to give you I think you'll like better than dessert. Today there were representatives of the Avenue Street Dancers at your dance class. They want you as an apprentice. After a year, if everything works out, you'll become a full-fledged member of the company."

His words reached her, but their meaning was beyond her grasp. She could only repeat, "That was an audition for the Avenue Street Dancers? How? Why?"

"Why! Because you have more natural talent in one foot than most dancers have in their whole body. How? Your dance instructor thought you were ready and we set it up. And finally, yes, that was an audition, and you passed with flying colors."

Way down deep inside where she'd hidden all her secret hopes and dreams, joy stirred to life. Through all the long years in the old neighborhood and all the time in Elmwood, she'd never let go of the dream. It had only been buried deep and safe where no one could harm it or take it away. Now her dream was at her fingertips.

She burst into tears. Loud, watery, streaming tears that would have horrified her yesterday, but didn't matter now. She was Cinderella, Snow White, every fairy-tale princess she'd ever read about.

Through her haze of tears David's face swam closer. "My God, Angel, I thought you'd be happy."

"I am happy!" she cried, throwing herself against his hard chest, wrapping her arms tightly around his neck and drenching the front of his sweater with her tears.

He smelled so good, like soap, and it felt perfect to be here safe in his arms. She'd only begun to dream of this, too, of having David hold her with such tenderness. His large hands stroked her hair and his deep voice murmured softly in her ear.

She shouldn't be greedy and ask for too much. One dream come true was more than most people ever got. Reluctantly she pushed herself away from him.

"I'm sorry," she hiccuped. "I just want you to know what this means to me. I don't know how to thank you for everything."

"Consider me thanked." His voice was quiet and his green eyes glinted in the firelight.

"Okay, I understand." She nodded, swallowing down another hiccup. "I mean, I understand how you feel. What would a guy like you want with someone like me? You've probably been with dozens of women. Movie stars, rock stars and stuff."

"Oh, yeah, I have a regular chorus line. And a girl like you, Angel? A male chorus line?"

"Me? Well, when you're Santos's girl you only have Santos."

She wasn't prepared for his response.

His strong fingers gently brushed her hair off her face and lifted her chin. He scrutinized her features. "Are you telling me you've never been with anyone but that punk?"

At her small nod his thumb caressed her full lower lip. Excitement mingled with joy, making her lightheaded.

"Then no one's ever made love to you."

Although she hated to admit it, it was tempting momentarily to tell him he was right, she couldn't lie to him. "David, Santos and I did make love."

"I seriously doubt it!" he growled, replacing his caressing thumb with his lips. It was so different from their kiss at Christmas! His mouth teased, coaxing hers open, then stayed to play ever so gently, nibbling at the corner and nipping her lower lip.

Her heart in her throat, she gazed into his eyes as he pulled away. "Why did you do that?"

"Because I want to. Why did you kiss me back, Angel?"

"Because I've wanted you to kiss me like that for so long."

Her honesty was rewarded. He rose slowly and pulled her into his arms. Cradling her gently in his arms, he strode effortlessly down a darkened hall and into his bedroom. At the side of the king-size brass bed he stopped.

"Not gratitude. Not because you think you owe me," he stated quietly, his eyes, for once, wide open.

"Not gratitude. But because I want to. For you, why?" Her pulse hammered again as he took her mouth in another sweet, teasing kiss.

"Because I want to be the first man to really make love to you."

Making love. Lovemaking.

He was right. It was her first time.

This afternoon the music had been with her stronger and more powerful than ever. That night David led her into a world with new cadence; love flowed through every cell of her body, making her one with it, filling her with a soaring breathless joy. If she was one with this music, she was the very creation of love, and joined with David, became the essence of all she had ever dreamed.

The steady heartbeat beneath her ear had lulled her into sleep, safe in David's arms. Even now, after the night they had just spent together, she couldn't find the words to thank David for everything he'd done for her.

I want to be the first man to really make love to you, he had said, and now at last she fully understood. Real love was the joy of music, of dancing, multiplied a million times over, endlessly soaring higher and higher until you became lost in its beauty, its magic.

Light filtered in through a crack in the heavy linen drapes covering the windows. Quietly she slipped around the room, pulling on her clothes as she found them in the near darkness. She couldn't resist one last touch.

Totally relaxed in deep sleep, his pug-nosed face was even smoother and younger. If it weren't for the frosting of gray at his temples and the heavy shadow of a morning beard, it could be a little boy's face. Its sweetness tore the words from her throat.

"I love you, David."

The whisper hung in the hushed room, echoing in her mind. Never, ever would she have the courage to tell him aloud. Instead she drew her love into the dream place inside her. But dreams do come true, she reminded herself, courageously feathering his mouth with a farewell kiss. David had the power to make her dream come true.

Outside the brownstone she found the temperature had risen several degrees. Sometime during the night light snow had begun to fall. It covered everything— grass, fences, trees, cars—until the city was a glistening fairyland in the bright winter sunlight.

Although she carefully looked in every direction, there was no sign of Santos and the gang. Another reprieve. But even that threat looming over her couldn't spoil such a beautiful day!

The long walk home was accomplished on feet buoyed by happiness. Angel pirouetted through the condo doors. No one was around, so the elevator went straight up. Fumbling in the dance bag for the key she never used, she was startled when the door opened on its own. Heidi looked at her with fatigue-heavy eyes.

"Heidi, you look like you haven't slept all night!"

Her lips curving in a tired smile, Heidi shook her head. "I haven't. I've been waiting for you."

Angel's laugh had a nervous little catch in it. Funny, she'd never heard it in her voice before. Could last night have changed *everything* about her? "You're too young to be my mom."

"I'm getting older by the minute. And colder. Aren't you coming in?"

Heidi stepped back and Angel lifted her bag from the carpet where she'd dropped it. Following Heidi inside, Angel racked her tired mind for inspiration. How did she begin to explain to Heidi where she'd been and what had happened between her and David?

Only after Angel silently hung up her coat and placed her dance bag beneath it in the hall closet did she join Heidi on the couch. "I've got something real important to tell you," she declared with uncharacteristic seriousness.

"I know. David told me last night about the Avenue Street Dancers." She clutched Angel's cold fingers for an instant. "I always told you I'd never seen anyone dance more beautifully than you do."

"Yeah, well, I gotta admit it's all still kind of unreal," Angel said earnestly, curling into a tight ball, her hands wrapped around her bent knees. "But that wasn't what I was going to tell you." Angel buried her face on her raised knees before peering up, almost shyly. "What I want to tell you is that David and I spent the night together."

Heidi experienced a small jolt of shock. She'd assumed Angel slept at David's, and she surely wasn't blind to their mutual attraction, but she was stunned, knowing David as well as she did, what this must mean to him.

At her silence Angel's face paled. "Pretty stupid, huh? I mean, why spoil a good friendship? But, hey, we can go back to being pals! David probably has a parade through there and probably still does lunch and stuff with the girls afterwards."

Heidi took both of Angel's hands tightly in hers. "You misunderstand me. I'm surprised because I hadn't fully realized how much David cares for you."

Angel's color returned, brighter than ever, and her eyes shone. "You really think so? You don't think it was just hormones? You know, me being stuck away for so long and...well, David just wanting to be *nice*."

"David's hormones never get in the way of David's feelings." They were perfect for each other, Heidi realized suddenly. And David, brilliant, shrewd, cut-right-to-the-heart David, had recognized it before anyone else. "If you and David made love, then you are very, very special to him."

"Yeah, we did. We really made love," Angel whispered, a faraway smile on her face. She rose and floated down the hall, and Heidi heard the bedroom door click quietly shut behind her.

Heidi grabbed the phone on its first shrill ring. David's voice was so wild she almost had to shout to stop him. "David! She's here! Safe! Calm down!" Not only had her own life been totally changed by the path she'd taken, so, obviously, had David's.

"Yes, I think a celebration tonight would be great. We're shopping for gifts to send to friends at Elmwood, but be here at six. We'll be finished by then." She took a deep breath to make sure her voice was normal. "No, I'll ask Luke. Goodbye, David."

She carefully replaced the receiver and then twirled around the room with none of Angel's grace, but a great deal of enthusiasm. At the end of this dark, unhappy year there really might be happiness.

She came to a halt in front of the mirror and stared at her own reflection. A faint shadow still lurked in the depths that only Luke could banish. She retraced her steps and stared at the phone, wishing she could make the call right now.

LUKE RAN his palm over his rumpled sheets. If he closed his eyes, he could still picture Heidi sinking back into his bed, see her glorious body arching toward his, her face so piercingly beautiful he ached just looking at her.

"Damn!" He lunged out of bed. No more imagining! He was determined to have the flesh-and-blood woman in his arms again.

Even after Luke showered and dressed, Peter was still asleep in the spare bedroom, so he scribbled a note before leaving for the office. Today he would see Heidi and give her the answer she wanted. It didn't matter that it wasn't true. He'd learn to live with it, bury it so deep she'd never realize he was living a lie. It wasn't cheating her, he rationalized. In every other aspect of their life together he'd open up to her completely. He'd give her everything he was capable of giving, including himself; all the love he now realized he could give. Everything . . . except for this one truth.

Struggling with his innate honesty, he still hadn't called her by the time he left for the office. Why couldn't he let it go? Why wouldn't his mind just accept her choice? God knows, his feelings for her had caused him to abandon everything else that had defined his life until that fateful moment of confrontation in the prison.

With Heidi he experienced emotions he hadn't known he was capable of feeling. His controlled world of good and bad, right and wrong, had left nothing to the imagination—no heights or depths or doubts. Now that he had touched a new kind of world, he wouldn't allow anything to destroy his chance at happiness.

The first chance he got during a busy day, he reached for the phone to dial Heidi's number, but it rang as his fingers touched the receiver. Hearing Heidi's voice brought sweet pain to lodge in his chest. There was so much he needed to tell her. But her voice was so full of joy and excitement he couldn't interrupt.

Finally she stopped for air and Luke whistled softly. "The Avenue Street Dancers! That's great. Angel must be good."

He chuckled, warmth coiling through him, and he held the receiver closer to his ear, wishing he could reach through the wires to touch her as she went into raptures over Angel's talent.

Her surprise invitation fanned the fire in his gut. "Yes, I'd like to celebrate with all of you. I'll pick David up at his office and be at your place by six."

Tonight he would tell her. After the celebration dinner for Angel, after all the others were gone, he'd take her into his arms, touch her petal-soft skin with his lips and whisper everything that was in his heart.

As Luke put down the receiver, he noticed Peter standing in the doorway to his office.

"Your secretary wasn't at her desk, so I came right in," he said. "What was that all about?"

"I'm seeing Heidi and Faith tonight for dinner."

"Have you had a chance to talk to her for me?" he asked eagerly. "Maybe I could come along tonight?"

Luke knew he was being totally selfish, but for once he didn't want to think about Peter and Faith, or their problems. He needed to concentrate on Heidi and what he could say to her.

"Back off, Peter. It's still too soon."

Peter's blue eyes hardened. "I don't know how much longer I can, Luke!"

It wasn't a threat, Luke told himself as Peter turned and stalked out. On one level he understood Peter's frustration. He'd do what he could for the kid, but not tonight.

Swiveling his chair to the right, he glanced at the brass wall clock. Two o'clock; only four more hours to wait.

"OH, MY GOSH, it's two o'clock already! We've got to hurry if we're going to shop, pack and mail everything by five-thirty. Let's hit the candy department first," Heidi decided, a list clutched tightly in her hand.

Faith wasn't really into this shopping spree at Marshall Field's, because the people they were buying for were all strangers to her. But she needed to keep busy. Soon enough she'd think about finding the courage to face Peter. Meanwhile she merely tagged along behind Heidi and Angel as they selected two boxes of chocolates for Letty.

While Angel paid for the candy, Heidi dashed to the perfume counter and bought a bottle of Oscar to go with Letty's gift. They were both so excited that they giggled like a couple of kids. When they swept into the toy section, Faith just couldn't get into the mood, so she hung back until she was bumped from behind by a man who didn't even bother to excuse himself.

Heidi and Angel were purchasing dolls when she caught up with them. One each for Dottie, Sissy and Joyce. Heidi had already stopped at the music store and bought two piano books and a small laptop practice keyboard.

In the sewing section they argued over which embroidery kit to buy Coralee. Wandering away from their friendly bickering, Faith looked up and noticed the man who had nearly run her over. He looked ridiculous pawing through the needlepoint. Downstairs in the book department Faith saw him again. Here he didn't look so out of place, but she finally mentioned the coincidence. "Have you two noticed that guy who seems to be in all the same departments we are?"

The huge smile Angel had been wearing all day vanished. "Where?" she bit out.

"Over there in the magazine section."

All three turned to look, but the stranger was gone.

"Well, it was probably just my imagination." Faith shrugged. "We'd better hurry. It's after four."

The stranger forgotten, they decided to pick out a dozen romance novels for Doreen. Even Faith got caught up reading the back of each jacket, trying to decide.

"This one sounds really good," Angel held up a book. "*Chains of Time*. It's a mystery about suspended animation."

"Oh, that sounds great!" Heidi agreed, adding it to the stack of books in her arms.

Finally finished, they headed for home laden with packages. For some reason Faith kept feeling the need to glance behind her.

"What are you looking at, Faith?" Angel demanded, her thin face sharp with fear.

"Stop worrying. It's nothing." She dismissed Angel's anxiety with the wave of a hand. "Let's hurry. I'm freezing."

Walking rapidly, she kept a few paces ahead of Angel and Heidi all the way home. She wasn't going to get paranoid because some guy stepped on her heels and then reappeared a few times. Besides, she didn't want to get everyone else worked up over nothing. Especially Angel. This was her celebration night. Today was for forgetting and fun.

Tomorrow she would think some more about Peter. Tomorrow she'd try to come to some decision about seeing him. She wasn't sure how she should deal with him, or how she should deal with the rest of her life, for that matter.

Rushing everyone along, Heidi felt like a mother hen. A flurry of activity kept them busy for the next half hour as they packed up all the presents they'd bought. Heidi glanced at her watch. They'd just make it to the post office in time. She'd noticed Angel's enthusiasm had decreased somewhat since Faith had mentioned the stranger. Now she watched Angel scan the street as all three of them walked the short distance to the post office. She was clearly nervous, and Heidi remembered her cryptic phone call the night before.

"Is something wrong, Angel?"

"No, nothing." Angel quickened her pace. "We'd just better hurry if we're going to get there before they close."

They made it with little time to spare. And by the time they finished they had to rush to get back in time to change for dinner. To save steps they cut through the parking garage. Now it was Heidi who looked around nervously. She hadn't been completely comfortable in the garage since the night she'd heard noises. She couldn't put her finger on what had changed, but something wasn't quite the same. She didn't want to worry the others, so she'd said nothing. But the vague uneasiness hadn't gone away.

The elevator came, and she felt greatly relieved when the door closed them in safely.

She glanced at her watch when they stepped out at their floor. "Five-thirty. We have a half hour to get ready."

Thoughts of seeing Luke made her fumble in her purse for the key. "Darn! I know they're here!"

"Here, I have mine," Faith offered.

"Oh, no! I was the last one out and I forgot to lock. I should have this time!"

"Angel, I've told you what a really bad habit that is," Faith scolded.

"Let me go in first!" Angel said, slowly opening the door and flipping on the foyer light.

Everything looked exactly as they left it.

"Okay," Angel sighed, color returning to her cheeks. "I'm getting as bad as Faith, worrying about everything."

Heidi watched Angel's strained face while they hung their coats in the hall closet. Despite Angel's reassurances, Heidi glanced both ways down the dim hall before walking into the living room. She came to a dead stop.

Behind her she heard Angel's gasp and Faith's faint "Oh." A hot rush of fear tightened around Heidi's chest so that it was hard to breathe. She blinked, not quite believing her eyes.

"Surprise, Angel! I've come to get ya just like I promised."

Santos was sprawled on the couch, his booted feet crossed on a cushion. Behind him, leaning against the wall, were two men, each with a bottle of the wine she'd been chilling in the fridge. She'd never seen them before.

The taller one straightened as his eyes roamed up and down her body. "Hey, Santos, who's the looker with the great knockers?"

"Shut up, Ric," Angel snapped, stepping in front of Heidi.

"Me, I like the little dark one. Hiya, honey. Remember Juan from this afternoon at the store? Let's you and me get better acquainted. We could be real tight friends," the shorter one mocked, moving around the couch toward them.

With a gasp of terror Faith cowered at her side, and Heidi reached out a protective arm. Finally she found her voice. "Santos, this has gone far enough!"

To Heidi's surprise he sprang off the couch and waved his thugs back. "Doll Face is right. Ain't got no quarrel with her or the little one. We've just come to take Angel back where she belongs. See, we found yer room and packed up yer stuff. Isn't that nice?"

There was a brown suitcase next to the chair. Part of Angel's red dance leotard hung out of one corner. The idea of those three pawing through their things angered Heidi. She felt a sudden rush of adrenaline, but before she could speak Angel stepped forward.

"Okay, Santos. You, me, Ric and Juan, we'll just leave now," Angel said softly as she moved away from Heidi and Faith. "We don't want any trouble, do we? We just want to leave here and go home."

Angel was within touching distance now, and Santos reached out, grabbing her cheek in what looked like a painful pinch.

"My smart Angel. That's right. No trouble. Just me gettin' what's mine."

A sick look crossed Angel's face, but she said, "That's right. I've always been your girl, you know that. So let's just get out of here and go back where we belong."

It was Maxime and the Honor Cottage all over again—Angel sacrificing herself to keep Heidi safe. She hadn't let her do it then, and she certainly wasn't going to let it happen now!

Pushing Faith to safety behind one of the overstuffed chairs, she ran forward, jerking Angel behind her so quickly that no one was alert enough to stop her.

"Heidi, don't try—" Angel cried, but Heidi cut her off.

"Quiet, Angel! You're not going anywhere!" she shot over her shoulder, keeping her eyes on Santos's swarthy face. "Santos, you don't honestly think I'm going to let you waltz in here and take Angel away against her will?"

"Don't want no trouble, Doll Face." Santos smirked, although his eyes shifted nervously. "Ain't forcin' nobody. Angel's comin' of her own free will."

"Yeah, that's right! I *want* to go," Angel pleaded, pushing past Heidi.

Heidi pulled her back. She knew Angel could easily detach her grip, but she also knew why she wouldn't. As tough as she was, she couldn't disguise the tremble quivering through her thin body.

Heidi wouldn't give in to her own fear. If she could buy a few minutes more, Luke and David would arrive. She played her trump card. "You say you don't want trouble, Santos. Well, I say you'll have to go through me to take Angel out of here. And to go through me you'll have to use force. Assault and battery is big trouble. I'll make sure you pay."

"Hey, Santos, I'm not messing with any uptown bitch." Ric fell back a step, shaking his head.

"Ric's right. Don't want no cops after us. Not when we got such a sweet business deal going," Juan whined, taking another long swig from the wine bottle.

"Santos, listen to me—" Angel pleaded, but Santos cut her off.

"Shut up, all of ya! Angel, if ya open that sweet, lyin' mouth of yours again, someone's gonna get hurt, definite!" Santos stepped close enough for Heidi to see the beads of sweat on his forehead. "Listen, Doll Face. Ain't got no quarrel with ya. Ya don't understand the rules we're playin' by here. A looker like you shouldn't be risking that beautiful face for the likes of Angel. She belongs with us. Not your kind."

"You're wrong!" She spit the words at him, as angry as she was frightened, for beside her, Angel choked back a sob. "Angel doesn't belong with you! You're on my turf right now and you'll play by my rules. I'm telling you to leave! Angel has friends, people who love her, who will *never, ever* let you victimize her again!"

As if on cue, there was a loud knock at the door.

"Shit!" Ric hissed, backing up another step, his eyes darting around the room, looking for escape.

"We got trouble," Juan whined.

"Shut up! Everyone keep still if ya know what's good for ya," Santos snarled in a hoarse whisper.

Heidi kept staring into Santos's face. On the fifth knock Luke shouted through the door. "Hey, it's us! What are you doing in there?"

Recognition dawned in Santos's dark eyes. And in that instant terror such as she hadn't known since Timmy's illness spiraled through Heidi.

"It's that smartass lawyer! Got a score to settle with him," Santos sneered.

"Shit, no, Santos! What are you...?" Ric protested, only to be stopped by Santos's switchblade waving in his face.

"Get behind the door!" he commanded.

Instantly Ric did his bidding. Reaching into his shirt, he pulled out a small gun as he ran into the hall. Heidi felt Angel stiffen at her side, or was it her own reflexes?

"You! Answer the door and don't make no trouble!"

Faith rose like a puppet from the deep chair and walked toward the door. Again Heidi felt Angel tense, ready to take some action, but suddenly on a signal from Santos, Juan had her in a neck hold. With a perverse smile he opened his knife, the light glistening off the long, thin blade.

"Should have let us take her, Doll Face," Santos cackled, his mouth an ugly sneer as he twisted her arm behind her back. His switchblade hovered at her throat, preventing her warning scream.

"What took you so long, Faith?" David's voice boomed in from the hallway. The door slammed.

There had to be something she could do. After all, it was five against three. Heidi waited, afraid to even breathe until the men appeared in the doorway. At the slightest signal she'd...

Luke's eyes found her immediately. In the midst of her fear joy flickered to life. With that look the last lingering doubt about his feelings for her fled.

"Well, well, isn't this my lucky day?" Santos breathed in her ear. "It's our big man with the brief-case. He ain't goin' to cause us no problems, is he? Don't want to see his Doll Face hurt."

Heidi now realized they had played right into Santos's hands. Ric waved the gun at Luke, stopping him from lunging across the room to free her.

"Santos, why don't you let the women go? Then it will be just you and me, the way you wanted." Luke spoke quietly and took a tentative step forward.

Heidi felt Santos's silent laughter. Now he would play with them, taunt the men by threatening the women. They both knew it. Heidi felt the excitement quivering through him an instant before he thrust her away from him, demanding, "Juan, give me Angel!"

Before she could think the switch was made. Now Juan held her captive, his knife open and ready in his left hand. His wine-soured breath fanned her cheek, making her nauseous. Luke stepped toward her, his eyes dark with menace. Laughing, Juan pressed the knife deeper, where the pulse hammered in her throat, and Luke stepped back, his face carved in granite.

"That's right. Our two heroes don't want to see their women get cut now, do they?" Santos mocked. "You like my Angel, muscle man?" Santos held Angel to his side, his arm crushing her breasts. "She's a lot of woman in this skinny little body, ain't she? Me and the briefcase man don't gotta fight. I already win! I got the girls!"

Rage quivered across David's face, and he clenched his large, powerful hands at his side. "If you hurt any of them, I'll kill you with my bare hands," he spit. Ric drove the nose of his gun deeper into David's back. Heidi saw a look cross between David and Luke. Then Luke shifted slightly on his feet, studying Ric.

"If ya cause me trouble, Angel here is gonna have trouble, too. Ya don't want that now, do ya? Anyways, ya ain't gonna find us," Santos said, smirking.

"This city isn't big enough for you to hide from me, punk!" David bit out.

"But I ain't gonna be here, big shot! Me and the gang got connections. Know what I mean? Me and my Angel gonna be real happy together again. But before that, me and the boys will have a little fun." Smirking into David's scarlet face, Santos squeezed Angel's breast. Although she had her eyes tightly shut, a tear escaped to roll down her cheek.

Heidi knew by David's face that was the last straw. Ignoring the gun, he lunged. In the blink of an eye, Santos's switchblade sliced deeply through David's jacket and blood spurted from the cut on his arm. But Luke had leaped toward Ric, preventing him from getting a shot off. They scuffled briefly, then the gun brought Luke to a standstill. Heidi sobbed once. Her heart pounded so hard that she could hardly breathe. She saw Luke's body tense as he gauged the distance between them.

Yanking Angel back with him, Santos retreated, but David kept going, his fingers over the cut. Ric raised the gun to fire.

Heidi screamed at the same time Luke knocked Ric's arm aside so that the bullet buried itself harmlessly in a wall. Desperately trying to free her arm from Juan's vise grip, another scream died in her throat as Ric struck Luke a glancing blow with the butt of the gun. She only started to breathe again when Luke rose slowly to his knees, shaking his head to clear it.

The gunshot stopped David long enough for Santos to pull his own gun and point it at Angel.

"Let's get the hell out of here!" Juan insisted, his hand trembling. The tip of the knife nicked her throat, and she felt something wet roll down her skin. It didn't really hurt, but it proved how nervous Santos's followers were getting.

Seeing the blood on her throat, Luke cursed. "Listen, Santos, this has gone far enough. How much do you want? Name a price, I'll pay it. If you let the women go, you walk out of here free and rich."

Heidi saw the idea click in Santos's eyes.

"Hey, briefcase man, ya ain't so stupid after all. But neither am I." He laughed loudly. "The boys and me got our price. I'll be in touch and let ya know what it is. Now, Ric, lock our two heroes in the closet!" Santos ordered, coming around to stand beside Juan. "Don't try to follow us or Doll Face and Angel ain't going to be so pretty."

Heidi met Angel's wide, terrified eyes. There were no words of comfort, but Heidi tried to signal a silent message of hope. They had survived so much together; somehow they would survive this. After an almost imperceptible nod, Angel looked back at David.

Using herself and Angel as hostages, Santos exacted his revenge. Luke and David had no choice but to allow Ric to prod them with knife and gun toward the closet.

"Santos, if you hurt them, there won't be any hole deep enough for you to hide in," Luke promised in a voice full of rage and revenge. His face was pale, and a line of blood ran across his temple, but his eyes were alert, reassuring her. It was the last thing Heidi saw before Ric slammed the door, locking them in.

"You! Don't let them out for an hour or more. Tell them I'll be in touch. If they call the cops, it means big trouble. Understand? Remember, I've got your sister."

Santos was almost screaming at Faith, but Heidi wasn't sure Faith heard him. She continued to cower in the chair, unmoving, her eyes glazed with terror.

"Don't worry. That one won't let them out. She hasn't moved a muscle since I shoved her in that chair," Ric sneered.

"Faith, don't be afraid!" Heidi tried to rouse her out of her stupor, but Faith didn't acknowledge her words in any way. Frantic, Heidi tried to twist out of Juan's grip, disregarding the knife hovering at her throat. He cursed, jerking her arm so high up her back that the pain took her breath away. She stumbled out into the hallway.

Ric kept his gun trained on the closed condo door as Santos pushed the elevator button. Unfortunately Heidi could see it was already on its way up. Even a little delay might have provided some diversion. But it opened almost immediately, and a man stepped out.

"Peter!" Heidi gasped, fresh fear ricocheting through her chest.

His face puzzled, he stepped toward her. "What the hell's going on?" he demanded.

In answer Santos raised his gun and, with a vicious swing, struck Peter on the temple. His eyes widening in faint surprise, Peter crumpled to the floor, unmoving. Heidi screamed, renewing her struggles to break free.

Thrown off balance by his attack on Peter, Santos had to loosen his hold on Angel. Suddenly she twirled out of his arms and, raising one leg in a high, powerful dancer's kick, she sent the gun flying out of Ric's hand.

Her heart in her throat, Heidi watched both Ric and Angel dive for the gun, but Santos grabbed Angel by her hair and threw her against the wall, knocking her senseless.

Rage replaced fear. Heidi used one of the tricks Angel had taught her. Buckling her knees, she forced Juan to lean over, trying to support her weight. At just the right instant she elbowed him sharply in the groin. His scream of pain was lost in the uproar, and Heidi was free as he doubled over, writhing in agony.

"You bitch!" Santos snarled, raising his gun. Just then the door crashed open and David came flying through, catching Santos in a tackle that sent him crashing against the wall, knocking the gun from his fingers.

Ric flung her aside, but an instant later he was slammed against the wall himself as Luke landed his first punch.

Heidi crawled toward Ric's gun, which lay almost within reach. With one desperate lunge she nearly had it in her grasp, but steel fingers locked around her wrist. Juan, his face chalky white from pain, glared at her with murder in his eyes.

She acted without thought. Leaning over, she bit his hand as hard as she could. Screaming, he let the gun drop, and she scrambled forward, grabbing it. She rolled up onto her knees. Shaking so hard she had to use both hands, she took careful aim.

Juan saw her first. He slid back down on the floor, sucking one hand, with the other resting protectively between his thighs. Ric succumbed to Luke's punches and fell to the floor.

Then Luke turned his head and looked at her. His heart was in his eyes, and an aching tenderness washed over her. He gathered her tightly in one arm as he took possession of the gun. Holding back her sobs, she leaned against him. It was over.

"David! David! Stop before you kill him!" Luke shouted. David stopped pummeling Santos and let his bloody body drop. A heartbeat later he picked a dazed Angel up off the floor and cradled her protectively in his arms.

"David, grab the other gun and call the police," Luke ordered sharply, his heart beating a rapid rhythm under Heidi's cheek.

"I've already called them. And an ambulance." Faith's hushed voice quivered in the hallway. All eyes turned to where she knelt, Santos's gun safely in her hand, the other stroking Peter's head as it rested on her lap.

CHAPTER FOURTEEN

THE FOCUS of Luke's life now was waiting. Waiting for a miracle. Waiting for some glimmer of hope. Waiting for Peter to open his eyes and yell at him, be irresponsible and sarcastic, do anything but lie here so utterly still in the hospital bed. It was hardly reassuring to see the equipment monitoring his heartbeat and brain waves.

Peter was alive. That was what mattered. People came out of comas every day. They woke up and were fine, he told himself time and time again.

He was doing everything he could for Peter. This was the best hospital in a city known for health care. Peter had the finest doctor. Everything that could possibly be done was being done. That was what he had told his mother when she joined him in his hospital vigil. Thank God he'd finally convinced her to get some rest while he kept watch.

So far there was nothing new. With each passing hour Luke's sense of helplessness grew. He'd never been so frustrated in his entire life. Except maybe when he'd watched those punks paw Heidi. He knew at last how deep his feelings for her ran.

Through the window he saw his friends returning with dinner. He wasn't sure he'd survive this without them. David, his arm in a sling, held Angel's hand, while Heidi, carrying food from a local deli, walked behind with Faith.

Faith had amazed them all. Somehow she'd come out of her stupefying fear and unlocked the closet door almost immediately. She'd also had the good sense to call the police, grab up the stray gun and help Peter while he and David were exacting revenge on those hoods.

They would be put away behind bars for a very long time.

A cold chill knotted his stomach. He knew exactly what that meant. Heidi had suffered that punishment for a different crime—the crime of loving. The fact he once thought she deserved it would forever scar his soul.

As if she felt his eyes on her, she looked up and smiled. The ache inside grew as he leaned into the window, his palms on the glass, wishing he could touch her. But she'd be here soon. Just as she'd been by his side through all the interminable hours since the attack. How had she stood this alone? For months and months she had been alone. He'd only had two days of indecision.

He feared making the wrong move. He struggled with the heartache of seeing someone he loved so helpless in a hospital bed. What would Peter want him to do? Luke's decisions would chart the course of his treatment. There were so many options to consider....

Once, in his arrogance, Luke had believed there was always one correct answer to such a problem. That belief had been shattered along with nearly every other dictate that had governed his life. The new foundation he was slowly, painfully, building filled him with humility.

FAITH HATED HOSPITALS. There had been too many of them in her life. While the others grabbed a quick cup of coffee in the waiting area, she crept quietly into Peter's room for just a few minutes alone with him. It was the first chance she'd had in the past three days, and she needed it.

Usually Luke was here, sitting beside his brother's bed, as if his vigilance could somehow make Peter well. Just as Heidi had sat beside Timmy's bed. The old pain made her tremble, but she was determined to conquer her fear. She wasn't the same weak girl who had entrusted all her problems to Heidi. She had proven it by her actions the night Peter was hurt. For once she had known what had to be done.

She stared into Peter's pale face. Nearly a year ago this man had changed the course of her life forever. Her world had disintegrated before her eyes when he denied the baby she carried was his. He'd refused to listen when, in shocked pain, she reminded him she'd been a virgin when they met. Not only had he refused to listen to her protestations of love, he'd refused to deal with anything. He'd simply gone away. Leaving her alone, frightened and more deeply wounded than she'd even realized at the time. Wounds so painful she, like Peter, couldn't deal with them. So she, too, disappeared—into her mind. She'd locked herself away so no one and nothing could ever hurt her again.

With help she had fought her way back. But she still felt that old pain when she looked at Peter, even though feelings of love were gone. Her pain had dissolved into sadness for the children they had been, playing at life but unable to deal with its cruel realities. Once she'd been afraid she'd never find the courage to face him; now she feared she'd never have the opportunity.

She picked up Peter's limp hand, holding it tightly between her warm palms. "Peter, it's Faith." The words sounded loud in the silent room. "I don't know if you can hear me, but I want you to know I'm here. As soon as you're better, we'll talk. I know you want to. So do I." She squeezed his cool hand tighter, wanting to emphasize that she spoke the truth.

"A lot has happened this past year that we need to talk about. You need to hear about... Timmy. I'll tell you everything. We'll talk and talk until you're sick of hearing me. I promise you we'll talk through everything. Maybe, if we do, you'll understand about Timmy, about Heidi, about us. I want that for you, Peter. I really do. No matter what's between us I want you to understand."

She broke off in a sob and closed her eyes, letting her tears flow. She'd face this herself—she'd burdened Heidi enough. At last Faith knew what it was to be grown-up.

THE SOUNDS of the hospital were becoming familiar to Angel now. They had a certain rhythm of their own. How could four days so completely change her life? It had, Angel realized, stretching the muscles in her tight back by getting up from the chair beside Peter's bed. She didn't even know this man, yet she stayed to help Heidi and Luke.

Then was no change, nothing to report, no flicker of hope, nothing. Tired, she stretched from side to side. She needed to stay alert, to give the others more time to rest.

She had finally talked Heidi into going home for a shower and change of clothes. David had forced Luke into a room the hospital provided down the hall for some much-needed rest.

Luke had refused to leave his brother, and Heidi didn't want to leave Luke. Angel understood. If it were David going through this, she wouldn't budge, either. A shudder rippled through her as she remembered how close Santos had come to taking her away from him. She would have gone. She would have done anything to get Santos out of the condo, leaving Faith and Heidi safe.

But Heidi refused to let go, refused to let her give up.

She moved to the window, staring out at the snow-covered rooftops. Without Heidi there would be no David. She felt his arm encircle her, smelled his light, tangy soap an instant before he pressed a kiss on the top of her head.

"What are you thinking about?" he asked softly.

"Heidi." Twisting in his arms, she rested against him, her cheek next to the strong, steady beat of his heart. "I think that all these good things are happening to me because Heidi came into my life."

"I know what you mean, Angel," he said, drawing his fingers slowly through her hair.

"Do you?" Pushing away, she went back to look at Peter lying so helpless in the hospital bed. It could be her lying here. She had no illusions about what Santos had planned for her. Heidi had stopped him. She had told Santos there were people in Angel's life who loved her. She'd had no one until Heidi had believed in her.

David sat in the chair and pulled her down on his lap. His clear green eyes promised understanding. "Tell me what's bothering you."

"It's just that everything started in a hospital room like this. But Heidi didn't have all of us around to help her. She was alone and afraid. Because of the choice she made, she was punished. And because she was punished, I have *everything*. It doesn't seem fair, does it?"

His large hand cupped her cheek, and she turned her lips into his palm.

"Once I would have said no. But then I saw everything as black or white. Now I see it as a balancing of the scales. Something good coming out of tragedy."

"Yeah, me, too!" She held the fingers of his injured hand to her lips and pressed a kiss to his bruised knuckles. "It sort of evens everything, doesn't it? It's like because Timmy had to have such a short, sad life, we all have a second chance with ours. We have the chance to have everything we've ever wanted."

Unsmiling, he stared at her for an instant. "I love you, Angel."

It was so typically David—blunt and to the point—that she wanted to cry with happiness.

"I recognized a while ago that you're my chance for happiness. I can't predict the future, but I can promise you I won't let anyone or anything take this chance away from us."

"I can predict the future." She had to whisper the words through the tears of joy gathering in her throat. "Fairy tales *always* have happy endings." She drew his head to her breast so that she could feather kisses across his adorable pug nose.

"I want this happiness for all of us, David. But especially for Heidi."

PAIN KNOTTED her insides and forced her to press her back flat against the wall of Peter's hospital room. If Heidi closed her eyes, she would be back in Timmy's room. There were the same brisk, efficient voices barking commands, the same sounds of machines helping the lungs to breathe, the heart to pump blood. Everything was working together in this moment of crisis: Peter's vital signs had dropped alarmingly.

She had to be strong now, as she had been then. Luke needed her. He was locked in his own private hell as the doctors frantically tried to revive his brother. She touched his shoulder, reminding him he wasn't alone. She was here to help him face whatever came. "Luke, come away and let the doctors do their job."

Somehow her quiet voice penetrated his pain, and he gazed down at her with bewildered eyes. "I can't just stand by and let him die, Heidi! I can't! I won't!" His hands balled into fists at his sides as if he could defy death itself.

Grasping his hands, she insisted, "Luke, look at me!" When his eyes focused on her face, she nodded. "We're doing everything that can be done. You know that."

Finally he sucked in a ragged breath and gathered her close to his side. "I know. But it's hard. It's so hard," he whispered, crushing her to him.

Tightly wrapping her arms around him, she rested her cheek against his shoulder. She understood his pain. For a man like Luke who stalked through life with utter confidence and boundless energy it would be devastating to come face-to-face with the reality that none of his courage, none of his strength could be brought to bear to help his brother. For her, that realization had been the most painful of her life.

She held his rigid body between her hands, her heart aching for him as his eyes scanned the monitor screens. When Peter's vitals kicked back in, Luke buried his face in her hair. "Thank God," he murmured. "Thank God..."

His fingers captured her chin, tilting it up, his blazing blue eyes boring into her. There was no need for words. That would come later. To be together was enough.

The monitors beeped reassuringly and the wait began anew.

IT WAS THE SIXTH DAY, or was it night now, since Santos had invaded their safe circle of new beginnings. Heidi had lost track of time. She only knew she had come full circle, waiting beside Peter's bed. A year ago she had been the one hunched over a hospital bed, willing the person there to fight to live.

She suffered for Luke, trying so desperately to sort through his feelings. "Why?" He asked unknowingly a hundred times a day. She never offered an answer—that was useless. She never offered an opinion when the doctor discussed treatment. She gave what she knew Luke needed most—her unflinching support for whatever decision he made.

Suddenly Luke tugged on her hand, entwining their fingers together, rising to pull her away from the bed and to the window. There was no park beneath Peter's window. The lights of the city twinkled like a million stars in the darkness. Reflected in the glass, she saw first Luke and herself, and beyond them, Peter, tucked under a white sheet.

"We haven't had much chance to talk since all hell broke loose." He laughed, but there was no mirth in his

tired voice. "That's funny, isn't it? We've been together constantly, but we haven't talked about us."

"Luke, talk isn't necessary now. You have Peter to
think about. When this is—"

He stopped her with two fingers over her lips.
"Heidi, I have to say this. It *is* necessary now. I
want . . . I need to ask your forgiveness."

"My forgiveness?" Of everything he might say, this
was the last thing she'd expected. "Forgive you for
what? I'm the one who should—"

"No!" He captured her hand tightly in his fingers.
"You don't need forgiveness for anything. Everything
you've done has been out of love. I should have accepted it earlier. Deep down I knew it, but I was too
stupid, too stubborn to listen to my instincts.

"You confused me. You weren't what I thought you
would be. And the more confused I became, the more
determined I was to evaluate the situation, as I'd always done, and set the proper course of action." He
gave a short bark of self-condemning laughter.

"What I discovered was that I had to help you. I finally learned that your pain, your sense of loss when
Timmy died was greater than mine could ever be. But
the walls between us were so high. I was in love with the
one woman I thought I shouldn't want."

His words filled her with a wild joy. She wanted to
say something to ease the unhappiness in his eyes. She
tried to speak, but he wouldn't let her.

"No. Heidi, you don't understand. I knew what you
wanted me to say. I was going to do it. I love you so
much that I would have lied to keep you. I would have
told you I understood all your choices, that there was
nothing but love between us. I would have cheated you,
Heidi. That's why I need to ask your forgiveness."

She pulled her hands away so that he couldn't feel their trembling. "You love me more than your honor? You would have lived a lie for me?"

"Yes. I was arrogant enough to think it would be enough for you. But I know now it wouldn't be." Pacing to the bed, he stared at his brother for a long minute before turning back to where she stood, afraid to move.

"How did you do it?" he asked with such feeling she felt tears welling behind her eyes.

"How did you know what to do? What would Peter want? To be a vegetable? A cripple? To lie here for months? Years? Or maybe he'll wake up tomorrow. The choices I make for him may have disastrous outcomes. How do I know what's right?"

"You can't. Search your heart. It will tell you what you have to do. And once you know, believe it, accept it. Don't doubt your instincts." She gave her answer as simply and truthfully as she could, all the while fighting the urge to go to him.

For the longest moment of her life he stood there, staring into her face. He looked so alone. Finally his voice broke the silence that stretched between them. "There is no right answer, is there, Heidi?"

Tears broke free to trickle down her cheeks. "No, Luke," she whispered. "There's only the best answer for the one you love. You must accept that once and for all."

"I know that now. I understand, Heidi. I do." He stepped closer, his eyes pleading. "Can you ever believe me?"

His words were unnecessary; it was all there in his eyes, the love and understanding that were her dream come true.

In answer she opened her arms. He came to her gently, holding her, allowing the walls to crumble and the true healing to begin.

Finally she opened her eyes, and once again she saw them reflected in the glass: two people who after traveling down a long and tortuous path had come together in love and understanding.

Beyond them she saw Peter move his head ever so slightly. Blinking, she saw him move again. "Luke, look!" she cried.

He turned in alarm at the note in her voice, then joy filled his face as he dared to hope for a miracle.

After pulling the bell cord to call the nurse, Heidi looked into her own eyes, reflected in the glass. At last the shadow was gone. She turned to Luke and joined her hand with his, offering him all her strength and love for whatever lay ahead.

Harlequin Superromance
Family ties...

SEVENTH HEAVEN
In the introduction to the Osborne family trilogy, Kate Osborne finds her destiny with Police Commissioner Donovan Cade.

Available in December

ON CLOUD NINE
Juliet Osborne's old-fashioned values are tested when she meets jazz musician Ross Stafford, the object of her younger sister's affections. Can Juliet only achieve her heart's desire at the cost of her integrity?

Available in January

SWINGING ON A STAR
Meridee is Kate's oldest daughter, but very much her own person. Determined to climb the corporate ladder, she has never had time for love. But her life is turned upside down when Zeb Farrell storms into town determined to eliminate jobs in her company—her sister's among them! Meridee is prepared to do battle, but for once she's met her match.

Coming in February

1992

Celebrate the most romantic day of the year with
MY VALENTINE 1992—a sexy new collection of four
romantic stories written by our famous Temptation
authors:

GINA WILKINS
KRISTINE ROLOFSON
JOANN ROSS
VICKI LEWIS THOMPSON

My Valentine 1992—an exquisite escape into a romantic
and sensuous world.

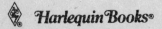

Harlequin Books®

VAL-92-F

Janet Dailey
Americana

A romantic tour of America through fifty favorite Harlequin Presents novels, each one set in a different state and researched by Janet and her husband, Bill. A journey of a lifetime in one cherished collection.

Don't miss the romantic stories set in these states:

February titles	#25	**MISSOURI** *Show Me*
	#26	**MONTANA** *Big Sky Country*
March titles	#27	**NEBRASKA** *Boss Man from Ogallala*
	#28	**NEVADA** *Reilly's Woman*

Available wherever Harlequin books are sold.

JD-FEB

HARLEQUIN
PROUDLY PRESENTS
A DAZZLING NEW CONCEPT IN ROMANCE FICTION

One small town—twelve terrific love stories

Welcome to Tyler, Wisconsin—a town full of people
you'll enjoy getting to know, memorable friends and
unforgettable lovers, and a long-buried secret that
lurks beneath its serene surface....

JOIN US FOR A YEAR IN THE LIFE OF TYLER

Each book set in Tyler is a self-contained love story;
together, the twelve novels stitch the fabric of a
community.

LOSE YOUR HEART TO TYLER!

The excitement begins in March 1992, with
WHIRLWIND, by Nancy Martin. When lively, brash
Liza Baron arrives home unexpectedly, she moves
into the old family lodge, where the silent and
mysterious Cliff Forrester has been living in seclusion
for years....

WATCH FOR ALL TWELVE BOOKS
OF THE TYLER SERIES
Available wherever Harlequin books are sold

TYLER-G

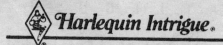 *Harlequin Intrigue*®

43 Light St.

It looks like a charming old building near the Baltimore waterfront, but inside 43 Light Street lurks danger...and romance.

Labeled a "true master of intrigue" by *Rave Reviews*, bestselling author Rebecca York continues her exciting series with #179 ONLY SKIN DEEP, coming to you next month.

When her sister is found dead, Dr. Kathryn Martin, a 43 Light Street occupant, suddenly finds herself caught up in the glamorous world of a posh Washington, D.C., beauty salon. Not even former love Mac McQuade can believe the schemes Katie uncovers.

Watch for #179 ONLY SKIN DEEP in February, and all the upcoming 43 Light Street titles for top-notch suspense and romance.

LS92

● HARLEQUIN

A Calendar of Romance

Be a part of American Romance's year-long celebration of love and the holidays of 1992. Experience all the passion of falling in love during the excitement of each month's holiday. Some of your favorite authors will help you celebrate those special times of the year, like the romance of Valentine's Day, the magic of St. Patrick's Day, the joy of Easter.

Celebrate the romance of Valentine's Day with

#425 VALENTINE HEARTS AND FLOWERS
by Muriel Jensen

Read all the books in *A Calendar of Romance*, coming to you one each month, all year, from Harlequin American Romance. COR2